All That
Lives
Must *Die*

All That *Lives* Must *Die*

To Kate.

IVOR EISENSTADT

Best wishes.

T

Troubador Publishing Ltd
Unit E2 Airfield Business Park,
Harrison Road, Market Harborough,
Leicestershire. LE16 7UL
Tel: 0116 2792299
Email: books@troubador.co.uk
Web: www.troubador.co.uk

ISBN 978 1836281 214

British Library Cataloguing in Publication Data.
A catalogue record for this book is available from the British Library.

Printed and bound by CPI Group (UK) Ltd, Croydon, CR0 4YY
Typeset in 11pt Minion Pro by Troubador Publishing Ltd, Leicester, UK

MIX
Paper | Supporting
responsible forestry
FSC® C013604

Dedicated to all who love and cherish our natural environment, practitioners of ecotherapy who support those suffering from anxiety and depression, everyone fighting to preserve the special place that is the Suffolk Heritage Coast, lovers of a murder mystery and those who simply like to know what their neighbours are getting up to.

All That Lives Must Die

'Thou know'st 'tis common; all that lives must die,
passing through nature to eternity.'
(*Hamlet*, Act 1, Scene II, Line 73, William Shakespeare)

Gertrude

Cold wind bites into Gertrude's face. Driving rain soaks her hair and nightdress. She knows her lodge is close; she stumbles but manages to stay on her feet. She tries to work out which way to go, but the moon is weak and there is little light to guide her. Ahead, she hears the roar of waves breaking on the beach below the cliffs telling her to go back. To go inland. Something strikes against her shoulder. She turns, brushes away a leafy branch and begins to walk. Slowly, carefully, full of fear, full of dread. She needs to get back to the safety of her lodge, but where is it? And where's Mike? Why isn't he here? And Gertrude's mind is full of what that woman had said. Horrible, senseless things. Why wouldn't she help? She was so unkind. So… just so… she didn't know, so… the words won't come. And that man. He didn't need to shout. What was wrong with him? People can be so nasty.

A gust of wind blows her forward; she almost loses her balance. Where is she? Where is the cliff? The wind and rain ease for a moment. She stops, stands motionless, tries to gather herself. Tries to think. She can sense someone else there now. A bright light shines, blinding her, confusing her. She flinches, turns away, looks back and sees a face she thinks she knows. She just can't put a name to it. Gertrude taps the side of her head, forcing herself to think. *Who is it? Come on, who is it? Think, woman, think. Oh, I know, I know…*

Chapter 1

I wake slowly, clutching to a vivid dream of Kathy. The one that convinces me she's still alive, still here with me. The one I never want to wake up from. My mind is unsettled, my stomach churning. It's almost two years since I lost her. Two years of going through the motions. Getting by years.

Dragging myself out of bed, I wrap my dressing gown around me, pull back the curtains and welcome in early morning spring sunshine. I emerge from my bedroom cocoon into the open-plan living area, command virtual assistant Alexa to play Rodrigo's *Concierto de Aranjuez* and am lifted by its "fragrance of magnolias, singing of birds and gushing of fountains". Grabbing a decaffeinated coffee, I step through French doors on to the raised decking of my lodge to look out over Dunwich Cliffs and a gently rolling North Sea. Already, the sun shining towards me from the east plays low across the water, creating shimmering dark blues, glistening pale blues and sandy shallow blues.

The sea shows no sign of the storm that raged through the night, although branches and leaves strewn over the ground tell a different story. Birds flit on and off feeders hung from a small sycamore close to the cliff edge about a hundred feet away. I walk out to the balustrade to get a closer view. The contented coos of a self-satisfied wood pigeon accompany the sound of waves breaking on the beach. Close to shore, gulls bob on a calm sea, riding smooth swells as toy boats in a bath. Taking a sip from my mug, I think, *Kathy would have loved this.*

I peer across at the lodge opposite and note Gertrude's doors are wide open. There's no sign of my neighbour or her brother Mike. They would usually be sitting on their decking having breakfast, watching the birds, gazing out to sea. Especially on such a sunny morning. I hear a shout and turn to see a figure jogging my way. It's James, owner of the lodge next door to mine further away from the cliff.

'Max, Max, have you seen Gertrude?'

'Good morning to you too, James.'

'She's missing, we can't find her.'

'Sorry. I just stepped out, you're the first person I've seen. What do you mean "missing"?'

James holds on to the other side of my balustrade, trying to catch his breath. He looks up at me. He's agitated, his eyes more lively, more intense, than usual. I watch as he wipes away sweat from his forehead before giving me a rapid-fire response.

'Mike found her bedroom door open this morning. She wasn't in the lodge or the garden. He couldn't find her anywhere. He's worried. You know how confused she gets. We've been searching for over an hour. There's no sign of her. She could have wandered off. She might be anywhere. With the storm last night, she'd have been terrified. Anything could have happened. We need to find her.'

'She probably woke up this morning, saw the sun and went for a walk,' I say in my best casual, "it's nothing to worry about" GP manner.

'Yes, that's what I thought, but Mike says her cocoa wasn't drunk last night. She always drinks it. She was in her nightdress and hasn't taken her tablets. He thinks she may have wandered off before going to bed.'

I immediately pick up on "she hasn't taken her tablets".

'Hang on, I'll join you.'

I slip back inside my lodge, dress and swap my comfy sandals for a pair of sturdy walking boots. Although the sun is shining, there's a chill in the air, so I pull on a fleece before heading down my decking steps back to James.

'Where have you looked?' I ask.

'I've been checking this side of the site and the road, Mike's covering the far side and the beach. Could you do the path along the cliff edge?'

'OK. She can't have gone far.'

I suspect we might find her asleep under a bush or in one of the camper's tents. I picture a disturbed caravan owner finding her and wondering what an old lady's doing in their awning.

'I'm sure someone will have seen her.'

'Yes, I'm sure she'll turn up, but she could be in a bad way. I'll call when we find her. You're a GP, maybe you can check her over, make sure she's OK.'

'Ex-GP, James,' I fire back. It's a nervous tic of a response.

He gives me a look that seems to say, "once a GP, always a GP", and heads off, leaving me remembering when being a GP was my vocation. How I loved looking after my patients, was never happier than when managing and caring for them. How satisfying it had been to be needed, appreciated. Then, when I couldn't continue. The worry and dread each time a patient walked through the door. Trapped, not wanting to give up, unable to keep going. Turning up at my surgery in the morning not wishing to let my patients down, but afraid to treat them. Paralysed by the fear of getting it wrong... again. I shudder and set off in search of Gertrude.

Chapter 2

I met Gertrude the first day I moved into Sunrise Park. I introduced myself, we chatted, she seemed pleasant. She told me that she and her husband had a photography studio. I told her that I had been a GP. The next morning, she asked me who I was and what I did. She offered to make me a coffee, disappeared into her lodge and failed to reappear. The signs were clear; you didn't need to be a doctor. Her husband Derek had been killed in a hit-and-run a few months before and her brother Mike was looking after her. Derek had been her rock. Mike had come up from London and stayed, only occasionally returning to the capital. I've watched him care for Gertrude as her dementia's progressed and she's become increasingly confused.

I head north along the cliff path with the sea on my right. Leaves and branches, having fallen from the trees during the night, lie across the sandy path as evidence of what was more than just a late-April shower. Using a stick, I check bushes that stand guard either side of me before arriving at a grass clearing. To my left are daffodils and to my right is a view of the sea over felled tree trunks that act as a barrier to the crumbling cliff edge. Hopefully, sufficient barrier for a confused old lady in a storm.

Looking out over the sea, then up and down the long pebble and sand coastline, I see couples strolling along the beach. A man is walking with a dog and a small group, probably teenagers, are playing in the water. To the north, Southwold juts out as if protecting the bay, its lighthouse repeatedly flashing a bright light warning to those at sea and bright light welcome to those approaching by land. To the south sits Sizewell B nuclear power station. It's as if a gigantic ice cream scoop has been dolloped onto an idyllic coastal scene as a human practical joke, or an alien spacecraft has chosen the most scenic place it could find to take up residence. I scan back and forth between these landmarks, but there's no sign of an old lady.

Stepping carefully over the horizontal tree trunks, I look down at a sixty-foot cliff face. It's not an entirely sheer drop but it would be a fatal fall for someone like Gertrude. Or me. It's inviting; I think about it, but I'm too much of a coward.

I peer over the edge. There's an initial steep section covered in rough grass and bracken that gives way to wild privet, spiky blackthorn and a mosaic of impenetrable bramble that blankets a gentler descent down to the pebble upper beach. I lean out further. There's nothing suspicious. Crows caw loudly overhead; harsh scolds telling me not to be so stupid. I pull back, walk on, and reach a stand of beech trees. Pushing aside low branches to check the undergrowth, I see clusters of bright bluebells, clumps of warm-hearted, yellow-petalled primrose and delicate sweet violets. But no Gertrude.

8

The loud, high-pitched reeling of a wren bursts out and I briefly catch a glimpse of the tiny bird with its provocatively pert, two-fingered tail telling me where to go. *Aggressive little bugger*, I think, smiling to myself. It's only a moment, but it helps ease the tension. Nature's pressure-relief valve.

At the end of the path, a four-foot-high wooden fence sits in front of dense shrubs. It's punctured only by a gate that's overgrown with ivy and not been used for years. I can't see Gertrude having scaled her way out of Sunrise Park here. Turning around, I'm startled by the explosive blast of a shotgun in the near distance. I picture an abruptly lifeless crow or wood pigeon falling from a tree. Pest control by local farmers. Then I think of Gertrude, alone and confused.

Retracing my steps, I pass my lodge on the right and arrive at a clearing with the cliff edge on my left. In front of several protective logs is a rustic sign that reads "Dangerous Cliffs". Recalling only one Cliff, I'm reasonably sure that one of the country's favourite Knights of the Realm isn't a Sunrise Park resident. I reflect that this is no time to be flippant. My defence is that it's a coping mechanism. Years of dealing with patients has led me to find humour in the most unlikely places. It's kept me sane – well, almost.

I repeat the previous exercise. Once again, the cliff face falls away sharply before reaching a less steep drop covered in scrub running down to the beach. It's hard to get a good view, as the vegetation is dense. I move closer to the cliff edge by holding on to a laurel precariously perched on the cusp of the descent. The crumbling ground momentarily gives way, and I lose my footing, feel myself toppling, think about going with it, then grip more tightly onto the tree.

Heart beating hard, I peer down at an unforgiving drop, equally unforgiving sandstone, and impenetrable, white-flowered, spiky blackthorn. I see nothing unusual and am about to pull myself back to safety when I glimpse something red where the steep slope ends. It's hard to make out what it is, as it's obscured by vegetation. I squint to get a better view. I do this when I see a bird that I can't identify but don't have binoculars. Of course, it rarely works, and I invariably put the bird down as an "unspecified little brown job". I decide not to put this down as an "unspecified little red job", extricate myself from the cliff edge and head back to my lodge to get binoculars. When I return, I repeat my previous trick with the laurel. With one hand holding tightly onto the tree and with heart in mouth, I raise the binoculars to my eyes. I'm unsteady, but I can just about make out the red object. It looks a lot like a lady's shoe. It also looks like it could be connected to something further into the dense bush. Not good. I can't make out anything else, so I pull myself back to safety. I suspect now is the time to give James a call.

'Have you found her?' I ask.

'No nothing.' He sounds worried. 'Mike's wondering whether to call the police.'

'Might be a good idea, and mountain rescue. I think there's a red shoe possibly attached to a person halfway down the cliff close to my lodge.'

'What?' Now he sounds alarmed. 'What do you mean you think there's a red shoe possibly attached to a person?'

'Hard to say for sure as it's in an awkward place to get a good view. I'm not great with heights; even with my binos, it's not clear. There's a red object and I think it's a lady's shoe. What colour was Gertrude wearing?'

'Hopefully black. I'll call Mike.'

It seems a long time before he gets back to me. He sounds breathless.

'Mike has no idea what colour shoes she's wearing. She does wear red now and again. He's on his way up from the beach, I'm on my way back.'

'Might be time to call for help.'

'Yes, Mike's on it. God, I hope you're wrong. I hope it's just an old shoe someone's thrown away, or something else red that's been blown there. Maybe an umbrella or a kite.'

'Do they make umbrellas and kites shaped like shoes?'

'You know what I mean.'

'I'm pretty sure it's a shoe, James. I just hope it's not her shoe.'

Chapter 3

I take Mike and James to the clearing where I repeat my trick with the laurel and the binoculars. Mike peers down intently, taking his time. James is reluctant; it seems he's not good with heights.

'Do you think it's her?' Mike asks, his voice shaky, his face flushed.

'I don't know, it just looks like a red shoe,' I say, trying to hide my concern.

'It must be her; it must be. It's my fault, I can't believe I let her wander off. How could I be so stupid, so bloody stupid? My own sister, for heaven's sake. I'll never forgive myself, not if it's her. Never. I need to get down there, I need to see.'

'Going down there would be suicide. There's nothing you can do. You need to wait for the police. Try not to worry, it's probably just an old shoe that someone's lost.'

Mike crosses the track to his lodge and sits on the top step leading to his decking. He's slouched, his paunch accentuated by his striped shirt. He blows out his cheeks, puts his palms behind his head and looks across at me.

'It's her, isn't it?' He rocks back and forth. 'I just can't help thinking, with the storm, if only I'd locked her in or just checked on her. If I'd left my door open so I could hear if she was going for a walkabout. I'm so stupid. So bloody stupid.'

'It happens, Mike. Elderly dementia patients wander off. With the best will in the world, you can't keep people locked away just in case they go and do something silly.'

James takes me to one side. 'Max, you're a GP, can you calm him down? Give him a sedative or something?'

'Ex-GP, James, and I don't have a temazepam with me. Tea with lots of sugar might help. It's good for shock.'

He offers to put the kettle on, and I realise I've not yet had my essential, 'keeps me regular' breakfast porridge.

'I need to go to my lodge, Mike. Is that OK? I'll be back when the police arrive.'

He's deep in thought. I repeat the question and this time he answers.

'Yes, of course, there's nothing more we can do for her.' He pauses and adds, 'Not now.'

As I head back to my lodge, a text arrives from Emma. *How are you? Can we talk? OK if I call around 8.30pm? Love you. Em x.*

Fine, speak then. Dad x, I text back.

Emma likes to check I'm OK, often calling in the evening after work. It's unusual for her to text first, so she must want something. I guess I'll find out tonight. I'm edgy and need calming, so I ask Alexa to play Schubert's *Impromptu No. 3*, take my breakfast outside and sit on the decking looking out to sea. I think of Kathy, accompanied by one of the piano pieces we both loved. A gentle breeze washes my face and sunshine warms my body. When the music ends, it gives way to the rhythmic rumble of waves gently breaking on the shore beneath the cliffs. I hear the distant sound of children playing. My mind fills with images of past holidays spent here in Dunwich. Emma and Greg on the beach with buckets and spades, building sandcastles, running away from the waves breaking on the shore, crouching down behind windbreaks, swimming in the cold water… with Kathy.

Chapter 4

I notice my neighbour Julia standing outside on her decking. She and her husband George have the lodge next to mine. They are closest to the cliff, set well back so as not to spoil my precious sea view. She sees me, approaches the balustrade opposite mine and leans across for a word.

'Morning, Max. James says Gertrude's gone missing.'

'Yes, she's not been seen all morning. We've been out looking for her. I don't want to cause alarm, but I think there's a red shoe in the bushes halfway down the cliff.'

'A red shoe?' Julia asks, eyebrows raised.

'You haven't lost one, have you?'

'Red's not my colour, darling,' she says, smiling.

'You don't know whether Gertrude's been wearing red shoes?'

'No idea. Wouldn't surprise me.'

'And why wouldn't it surprise you?'

Her smile fades. 'Oh… nothing, just kidding,' she answers, looking down at the unmown grass between the balustrades.

'What is it? Come on,' I prompt.

Sensing from my tone that it's important, she opens up.

'You've not been here long but some of us go way back. Gertrude was quite a flirt when she was younger; she had a bit of a reputation. She came on to a few of the guys. Came on to George. Red shoes would fit.'

I've never been particularly nosey but living in a lodge at Sunrise Park has opened my eyes to the enjoyment people get from gossip and rumour. I'm about to explore the topic of Gertrude's flirtations further when a police car turns up. There's no siren and initially no one emerges. The two uniformed occupants sit for a while, making notes and taking calls. Gertrude, it seems, is not a particularly high priority. When one of them eventually gets out of the car, he looks around before asking which of us is Mike. They have a brief conversation before the officer comes across to where I'm sitting on my decking. He looks up and examines me.

'I understand you think you've seen a shoe halfway down the cliff belonging to this gentleman's sister?'

'Not exactly. I think there's a red shoe halfway down the cliff and his sister Gertrude is missing. I wouldn't necessarily want to put the two things together.'

'Yes, of course. Show us. Let's have a look at this shoe.'

I nod, leave my lodge, walk towards the cliff edge and step over one of the horizontal log barriers. The police officer follows. He's not happy.

'Just a minute. Can't you read the sign? "Dangerous Cliffs".'

I get the image of Sir Cliff again in my mind and this time he's precariously perched in the front row of the

16

royal box at Wimbledon, leading a singalong with the crowd while rain interrupts play.

'Do you want me to show you or not?'

'Well, be careful,' the officer replies, giving me an impressively firm glare.

I would normally be tempted to answer, 'Thanks, useful tip,' but he doesn't seem the sort to mess with. I find a foothold, grab my trusty laurel, and point to the shoe.

'It's there. You can just see it sticking out from under the bush. I think there might be something else further in. I can't be sure.'

I step back and the police officer takes my place. He scrunches his eyes, squinting. For a moment, I have the urge to ask him if he's seen a rare, "unspecified little red job".

'I can't see anything much. Maybe there's something red down there, but it's not obvious.'

'You need binoculars,' I reply helpfully.

'I don't have any,' he says, examining the pair around my neck.

'Here, you can use mine.'

It's an automatic response and immediately after I've said it, I can't believe what's come out of my mouth. He steps back from the edge, holds his hand out and I reluctantly give him my beloved, treasured last present from Kathy. If he lets them fall, even though it may be hard to justify in front of another police officer and what must now be half of the park residents, I will personally push him after them.

He steps gingerly up to the cliff edge, grabs the laurel, juggles my precious binos with one hand and looks down at what should now be a more visible red shoe.

17

After a while, he returns to announce, 'It's not obvious. You may have something, but there's no way we can get down there without support.'

He then shouts to his so far uninvolved colleague, who is leaning against the police car looking at his phone screen.

'Roger, call it in, we need support. Possible person not moving sited halfway down the cliff at Sunrise Park.'

'Roger, Cliff,' his colleague responds.

I can't help smiling; in fact, I almost laugh out loud. What are the chances? If it were not for the seriousness of the situation, I would be cracking up. Cliff hands me back my binos and wanders over to talk to Mike.

I return to my lodge to relieve myself before washing my hands and splashing my face with cold water. It's as much to make sure what's happening is real as to freshen myself up. I look closely in the mirror. Not too bad for just over sixty years on the planet. Full head of silver-grey hair; bushy but under-control eyebrows; trimmed, almost stubbly, beard; "characterful" bulbous nose; and, as Emma insists on describing it, emoji-like smiley face. Kathy used to try to convince me that I looked young for my age. I can't pretend it now. The past few years have taken their toll, as evidenced by my ever-increasing wrinkles, worry lines, drooping cheeks and dull, dry skin. What would she make of me now? Can it really be two years? I imagine her staring back at me in the mirror.

'Oh, Kathy.' I sigh and apply moisturiser to my face in the hope of disguising, even arresting, the attrition. I reflect that I could probably have as much as twenty years left, shudder, and head back outside.

Chapter 5

In time, an emergency recovery team, suitably dressed in blue overalls and helmets, arrives at the top of the cliff. They unload ropes, rigging and other gear and are soon ready to work their way down to the shoe… and possibly Gertrude. We watch as two of them disappear over the edge and then wait for news, sitting around Mike's decking table. He has his head in his hands; I'm aware that I'm biting my lip; James is annoyingly bouncing his right leg up and down. The rescue workers are gone for about half an hour before reappearing. The taller of the two calls across to the now five-strong police team.

'There's a lady down there; face up, no pulse, not breathing. She's dead. We'll need to recover her. The brambles are too dense to get to her from below; we'll need to bring her up.'

There is stunned silence. I'm not sure that it's quite the way one would have wished the news to be broken to poor Mike, but what's done is done. I look at him; he looks at me. He's like a little boy who has lost his mum. I get up and put my arm around him. I'm not sure what to say as there's still a chance it's not Gertrude. Slim, unlikely, but not impossible. We sit with him while the emergency services get on with what they need to get on with.

'It may not be her, you know,' James says, breaking the silence.

'It's her. Of course it's her,' Mike responds, turning his head away and looking out to sea. 'Confused old lady with dementia goes missing on a dark night in a storm not far from a dangerous cliff. Body is discovered the next morning having fallen down the cliff. It doesn't take a genius.'

He's got a point. James is just giving him some hope and Mike knows it.

'We can't be sure. The woman may have fallen a while ago or someone else may have been out walking last night,' I say, trying to help.

'In a raging storm?' mutters Mike, looking at me as if I'm demented.

'I guess we'll have to wait until they bring her up.' It's the best I can do.

Mike stares back out to sea. It's as though he's searching for his sister on the horizon.

'We've always been close. Since we were kids. Since my wife left me. Since we lost Mum and Dad. She's pretty much all I've got left.'

'Where were you brought up?' I ask, hoping to distract him, relieve the tension.

'Hertfordshire, Tring.'

'Tring?'

'Small town, pretty. The best thing about it is its museum of stuffed animals.'

Mike loves his birdwatching as much as I do, and I sense a way to take his mind from Gertrude.

'Is that where you got your love of birds?'

'I used to visit the bird section, gaze at the specimens, sketch the stuffed exhibits. Might seem a bit weird for a kid, but it was great. It taught me the names of the birds, how to tell them apart. They had a dodo egg, and hummingbirds. The hummingbirds were my favourite. Hundreds of tiny jewels in a tall glass case. Magical, they're magical… birds… it's why I love Sunrise Park, the lodge, being here.' Mike silently reflects for a while before being distracted by a magpie chuntering loudly in a high tree behind my lodge. 'One for sorrow,' he mutters, pauses, then continues, 'Gertrude loved nature but hated the museum. She used to tease me. Would tell my friends I was a nerd drawing stuffed dead birds. She thought I should have been outside watching the live ones. Probably had a point. She loved nature, was a real eco-warrior.' He stops, frowns, then corrects himself, 'Is a real eco-warrior.' Another pause. 'She never stopped ribbing me over my drawings, even here. Every time I went for a walk, she would have a go, "Off birding, are we? Don't forget your sketchbook. The stuffed ones are easier." She thought it was hilarious. It wasn't, it was annoying, and it's been getting worse. She was always feisty, but she's become mean. Not just confused. Since Derek died, she's been angry. Angry at me, at others, at life. She's not been easy.'

Well, that line of distraction went well. Police Officer Cliff comes over to where we're sitting and looks at Mike.

'We'll be bringing her up shortly. It would be good if you can confirm if it's your sister.'

Mike agrees, although I reason it would be better if he can't. The police officer turns to me.

'I understand you're a GP. I don't suppose you could take a quick look at her when we get her up top?'

'Ex-GP; I've retired. I'm happy to take a quick look, but I'm not exactly sure what you want me to check for.'

'Just to confirm she's dead. Perhaps see if there's anything unusual, anything we should be aware of.'

I will have no problem confirming whether the lady is dead but I'm still not sure exactly what else he's after. I would have thought being killed falling down a cliff would be unusual, but I suppose there's no harm in giving her the once over.

It's not long before a white body bag is brought to me so that I can "take a quick look". I unzip the package to reveal poor Gertrude lying face up. She's dead. I check anyway for breathing and pulse, look into her eyes, examine the rest of the front of her body. She's wearing her nightdress, which is soaked through, and her hair's a mess. She's covered in surface scratches and abrasions but there's no obvious major wound and nothing appears to be broken. In fact, she's remarkably free of injury. I assume the bracken and other vegetation on the cliff face must have cushioned her fall. I decide not to turn her over as I don't want to remove her from the bag; she will be thoroughly examined when they carry out the post-mortem. It's not my area of expertise but something does feel slightly odd. I can't put my finger on it, but it bothers me. I don't want to miss anything, not again, not like before. I turn to the police officer and let him know my findings.

'It's Gertrude; she's dead. No pulse, she's not breathing. Her pupils are fully dilated.'

'Anything unusual?'

'Not sure, nothing obvious I can see. She had dementia. I imagine she walked out of her lodge in the storm last night, became confused and fell down the cliff.'

He nods and zips her back into the bag. 'OK, thanks, we'll take it from here.'

By "it", I assume he means poor Gertrude. A practising doctor will need to formally confirm the death, the coroner will carry out a post-mortem and the funeral will be in a couple of weeks. I suspect many of the other lodge owners and some of the site staff will turn out, the same group who said goodbye to her Derek just a few months ago.

The police officer ushers Mike over to the body and unzips the bag once more. It's clear from Mike's face that he recognises his sister. He confirms it to the police officer with a brief but meaningful nod. I wait a short while before putting my hand on his shoulder.

'I'm so sorry, Mike.'

Mike's head is bowed. He whispers his response into the ground.

'Thanks, Max. I can't believe it, I really can't. And it was all my fault.'

I know how he's feeling, I know the guilt. I don't want him to suffer the way I have.

'Dementia is awful. Over the years, I lost many patients to it, often from pneumonia but some due to accidents. It's not your fault, it really isn't, it was the disease. You did everything you could for her, everything.'

'Maybe, perhaps, but I feel terrible. I keep kicking myself for not checking on her and making sure she was alright. With the storm, she would have been scared just being in her room. Out there, she'd have been terrified.' He pauses then adds, 'I let her down.'

The words make me flinch. I think of Kathy and bite my lip.

'I need a glass of water. Do you want me to get you anything?'

Mike looks at me, frowns and shakes his head just as James comes across to join us. I've not seen him since they brought the body up. He's looking pale. The sun is shining and the chill in the air has gone but my stomach is uneasy, my shoulders ache and I'm on edge. It's as if something bad is about to happen. It's a feeling I know well. The morning has taken its toll.

'Anyone fancy a walk across the heath? I need a dose of nature to clear my head.'

'I have to be here for Gertrude,' Mike responds.

James says, 'Yes, I could really do with a walk.'

James

James needs to take his mind from thinking about what's happened. Thinking about Gertrude. Thinking about Margaret. That moment, long ago, peering down from his window at his little sister lying crumpled on the ground. In her white socks and light blue polka dot dress. Not moving. A patch of crimson by her head.

And he hears himself shouting, 'Margaret, Margaret. I'm sorry, I'm sorry.'

It's brought it all back. His mum and dad, the tears, the shouting, the looks. The guilt. The way everything changed. He can't get Margaret out of his mind… or Gertrude.

His throat is dry; his hands are shaking; he feels nauseous. He recognises the signs. The fear, the interminable fear that something terrible is about to happen. The panic attacks. He couldn't go through all that again. He needs to be doing something, to be in the heath, to be in nature. To walk and to focus on the birds. Something, anything that can stop his mind thinking about it. Maybe he should talk to Max. He's a GP. He'd understand, be able to help. James straps on his boots. He needs to walk it all away.

Chapter 6

I return to my lodge, fill a pint glass from the tap, down it in one and collect my rucksack. It's already loaded with the essentials: sun hat, lotion, rain cover, bird guide, water bottle, chocolate. I add my journal notebook and pens. Within ten minutes, James and I are heading out of Sunrise Park to the sanctuary of Dunwich Heath with our trusty binos hanging around our necks. We walk side by side, maintaining a good pace, initially saying nothing, keeping our thoughts to ourselves. I'm struggling to get my head around what has happened, and I sense James is the same. Gertrude out in the storm, alone, confused, probably terrified, killed falling down the cliff. The cliff next to my lodge.

I'm shaken out of it by a woodpecker's loud, machine-gun drumming delivered from high up in a tree to our right. Instinctively, I label it out loud.

'Great spotted woodpecker.'

'Yes, up in the tall birch over there.' James points it out as he speaks. His hand is trembling.

The drumming repeats. I angle my binos towards the upper trunk from where the sound has reverberated.

There's no sign of it. I try to spot it with my naked eye and watch for movement. They can be elusive. James still has a view in his binos.

'There, on the large branch to the left of the main trunk, about two thirds of the way up.'

I do the eye squinting thing and spot something that's the general impression, size, and shape – "GISS" – of a great spotted. I focus my binos on it and, yes, it's a male great spotted woodpecker. Roughly the size of a blackbird, upright stance, black-and-white pied head and body, crimson back of the head and lower belly. Beautiful. Such sightings brighten the day and today certainly needs brightening. We watch for a good five minutes before walking on. My thoughts return to Gertrude.

'Shocking morning, it's hard to take it in. Poor Gertrude, poor Mike. I tried to convince him he wasn't to blame but he wasn't having it. I guess it's too soon.'

'Much too soon, it's going to take him a while to come to terms with it.'

'He'll need our support.'

'He will.' James seems to shudder, pauses, then repeats, 'He will.'

We walk out of the holiday park and cross narrow Minsmere Road, which runs alongside Sunrise Park. Passing through a small gate, we join the sandy, stone-impregnated path flanked by woodland and fenced fields that leads to Dunwich Heath. It's drying well after last night's storm, although our boots still make satisfying squelches as we step through the remaining wet patches. James, his eyes alert and constantly scanning for birdlife, continues to talk as we walk.

'Over the years, I got to know Gertrude and Derek quite well. Being on my own, I think they took pity on me. We would sit on their decking in the morning, drinking coffee, looking out to sea, chatting. Later, once the sun had gone, we might sit out on mine. Gertrude liked her white wine, Derek his gin and tonics. Sometimes we'd play Scrabble, sometimes we'd just sit and put the world to rights.'

'What was she like before her dementia?'

'Feisty. Always up for a good cause. She and Derek were actively fighting Sizewell C. The idea of a third nuclear power station here made her – them – very angry. They couldn't stand the idea of losing more precious wildlife habitat, rare species, beautiful landscape. She would get worked up, very emotional. Back in the day, she used to go on CND marches. She was one of those camped at Greenham Common protesting about the nuclear missile base. It's where she and Derek met. He was a freelance photographer.' James pauses, then adds, 'Apparently, she was quite striking in her day.'

It triggers a thought from earlier.

'Julia said something that surprised me. She implied that Gertrude was a flirt. Possibly more. Any idea what that was about?'

'I'm not sure now is the time to be delving into that corner of her life, not just yet. She may be able to hear us, you know, floating overhead, her brain still registering what's being said about her, taking it all in one last time.'

I smile at the thought.

'Interesting idea, James, not one covered in my medical training.'

'It just feels wrong, too soon.'

I catch a glimpse of a tiny bird flitting around in an oak tree to our right. It's greyish green with a pale belly. The wrong colours for a great or blue tit, wrong GISS for a goldcrest. I spot it in my binos.

'Chiffchaff; it flicked its tail.'

James watches it for a while before delivering his verdict.

'Not sure, stripe over the eyes is strong, legs maybe not dark enough, belly's very light. I reckon willow warbler.'

'No, legs are darkish and, there, it flicked its tail.'

'I've lost it.' James sighs.

'It's still there. Come on, sing, you bugger.'

We wait patiently for its tell-tale song and soon get lucky as it repeats, 'Chiff-chaff, chiff-chaff, chiff-chaff.'

I smile and we walk on. James sighs again before bringing us back to Gertrude.

'You know, it would have been best if she'd taken the nursing home place she was offered. I know Mike was looking after her, but she was ready for it. Her dementia was getting worse, she was an accident waiting to happen. I wouldn't say it to Mike, but she was.'

'Recently offered a place in a local home?'

'Yes, in Halesworth, close to where she lived. They have a unit for dementia patients that would have been perfect, though I imagine she would have had to sell the house and perhaps the lodge to pay for it. She was ready though.'

'Yes, it would have made sense. I wonder how Mike's feeling about it now?'

'Yes,' says James, 'I wonder.'

We arrive at Dunwich Heath and take the left-hand fork that leads to a row of adjoining clifftop buildings known as the Coastguard Cottages. The path is fine sand and to either side of us extends gorgeous brown, soon to be purple heather and spiky, yellow-tipped gorse bushes interspersed with lush green grass and dense bracken. I never fail to feel at ease here. It takes me outside of myself, grounds me in the moment and washes away any tension. I sense that it's the same for James. We keep scanning for birdlife; we know what we're looking for. James spots one.

'Stonechat, up on the bush to our left.'

I can't miss it. Robin-sized, raven-black head, white half-collar, orange breast. Male stonechat. I look for its mate and there she is, also on top of a bush, not as brightly coloured, but still lovely. We watch for a while and as we start to walk, the male repeats several short bursts of his thin, wispy, high-pitched song. It then sends us on our way with its distinctive "tapping two stones together" call.

James says quietly, 'I wonder how it will affect Felicity?' It's almost as if he's thinking to himself.

Felicity lives on her own in the lodge next to Gertrude's that sits further inland from the sea, her husband having died of a heart attack a few years ago. I don't know her well, but she seems pleasant enough. The question surprises me.

'Sorry, why Felicity?'

James stops walking and scans around for birdlife.

'Sorry, just thinking aloud.' He then adds, 'You do know what happened between them, don't you?'

It feels like he's about to confide in me.

'Er, no, not really.'

'How her husband, Peter, died?'

'Heart attack, wasn't it?'

'Yes, he'd had heart disease for a long time, a couple of operations and a heart attack several years before. He was told to avoid stress, but Gertrude and Derek would play loud music well into the night. It drove Peter crazy. I often heard them arguing. When he had his fatal attack, Felicity was convinced that they'd caused it. She's not spoken to Gertrude since, even when Derek died. She doesn't like to talk about it.'

I have a vision of ants, beetles, worms and assorted insects going about their business under a rock, unseen until someone flips it over and they're revealed in the sunlight.

'What goes on in holiday parks, eh, James. Don't you just love it?'

'Old people, don't you just love them?' he responds in kind. 'I never wanted to get old. At one point, I made a vow to myself to end it all before I started falling apart. Now it's happening, I can't seem to bring myself to do it.'

I know how he feels. Getting old and losing those we love. Life becomes so much harder. But ending it is so final, it takes such courage.

'We need to make the most of the quality time we get. A geriatrician once told me, "Any day you can wipe your own bum is a good day." I often remind myself of it, of the need to enjoy doing the stuff that makes us happy while we can. Talking of which, a Dartford warbler just came up in the tall gorse bush to the right about twenty feet ahead.' As I say this, I watch a wonderfully dainty rufus-grey Dartford warbler with its white patched belly, beady eye, and long flickering tail. 'Lovely bird. I still can't get used to seeing them here, not when there are so few elsewhere.'

'Gertrude used to say it was her favourite,' James says, pointing to a second one that's popped up on a smaller, more densely yellow gorse bush.

'Really?'

'Yes, she'd look for them whenever she walked across the heath. She told me she loved them because they were so delicate, had been so close to being wiped out, but had made a comeback. They proved that, given half a chance, nature can survive no matter what we throw at it. That there's still hope.'

We watch in silence until the rare warblers no longer show, then walk on.

'Will there need to be a post-mortem?' James asks.

'Yes, almost certainly, you need them for deaths that are sudden, unnatural, due to violence, or where the cause is unknown. Falling off a cliff comes into at least two of those. The coroner will decide but they will need to establish the cause of death. The coroner's officers issue the medical certificate of cause of death after the post-mortem.'

We walk on. He's deep in thought.

'When will the funeral take place?'

'It depends on the post-mortem. If her death was accidental, maybe a couple of weeks.'

'If? If it was accidental?'

I reflect on his question. I can't work out what it was that bothered me when I examined Gertrude but it's a relief to now share this with someone else.

'Well, yes, if. It probably was but I had a feeling something was wrong when I examined her. I couldn't put my finger on it… I still can't.'

'Really? A feeling something was wrong?'

'It's probably nothing.'

More silence. We walk on and soon arrive at a connected row of squat, white cottages that sit proudly on Dunwich Cliffs looking out over coast, marsh and glorious heathland. They are the northern contributor to a pair of bookends that flank Minsmere, my favourite bird reserve. We look south across reed beds to the distant Sizewell power stations that form the southern bookend. They feel incongruous.

'Sizewell A is such an ugly concrete block, and the ice cream dome of Sizewell B is so intrusive. Heaven knows what Sizewell C will look like,' I say.

James nods and adds, 'I've always thought of the Coastguard Cottages as Gondor and Sizewell as Mordor.'

We look out over the scene, not speaking, just taking it in. James breaks the reverie.

'I sometimes came here with Derek and Gertrude. Derek would take photos of the scenery, the flowers, the wildlife. They used to say that it was their favourite place. I guess that's why they hated the idea of another power station intruding on their paradise. It's why they got involved in the protests. They ran meetings, went on marches, that sort of thing. They even managed to generate national media coverage. Derek was planning a photo exhibition to highlight its potential impact when he was killed.'

'Losing him must have hit Gertrude hard.'

'Yes, the prospect of Sizewell C, then what happened to Derek. She became angry, bitter. It seemed to accelerate her dementia. She became more and more confused, more and more argumentative. With me, with everyone. Mike tried to look after her, keep her calm, but she can't have been easy. He did his best.'

Chapter 7

We secure one of the tearoom's outdoor wooden tables with a view across the heath and out to sea. James offers to get the teas, and I take out my notebook journal to jot down thoughts and observations on the day. It's been a habit since I first suffered from anxiety. A kind of diary. It helps me clarify things, keep track of my life, make sense of it all. Overhead, swallows and smaller sand martins rise and swoop in pursuit of insects. Newly arrived long distance travellers here on their Suffolk coastal holidays. James returns with a tray on which rests mugs of tea, pasties and packets of crisps. I examine him closely. He's younger than me. I'd guess mid-fifties, tall, slim, with intense blue eyes and a silver stubbly beard. He has the look of a walker, the look of a bird watcher. Well, my idea of a bird watcher. He places the tray on the table.

'Here, Max, something to keep us going. You do like their pasties, don't you?'

'Of course. Thanks. How much do I owe you?'

'No, this one's on me, you can get the next shout. Perhaps we can do Avocado in Aldeburgh?'

Aldeburgh is an upmarket seaside town just a few miles away and Avocado is a Michelin-starred restaurant with prices to match. It seems James has a sense of humour.

'Expensive taste, James.'

'Not really but Mary, my ex, she used to like posh nosh. I prefer junk food,' he replies, smiling as he opens one of the crisp packets and helps himself to the contents.

'How long were you together?'

'Twenty years. She left me for her boss at work. He could provide her with more of what she was looking for. Gucci shoes, Versace handbags, meals out at Avocado, that sort of thing. It took me a while to get over. We sold our house, split the money and I downsized to a place in Stevenage close to where I work. I bought the lodge at the same time to get away from it all. Well… her, them. Somewhere to go birding whenever I wanted. My way of making it up to myself.'

'Kids?'

'No, she never wanted them. Too expensive. You?'

I smile, appreciating the irony.

'Yes, two, Emma and Greg. Both grown up now, fully fledged.'

'What about your wife?'

'Kathy, we were married forty years. We met at university when we were eighteen and stayed together until she passed away. Cancer.' I pause then add, 'Almost two years ago.'

We sit in mutual silence reflecting on our misfortunes. We get so used to life going on with just a few odd bumps in the road that when a bombshell hits and the road collapses, we are completely unprepared. We can't drive around it. We need to get out and learn to walk again. It occurs to me that both James and I are literally doing just that, walking our way back to some form of normality, some form of happiness.

'Is it why you retired as a GP?'

I take a moment, thinking about my answer.

'Yes, partly. She was diagnosed with terminal liver cancer. I wanted time to support her… and I had anxiety.'

'You did? Me too, I had it a few years ago. It came out of nowhere. One minute I was running a successful business, the next I was a nervous wreck. Couldn't sleep, couldn't eat, couldn't concentrate. I couldn't even drive. Lost a stone in just a few weeks. I thought it would never end. Like there was no way out. Endlessly going over things, constantly on edge. My mind wouldn't settle. I was lucky my team supported me, covered for me. It's hard to think about it, talk about it. Even now.'

It takes me back to when I was suffering most. Having had anxiety and depression when I was in my early-fifties, I managed to come through it, only to have to face it again with Kathy's cancer.

'Just like me. Worst experience of my life. Well, apart from losing Kathy. I'd had it before, losing her set it off again. Continually being on edge. The gnawing feeling deep in my stomach as though something terrible was about to happen. Mind turning over and over with no let-up, not even to sleep. It was as though a motor in my head had been left running at full throttle with no way to slow it down or switch it off. Sometimes now, when I sit looking across the heath or out to sea and feel a sense of calm, I think back to those times and breathe a huge sigh of relief.

That I'm normal again. That it wasn't a life sentence. That I can just sit with the engine off and feel stillness inside me.'

'Yes, it's horrible.'

'And not uncommon. I had so many patients with it. I'm just thankful we're living now when we've got effective drugs. Drugs that work. They did for me, did for my patients.'

We fall silent, reliving past dark days. James stops eating his pasty, puts his knife and fork down and rests his hands on the table. Despite what he's just said about finding it hard, I can tell he's itching to talk more about it. He looks directly at me, leaning forward.

'I never worked out what set mine off. I had a bad fall and hit my head on the drive. It could have been that. Possibly a midlife crisis. Mary and I weren't getting on, we were arguing all the time. I was stressed at work, under a lot of pressure. That could have done it. What do you think?'

'It could have been any of those things, there's no way of telling. Not now. Maybe a combination, one thing on top of the other.'

'Maybe.' James pauses, hesitates as though unsure what to say next. 'I lost my sister when I was young. She fell from my bedroom window. What's happened to Gertrude, it's brought it all back. Made me feel anxious. Should I go back on the tablets?'

'Oh, that must be hard. Give it some time, it should settle. It's probably the shock. If you're worried, go and see your GP.'

'Yes, thanks. Do you know what triggered yours?'

'Work. Stress from work.'

'Overwork?'

Now it's my turn to hesitate. I weigh up what to tell him, how much to say. There was a time when I was ashamed and feared what others might think, so I would avoid talking about it. Apart from with Kathy. I'm stronger now.

'No, a patient, I misdiagnosed a patient. A child. He died.'

'Oh. I'm sorry. That must have been awful.'

There's more silence between us. This time, it's awkward. We avoid eye contact. He takes a bite from his pasty, I eat a few crisps, we look out to sea. It's a relief when James focuses us back on himself.

'After I came out the other side, I mentioned it to friends. Almost all had some experience of it, but they never said anything. Not to me, not to anyone.'

'Suffering in silence. If they don't come forward, we can't help them. Any idea how many consider finishing it? One study found over seventy per cent of attempted suicides had some form of anxiety. Seventy per cent. It's not uncommon and it's treatable.'

James nods, cradles his mug and stares into his tea. 'Yes, CBT helped. Thinking positive thoughts, putting things in perspective. But it was the tablets that did my heavy lifting.'

'Yes, the drugs sorted my acute phase, CBT helped – helps – keep it at bay.' I pause, look around and say, 'And ecotherapy. Nature, it's therapeutic, restorative. I'm a great believer. Spending time in nature, walking in it, being immersed in it. Like today.'

James also looks at the golden-yellow gorse bushes, the heather reaching to the cliff edge, the swooping swallows and buzzing martins.

'It does help. Being here. Dunwich Heath, Minsmere, the wildlife, the birds.'

As he finishes speaking, several starlings appear ready to pounce on our leftovers. James and I exchange glances. I'm not a big fan of these noisy opportunists.

'I once watched a starling pluck baby sparrows from their nest hole and drop them one by one to their deaths. It looked at me innocent as you like, as though nothing had happened. It then moved in, claiming the site for itself.'

James winces and then adds has his own anecdote.

'I've seen one kill a young blackbird by pecking repeatedly at its neck. Several blackbirds tried to stop it, mob it, frighten it away, but the starling just kept pecking. When it had finished, the starling left the dead juvenile on the lawn. There was no obvious reason for it. Spite? Protecting its food supply? Protecting its young? I guess that's what makes nature so fascinating. We're not so different.'

A more uplifting image comes to mind.

'I'm not a big starling fan, but I do love watching their enormous roosts as they fly in.'

'Yes, safety in numbers, tens of thousands in the air together twisting and turning as one. I love watching the shapes they form.'

I think of the starling patterns I've seen here at Minsmere. Dark, shape-shifting clouds swirling in the fading light of the setting sun, forming into balls, hearts, mushrooms and, once, even a duck. For some reason, my mind then pictures a shoe, a black shoe. It soon becomes a red shoe, Gertrude's shoe. I think of it lying in the bushes halfway down the cliff. I think of her nestling in the body bag with her nightdress soaked, her hair a mess and her scratched but unbroken face looking up at me. Why does it feel wrong? What am I missing?

Chapter 8

When we arrive back at Sunrise Park, we pop into the handy site shop to be greeted by a stout lady with short pink hair. Joyce has been serving here for years and is well known for being chatty, direct and the centre of most of the site gossip. I pick up a basket, fill it with essentials and approach the counter. Joyce continues to label some sweet packets, before weighing me up with what feels like an overly critical eye.

'Afternoon, Max. How are you?'

'Afternoon, Joyce. I'm OK. You?'

'Shaken. I'm shaken. Who would have thought it? Gertrude out last night in such a bad storm. When our time's up, it's up, but falling over a cliff? She must have been more confused than normal. Still, with her dementia she'd been going downhill for a while.'

I can't help being tickled by what she's just said about Gertrude going downhill. I'm sure that it wasn't meant to be funny and manage to suppress a smile.

'I hope it doesn't affect my trade,' she adds.

'Why would it affect your trade?'

'You know, people put off coming. Folk don't like being around death and they might wonder whether it's safe.'

'I don't think it's happened to anyone before, not here. I'm sure it won't happen again. It was just a one-off.'

'I suppose so. But still.'

'It was an unfortunate accident.'

'Maybe, but I wouldn't be too surprised if someone gave her a hand.' Joyce looks into my eyes as if studying them to see my reaction.

'What? What did you say? Someone might have pushed her?'

'Maybe.'

'What on earth makes you say that?'

'Don't get me wrong, I liked Gertrude, I'll miss her. She was a character. But she wasn't everyone's cup of tea. She was argumentative, spoke her mind, would cause ructions. She wouldn't be pushed around by the likes of Tim and George. Their kind.'

'It doesn't mean they'd shove her off a cliff.'

'Maybe.'

I recoil at the thought. I need to move the conversation to something more comfortable.

'I feel for Mike. He's going to miss her.'

'Really? They always used to bicker whenever they came in. He'd want strawberry jam, she'd want apricot. He'd want granola, she'd want muesli. He'd want milk chocolate, she'd want dark. He'd want white bread, she'd want granary. It used to take them hours. I guess I'll have fewer queues now.'

'Maybe.'

'You all done, Max? Anything else?'

'Not that I can think of.'

Joyce turns to James and smiles. 'Not buying any more boxes of fancy chocolates?'

James looks embarrassed. 'No, I'm still working my way through the last one.'

Joyce smiles at him again and puts my items through the till. I pay and turn to leave. As I do so, I brush against a lady who's just entered the shop. A red scarf partially covers her face, yet she seems vaguely familiar. My heart skips a beat, my stomach tightens. As I walk out of the shop, I realise I'm biting my lip.

It's just a short distance back to our lodges, initially past camping tents then touring caravans. We pass a toilet block and washing-up area before entering a section where static caravans and permanent lodges sit in their own small gardens. We ignore two turnings on our right before entering Sunny Drive with its six lodges paired either side of a short gravel track that leads to the cliff and our wonderfully panoramic view of the North Sea. Felicity's relatively modest dwelling sits first on our right, the more impressive, luxury lodge belonging to James is opposite hers on our left. Mike's place is next to Felicity's, mine faces his. Sitting beside my lodge, closest to the cliff, are George and Julia, while opposite them next to Mike, are Tim and Louise.

There's no sign left of the emergency services. Red and white barrier tape now runs along the cliff edge; otherwise, it's as if Gertrude's fall had never happened.

'I'm surprised everyone's gone. I would have thought they'd still be all over the area,' I say to James as we stop outside his lodge.

'They must be satisfied it was an accident. Confused old lady in a storm, open and shut case, not worth lingering over.'

'Yes, I suppose so. But it does seem quick. I wonder how Mike's doing. I think I'll check in on him.'

James heads up to his decking and I continue further along the track before climbing Mike's steps and ringing his bell. There's no response. He's either out or he's out for the count. As I cross over to my lodge, I see a green woodpecker probing for insects on the grass by the cliff where Gertrude fell. It's resplendent in Catholic-green vestment cloak and blood-red skull cap. The garments of life and hope. The image works on my mind and, as I turn the key in the front door, it comes to me. The woman I brushed into as we were leaving the shop, the one wearing the red scarf, she looked like Ann. The mother of Seb. The boy I misdiagnosed, the boy who died. Of course, it wasn't her, it couldn't have been her. Could it? I sigh, bite my lip and enter the sanctuary of my lodge.

Chapter 9

I'm unnerved by the events of the morning and the woman in the scarf. I need to rest. I ease into my "stress-free" comfy recliner, lie back with my eyes shut, and it's not long before I nod off.

Kathy's standing next to the cliff edge. She's facing me. She leans back, overbalances and, arms flailing, begins to fall. I reach out and catch hold of her hand. She looks at me, recognises me. We smile, then part. She plunges down the cliff. I shout, 'Kathy, Kathy.' She hits the ground and lies still in dense vegetation. Her eyes are fixed, staring up, drilling into me.

I wake, shaken, heart pounding, mouth dry. What was all that about? I try to work it through. Obviously, it was triggered by what's happened to Gertrude. But why Kathy? Is it guilt at missing her lymphoma? That by the time I suspected anything, it had spread to her liver. That I couldn't save her? I picture the scene again. Kathy's facing me, then she's falling. Falling backwards. Did I let go of her or did she let go of me? Am I telling myself I failed her? Is she telling me it's time to release her and move on?

If only she was here now, we could decipher it together. Like when we used to solve the cryptic crosswords.

I close my eyes and picture the two of us. I think of the good times we shared. I calm down, my mind settles. I see her falling again. That's when it comes to me.

Gertrude must have fallen backwards.

If she'd been confused and walked off the cliff edge, she would have fallen forwards, would have been face down when they found her. She would probably have had serious forehead, face and neck injuries. She would have had injuries to her hands and wrists from trying to break her fall. She would have had much worse injuries than I saw. I could be wrong, I'm no forensics expert, but otherwise, it doesn't seem to make sense. Backwards, she would have been unable to break her fall and would have landed on her back, probably smashed her coccyx, possibly her pelvis, maybe injured her spine. It's not what I checked for.

The image of Kathy falling and staring up at me returns. But why would someone walk backwards off a cliff? I lie in my recliner, going over it again and again. My legs are restless. I'm doing the thing with my lip. I need to relax. It's time for me to run through my well-practised routine. First, I concentrate on releasing the tension in my toes, then do the same for my feet, leg muscles, stomach, chest, neck, head and, finally, my mind. The last part is the most difficult. My brain likes to wander off into random uncontrolled thoughts. But I persist and eventually it settles. Well, almost settles. I'm brought out of my relaxed state by the loud ringing of a bell. I drag myself up out of my recliner and open the front door to find James standing on my decking.

'Are you OK, Max? What happened to Gertrude has shaken me. The walk helped, but I can't stop thinking about it. How was Mike?'

'I just had a nap, but yes, it's hard not to keep thinking about it. Mike didn't answer his door.'

'He's probably getting some rest. We should check again to see how he is. Find out if we can do anything.'

James and I walk across the track to Mike's lodge. I ring the bell, and a dishevelled figure opens the door.

'Mike, how are you doing?' I ask.

'I'm OK, thanks, Max. I've tried to get some rest but keep working things over in my mind. The police are coming back later; they need me to run through everything. I'm going to have to make a formal statement about how I was so stupid that I let a woman of seventy-one with dementia, who I was caring for, responsible for, wander off into a stormy dark night close to a cliff edge. I still can't believe it, I really can't. I'm so bloody stupid. It was all my fault. It makes me want to believe we are reincarnated so I can have another go, a second chance. Not have to carry it around with me for what's left of my time on this unforgiving planet.'

I'm not sure about the "I'm OK" bit, but the rest feels brutally honest and self-critical. I suspect Mike is another fellow anxiety sufferer, prone to catastrophising, a perfect case for CBT, possibly even medication.

'Don't blame yourself, Mike, I can't stress enough how often dementia patients go off on walkabouts. It happens all the time. It's just on this occasion, through no fault of yours, Gertrude didn't make it back. Please don't think like this; she wouldn't want you to think like this.'

He looks to the ground. 'I know. I can't help it.'

There's not much I can say. It's like me with Kathy, I can't help feeling the guilt. I try to focus his mind on more practical matters.

'Have you thought about her arrangements?'

'Not yet. Too soon.'

'Is there anything we can do?'

He looks at me, then at James, as though he's working out whether it's a serious offer.

'No, I'm sure I can manage.'

'Have you thought about seeing your GP? Getting some help with sleeping, short term, until the shock wears off.'

'Thanks, Max, I don't need help. I'll be OK.'

I sense he's drawing into himself, wanting to go it alone.

'What are you doing for dinner?'

'Dinner? No plans. I couldn't face lunch; I wasn't hungry.'

'I'm eating at The Six Bells, why don't you join me? Doctor's orders.'

The Six Bells is the Sunrise Park restaurant. It's friendly, welcoming, with a well-stocked bar, an extensive menu, and enormous portions.

'Doctor's orders?' He looks at me. He's torn, waivers, then relents. We agree to meet there at 6.30pm. James lets us know he can't make it, as he has other plans. He's a bit vague about them but I let it go. Sometimes it's best not to intrude.

I've been having problems with my outside lighting, so when I get back to my lodge, I give Paul, our site electrician, a call to see if he can come over to have a look. He's always prompt, helpful and usually manages to sort things out. He responds to the call straight away. He has another job on so can't come at once, but he will look at it later. He doesn't think he'll need me to be home, so I'm all clear for dinner with Mike tonight.

Feeling the need for a relaxing soak, I run myself a bath and lie in steaming bubbles, trying to let the events of the day wash out of my mind. It works and I'm soon nicely relaxed. I think how nice it is not to be dwelling on what happened to Gertrude. I think about what I might do over the Easter weekend. I wonder what Greg and Emma are up to. I let my mind wander. Let it drift.

It's then that another thought comes to me. A dark thought. A "you have to be joking" kind of thought. Maybe Joyce was right. If Gertrude fell backwards, if she fell away from the cliff, maybe someone did give her a helping hand. Maybe she was pushed.

Mike

He knew he'd feel bad. But he didn't expect to feel this bad. But now she was gone, he was safe. He wouldn't have to find somewhere else. He had the house in Halesworth, he had the lodge, and he had money. He could relax. Enjoy life. Not have to constantly pay the price. Her moaning, her goading. The nastiness. Not have to pick up all the pieces from her fallings out. Witness the arguments, the shouting. He no longer had to tread on eggshells. With her, with everyone she came up against. Not have to look after her. Be on call day and night. He could be himself. Do what he wanted. And he'd have more space. He was already thinking about moving into the bigger bedroom. He just didn't think he'd feel this bad. The guilt. He wasn't expecting the guilt. And the loneliness. Like an arm was missing. Already. He wasn't expecting that. But what's done is done. He couldn't reverse time and put her back in her room. It was over. Now he'd have to live with it.

Chapter 10

The double door entrance to The Six Bells gives way to a run of tables either side of the main walkway, each in their own dimly lit cubicle. This opens out to an area where tables sit on a raised platform opposite a long bar that is accompanied by several high stools. Turn left and there's a room with pool tables, turn right and you enter a large, well-lit café diner that leads to outdoor seating overlooking a children's play area. Already, most of the indoor tables are taken and it's a bit too chilly to eat outside. Anyway, I'm not keen on trying to talk over the screams of kids as they let off steam before bed. I have a lot to ask Mike, and I want to be able to hear what he says. I target barmaid Becky, who also doubles as waitress. She must be around nineteen, is always friendly, always helpful. Her pretty, oval face and long dark hair remind me of my first girlfriend.

'Hi, Becky, how are you keeping?'

She smiles at me. 'Fine thanks, Max. You?'

I'm not sure how to respond, as I don't know if she's heard about Gertrude, and I don't want to get involved in a long discussion about it. Not with Mike about to arrive.

'OK, thanks. Pint of the usual and something for yourself.'

'Will do. Thanks, Max.'

'Do you have a quiet table for two free for dinner? Mike's joining me.'

'Mike's joining you?' She frowns and continues, 'It's already busy, I think we might be fully booked. Let me check, I'll see what I can do.'

She disappears into the kitchen behind the bar. After a short while, she returns with a couple of menus.

'Yes, we can squeeze the two of you in. You can have Simon's table. He's got a better offer tonight.'

Simon's The Six Bells' manager. His table doubles as his office, where he often holds court with one or more of his team. Becky leads me, pint in hand, to his corner table tucked well away from the main seating area. It's perfect. I sit myself down and wait for Mike. He soon arrives, dishevelled and out of breath.

'Sorry, I had to take a call from London. I had a few issues to sort.'

'Gertrude?'

'Er, yes, and other stuff. Simon's table, hey, you must have pulled a few strings.'

I suspect that it was Mike who unknowingly pulled the strings, say nothing, and let him settle in. We both scan the now familiar menu. I go for my usual Six Bells BBQ ribs and fries. I take the half rack of ribs, as I once tried the full rack, and it beat me out of sight. Mike goes for The Six Bells version of chicken madras. In my experience, it's more like a pasanda than a madras but Mike seems keen. He also orders a lager. I take a sip from my pint and look at him.

'How are you doing?'

'Still trying to get my head around it all, coming to terms with it. It feels surreal.'

'I can imagine. You've had a shock.'

'Yes, I don't really know how I feel. Mainly numb, I suppose.' He looks down at the table, sees a beer mat, lifts it, slowly flips it and adds, 'Empty, sad, guilty. I feel guilty.'

'Don't torture yourself, it wasn't your fault. It really wasn't.'

'Perhaps,' he responds while flipping another beer mat.

I need to take his mind away from this line of thinking. I need to focus him on something constructive.

'I assume you'll have to wait for the post-mortem before arranging the funeral?'

'Yes, I'm told it won't be until Tuesday, what with the Easter weekend. The funeral won't be until the week after next at the earliest.'

'Do you know her wishes?'

'Not really. Mum and Dad are buried in the cemetery in Tring. It's where they were married.' He pauses, reflects on what he's just said and adds, 'The church, not the cemetery. But it's not where I would want to end up.'

I'm curious. 'Why not?'

'I'm not religious. Unlike them, I've always been a non-believer. Religion has never made any sense. I can't make myself believe there's a God any more than I can make myself believe I'll see Gertrude again. As far as I'm concerned, if there is a God, he's done a good job hiding it. No, I want to be cremated and my ashes sprinkled over Minsmere for the birds to have the last laugh.'

He's a man after my own heart. I want to know more.

'Hiding it? Has life been that hard?'

'I've had my share of misfortune. Losing Gertrude's one in a long line. I started out after Oxford wanting to be a writer but couldn't make it pay. I had a small PR company that went bust. My investments bombed. I ended up bankrupt. One failure after another. To cap it all, my wife Alicia left me, and I lost Mum then Dad within a year of each other. Not a great track record. Look at me, late sixties, I don't even own my own place.'

'I thought you had a house in London?'

'Not anymore, it was repossessed. I stay here at the lodge most of the time. I can do my freelance editorial work without interruptions. It's home; in fact, it's better than home, it's my refuge. The sea, the heath, the birds. They keep me sane.'

'I get that. I lost my wife Kathy almost two years ago. The lodge, Dunwich, Minsmere, they've been my sanctuary.'

There is silence. Mike flips another beer mat and then looks to see where his pint has got to. There's no sign of it. He looks back at me.

'It was the same for Gertrude and Derek. They spent as much time as they could here. They loved walking. Derek would take photos. He used to run wildlife photography classes down the road in Leiston.'

'What happened to him?'

'What happened?'

'When he was run over. When he died.'

'Hit-and-run. He'd just finished an evening class and was crossing the road into the car park.'

'In Leiston?'

'Just going out of the town, the car park opposite the cinema on the road to Aldeburgh.'

'Accident?'

'Maybe, no one knows. Whoever did it didn't hang around. No witnesses, nothing.'

'How could anyone do that? Just leave him.'

'There are some evil people out there.'

'And now Gertrude.'

'Yes, now Gertrude.'

'As they didn't have any kids, I suppose the house and lodge will be yours?'

He gives me a searching look. I can't help thinking it could be a "what's he driving at?" kind of look. The atmosphere between us suddenly feels uncomfortable.

'Yes, I suppose so,' he responds, before quickly adding, 'I wonder where our food has got to?'

Becky arrives right on cue carrying my BBQ ribs, Mike's pint, poppadoms, relishes, madras curry and rice. I breathe in the pungent mix of garlic, cumin and assorted spices.

'Smells good.'

'It is good, you should try it.'

I let him arrange his food on the table and I eye my large plate of sticky sauce-covered ribs.

'Are you planning to spend most of your time here at the lodge?' I ask.

He munches on a poppadom. 'I'll see. Maybe.'

I change tack.

'I haven't seen Felicity today. I wonder where she's got to?'

'No idea. She's been staying at her lodge. I heard that she was going to be here for Easter, but she disappeared last night.'

'James says Gertrude and Felicity didn't get on. Do you know anything about it?'

'It happened before I got here. Apparently, Felicity blamed Gertrude and Derek for causing her husband Peter's heart attack. Seems like nonsense to me. By all accounts, he had heart disease and would get upset with them playing loud music at night. As if that would trigger it. I don't think they spoke after Peter died.'

It confirms what James has already told me. I make a mental note to follow it up with Felicity. I also note that I seem to be transforming from thinking like a retired GP to thinking like a detective. I'm asking questions, probing, seeing where the answers lead. It's fun. It takes my mind away from thinking about Kathy. I look closely at Mike. He's sweating; I assume it's from the madras and not something to do with Felicity. Or Gertrude.

'What's Felicity like?' I ask.

'Pleasant, intelligent, bubbly, smiles a lot. Gertrude always hates it – hated it – when I used to chat to her, but it's hard to avoid each other around here. Why?'

'Oh, just curious. What about your other neighbours, Tim and Louise? How did Gertrude get on with them?'

The question sets Mike off. He stops eating, puts his knife and fork down and leans forward, looking directly at me.

'That's a whole different thing; they're nasty. Don't get me started. They insist on parking out front of their lodge and blocking our sea view. It wound Gertrude up, really got to her. They have a spot next to their lodge, their official space, but they never use it. Apparently, it blocks their sea view. Well, they knew that before they bought the lodge. They knew where their parking spot was, it was bloody marked out for them. Every time we complain, we get a torrent of abuse from Tim. It doesn't help that he drinks like a fish. Every night. He just had to see Gertrude when he was drunk for him to give her a mouthful. Mind you, she gave as good as she got.'

Mike's clearly not a fan of our neighbour, Tim. Although I've witnessed a few of their heated "discussions", I've hardly spoken to him since I've been here.

'I haven't seen his car for a while and don't see either of them around the site very often. Why's that?'

'No, you won't. Not now. Gertrude kept complaining and the park stopped them parking there. Tim wasn't happy. Then he lost his licence. Louise has their car.'

'Lost his licence?'

'Yes. Drink driving. Not very surprising. They have a house in Lowestoft where Louise lives with the kids. Tim stays here on his own, works at Sizewell. He's head of security or something. He gets taken back and forth by taxi, spends his time there during the day, drinking in the bar here at night.'

'How about George and Julia, did Gertrude know them well?'

Mike looks at me and furrows his eyebrows. 'Wow, this is turning into an interrogation.'

'Sorry, I didn't know Gertrude well and I won't now. I'm just interested.'

'It's OK.'

He's then silent and seems to be thinking about whether to respond to my question.

'Not much to say really. They go way back. I remember them being friendly years ago, but I don't think that they've been close for a while. I guess her dementia made it difficult.'

We finish our main course. I ask Mike if he wants dessert, he gives it a miss and I do likewise. It's been a long day, and I want to get back in time to take Emma's call. I realise I've not mentioned to Mike my suspicion that Gertrude might have been pushed. It feels too soon, too insensitive. It can wait until I feel the time is right.

Chapter 11

It's already dark when we stroll back to our respective lodges, guided by the subdued site lighting and our mobile phones. I'm climbing the steps to my front door when my phone rings. It's Emma.

'Hi, Dad. How are you?'

'Emma. Hang on, I'm just opening the front door. Two secs, let me get inside. I'm kind of OK. You?'

'Yes, I'm fine. What do you mean kind of OK?'

'It's been a traumatic day.'

'Traumatic?'

I enter my lodge and ease down in my living room recliner ready for a long conversation.

'One of my neighbours, Gertrude, the nice old lady opposite – you must have seen her – she fell down the cliff last night. She died.'

'Oh my God!' Emma exclaims. 'What… Gertrude, tall, grey hair, rambled on a lot? Angry about Sizewell C?'

'Yes, Gertrude. She had dementia; it's been getting worse. I think she was ready for a nursing home.'

'Oh, Dad, I am sorry.'

'To be fair I didn't know her well.'

'But it must still be a shock.'

'It was, it is. I spotted her body this morning. She'd fallen down the cliff by my lodge. They pulled her up and the police asked me to look at her and confirm she was dead. She must have been killed in the fall; there was nothing anyone could do.'

'You spotted the body?'

'Well, at first, I just saw one of her shoes halfway down the cliff. It was red and covered by vegetation. I nearly missed it. Now I'll never forget it.'

'Hadn't she recently lost her husband? Wasn't her brother looking after her? I met him the last time I was there. What's his name?'

'Mike.'

'Yes, Mike. Poor man, he must be devastated.'

'Yes, we just had dinner. He blames himself, feels guilty for letting her wander off in the storm last night.'

'Knowing you, you'll be comforting him.'

'I'm trying.'

'Do you want me to come down at the weekend for some company and a bit of support?'

'No need, I'm fine.'

'I'm free and was thinking of coming anyway. I may as well tell you now. Greg and I were going to surprise you for Easter. It's why I wanted to speak with you. I wanted to make sure you were going to be there. We wanted to be with you, and we've booked a concert on Monday in Ipswich. It would be great if we can use the lodge and go from there as it's so much closer. You don't mind, do you?'

'Of course not. It'll be lovely to see you both, especially over Easter. What's the concert?'

'Ed Sheeran. He's from Suffolk; he's doing a special, one-off gig.'

'Ed Sheeran, he did "The A Team". Kathy, we, used to sing it together. Of course you can stay. When will you be arriving?'

'Saturday mid-afternoon, if that's OK.'

'Can't wait.'

'Thanks, Dad. I've got to go. I've cooked dinner for a friend. He's about to arrive.'

'Anyone I know?'

'Just a friend. I'll tell you about him at the weekend. Bye, love you lots.'

'Bye, Emma. Love you too.'

The call leaves me feeling happy, even excited. It will be so good to see her and Greg over Easter. I put the kettle on to make myself a celebratory cup of tea. My eyes then catch sight of the collection of bottles that sit on my sideboard. The temptation is too great. I opt for the malt whisky, pour myself a large one, add several cubes of ice, take my first sip and savour the smoky, back of the throat bite. I then hear the familiar sound of the kettle turning itself off after having done its job and feel a pang of guilt at having wasted the energy. I'm just glad Emma's not here to witness it. Like Gertrude, she's a keen eco-warrior.

I tell Alexa to play Vaughan Williams before retrieving my journal out of my rucksack. I like to write notes on my day before bed. It relaxes me, allows me to work things through, helps me put things into perspective. Today, I need a dose of all three. I write for the best part of an hour, by which time I've finished three generous helpings of whisky and been soothed by *The Lark Ascending*, *Fantasia on a Theme by Thomas Tallis* and a selection of other wonderfully sedate, evocatively English classics.

I turn in early, happy to put the day behind me and, as usual, sleep for just a few hours before I need to relieve my bladder. I struggle to get back to sleep and lie in bed thinking about Gertrude. Was it an accident or was she pushed? I can't help seeing the image of her lying face up on the stretcher with no obvious injury to her forehead, nose, eyes, wrists, or hands. This doesn't feel right if she'd fallen forwards. She must have fallen backwards. She must have been pushed. I know I'll have to wait for the post-mortem, but I can't help thinking it. I'm searching for any small detail that might help me understand better what happened. And if she was pushed, who would have done it? Who could have done it? Is one of Sunny Drive's lodge owners a murderer? I try to take this in. It doesn't feel possible. It must have been an accident. But if it was one of my neighbours, which one? Who would want Gertrude dead? I need to find out. I need to spend time with them gathering information, piecing things together.

This isn't helping me get back to sleep. I'm obsessing, going over things again and again, just like before. When I was waiting for the result of the hearing, not knowing whether it was my fault. Whether I was to blame. Whether I'd missed anything, should have played it safe and referred Seb to hospital. Should have done things differently. I need to break the cycle. I close my eyes and run through my relaxation routine while listening to the sound of the sea through my open window. I'm walking with Kathy, barefoot, along the Dunwich shoreline. Waves are gently breaking, sun is shining on calm water, there is soft, warm sand beneath my feet. It takes me a while but eventually it works. This time, I sleep through until morning.

Chapter 12

I enjoy my coffee and porridge sitting outside, listening to Mozart's *Jupiter* symphony and admiring the sun blaze an orange shaft across the sea. It's warm, a kind April breeze blows across my face, several gulls pass overhead emitting grunts and squawks and squealy laughs. More gulls, and what looks like a red-throated diver, sit on the water enjoying the gentle ride.

The police barrier tape hangs loose, swaying back and forth in front of the cliff edge. It makes me think of Gertrude. It gives me the urge to do some detective work. I leave my decking, walk over to it and peer down at the surf fizzing back and forth as each wave washes on to the shore. I then look on the ground at the top of the cliff for anything unusual. There are numerous footprints. It's not surprising, considering how many people were here yesterday. I check the bushes and, lifting the tape, nip under it before grabbing my trusty laurel to peer down to where I first saw Gertrude's red shoe. The cliff face seems untouched, but just above where she was lying, the ground has been disturbed. It could have been where she landed and possibly bounced before coming to rest under the bushes. I can't tell whether the marks were from her back or her front. Then again, they could have been made by the rescue team. It seems odd that the police aren't here. I suppose when you have an old lady with dementia falling over a cliff, it's thought of as an accident unless there's good reason to suspect otherwise. I wonder whether the post-mortem will provide answers, and I wonder if, by then, the scene will no longer hold any clues to what happened.

My phone rings and I step away from the cliff edge to take the call. It's Greg.

'Hi, Dad, how are you?'

'OK. You?'

'Good. I understand Emma's told you we're planning to stay with you at the lodge over Easter. It was meant to be a surprise. It'll be great to see you and we've got an Ed Sheeran concert on Monday night. It is OK, isn't it?'

'It's fine, it will be lovely to have you around.'

'Great, thanks. Emma said one of your neighbours fell down the cliff or something. Is that right?'

'Yes, Gertrude, she died. It was probably an accident, she had dementia, but we're all shaken.'

'I'm not surprised you're shaken.' He pauses then adds, 'Probably an accident. What are you not telling us?'

Greg doesn't miss a thing. He's always been sharp. He takes after his mother.

'I'll tell you about it when I see you.' I don't want him to ask me to explain it now, so I quickly change subject. 'Are you OK if I arrange for us to visit Aunt Sally in Leiston while you're here? I'm sure she would like to see you and Emma. Perhaps on Easter Sunday?'

'That would be good; Mum would have liked it.'

'Great. Emma said you'll be arriving mid-afternoon.'

'Yes, if it's OK. I'm driving her up in my new convertible.'

'Mid-afternoon's fine, it will give me a chance to get some basics in. Don't drive too fast. I know you'll want to put the car through its paces but it's better for the two of you to get here later all in one piece. There's a key in the key safe by the BBQ in case I'm out.'

'Remind me, what's the code?'

'242526.'

'Great, do you need us to bring anything?'

'Just yourselves. Oh, and Easter eggs.'

'Of course, see you tomorrow.'

I ring off and immediately receive another call. It's Paul.

'Max. Sorry about last night, I was on the drag all day then my daughters needed me back home. I can come now if it's OK.'

'Yes, it's fine.' I have visions of him arriving off his head spaced out on dope. 'On the drag?' I ask.

'Sorry, running late. It's what we say in Suffolk.'

Paul

He should have been there with them. He knew how they hated storms. How scared Kylie got. He couldn't expect Karen to have to always look after her sister. She was still just a child. But he had to work. He had to put dinner on the table and make sure they had what they needed. Their school stuff, clothes, latest phones, latest games, music. All the things their friends had. But it was wrong. It wasn't natural. He shouldn't have to do this. If only they had Jean back. Kylie needed her, Karen needed her. He needed her. The job, the girls, everything. It was too much, and it wasn't fair. But now everything was such a mess. He couldn't keep doing this. *Come on*, he thought, *you need to hold it together. For the girls.* He had to be there for them. Jean's mum would help when she could. But she had her dad to look after. He had to accept things. That they'd play up, be wild. It was natural. But Karen was so argumentative, always in trouble. She was never like that when Jean was alive. And Kylie's so quiet. It wasn't natural. *Come on*, he thought, *you have got to keep going. They need you to help them through.* He had to make sure he would always be there. For them, for Jean.

Chapter 13

Paul is usually reliable, so, although he doesn't live on site, if he says he'll be here shortly, he will be. Sure enough, within ten minutes, Paul turns up. He must be in his mid-thirties, short, stocky, clean-shaven with dark hair and a thick Suffolk accent.

'Hi, Max. You alright? I have a few jobs on site this morning, so this works out nicely. What's the problem?'

'My outside lights aren't working. I think it started in the storm we had the night before last.'

'OK, let me have a look. It may be something's shorted. You've checked the fuse?'

'Yes, it keeps tripping.'

He heads to the fuse box and confirms it for himself.

'OK, let me check the outside switch,' he says, before unscrewing the faulty device by the front door and taking a good look. 'It's damp, probably got wet in the storm. I'll need to dry it out and seal it properly. Happens a lot with these newer lodges with their fancy outside switches. The storm did the same to Tim's. Leave it to me.'

Paul does what he needs to do with the switch and when he's finished, I offer him a mug of tea. We stand either side of the kitchen island unit, he's unlikely to want to stay long and it feels more informal.

I ask about the switch. 'Everything OK?'

'I'm fine, thanks, Max. You?'

It's not what I was expecting. As he's asking, I answer, 'To be honest, I'm shaken up by what happened to Gertrude.'

'Yes, I don't understand what she was doing out, especially on such a rum night. It was just as bad around my way in Leiston, it scared the hell out of my Kylie. She's ten, can't handle bad storms. Her sister Karen had to calm her down; she's just twelve. Since we lost their mother, she's had to step up.'

He has a sip of tea to check the temperature then takes a good gulp, looks at the floor and waits for me to respond.

'What happened to their mother?'

'Jean, she died. Not long ago.'

'Oh, I'm sorry. Must be hard.'

'We were expecting it but yes, it is, very. On me and the girls. We miss her.'

He turns away and stares out of the glazed doors while gently cradling his mug. I sense he would rather not talk about it.

'Do you spend all your time here at Sunrise or do you have other jobs outside the park?'

Paul looks back towards me, seemingly relieved with the change of subject.

'I mainly work here and do outside jobs from time to time. I've got a major rewiring job on now up at the Coastguards.'

'The Cottages, it's beautiful. So peaceful. My late wife

Kathy's parents were from Leiston. They loved Dunwich heath and often used to visit the Coastguards. When they died, we had a bench installed there dedicated to them. It sits up on the clifftop looking out to sea across Minsmere reed beds.'

'I know it. I used to sit there with Jean. We'd chat for hours, enjoying the view, making plans, putting the world to rights. It's where we got engaged, our special place.'

'It's where we scattered Kathy's parent's ashes. Then hers.'

'Leiston's a small place, my mum and dad probably knew them.'

'Eric and Olive Westleton, same spelling as the village. He was a local policeman based in Orford during the first half of the war, then Leiston after the war.'

'In Leiston?'

'Yes, Kathy's mum Olive looked after the police house where he was based. It's what police wives did. It's where Kathy was born.'

'She grew up in Leiston?'

'Yes, born and raised. Eric and Olive loved going to the clifftop overlooking Minsmere. They would take Kathy and her sister to enjoy the view and picnic where the bench is now. Sometimes Eric would go on his own and sit thinking about crimes he was working on. He said it was where he could think best, where his mind was most sharp.'

Paul looks back down at the floor. He's deep in thought. I let him reflect in silence, before he hands me his empty mug.

'I've got to head off, thanks for the brew. The switch should be fine. I'll check it again in a couple of days.'

I watch Paul go, thinking that I can't help liking him, feeling for him. It won't be easy bringing up a young family on his own. Life does throw up some terrible situations.

Chapter 14

I make my way out through the double doors on to my decking and almost immediately hear the ominous sound of the poo lorry. The poo team come around every few days to pump out the septic tanks and it's a sign for all in the vicinity to shut their doors and windows. There are few downsides to life at Sunrise Park; the poo lorry is one of them. Two members of the site team jump out of the lorry; one looks up at me.

'You alright, Max? Ready for cleansing?'

'Hang on, I'll just shut the windows and doors.'

'Squeamish townie, can't take the smell of the country? This is where Gertrude went over the cliff, isn't it? She hated us coming around, really hated it, called us all sorts. It's not like she didn't need to have the tank emptied. We're just doing our jobs.'

I realise that the sewage tanks need emptying, but the smell always gets to me. It raises my stress level, puts my blood pressure up. I know it shouldn't; I can't help it. I step inside, close the doors and head for my telescope. It's trained on the bird feeder close to the cliff edge where a pair of thick-set cheeky greenfinches are at work. I watch for a few minutes before giving the scope a gentle swivel and point it out to sea. A large tanker is working its way north far out on the horizon. The light is good and the sun shines across calm water illuminating a small yacht in the mid distance. A procession of dark forms fly past. From their shapes, size and flight patterns, I suspect a combination of rapid wingbeat cormorants and smaller common scoters. As I scan across the water, I lock in on a couple of red-throated divers bobbing on the surface. I watch for a while as they disappear under the water and reappear, often quite a distance from where they submerged. I'm completely absorbed and it's not long before the nature therapy has eased my blood pressure.

I open the doors, return to my decking and, although a whiff of the sewage lingers, the poo lorry has gone. Sheila, a lodge owner from one of the other site tracks, is walking past with Betty Boo, her Jack Russell terrier. A trickle of dogs and their proud owners pass by the lodge throughout the day. We usually acknowledge one another, and I've even got to know a few of the pooches that come in a wide variety of shapes and sizes. I've never been much of a dog person, but I can now tell a springer spaniel from a cocker spaniel (smaller, fluffy coat) and a Labrador from a golden retriever (longer nose, wavy coat). Sheila and Betty Boo are regulars, passing twice daily come rain or shine, followed at a discrete distance by Sheila's ginger cat, Sooty.

'Morning, Sheila. How are Betty Boo and Sooty today?'
'Fine thanks, Max. How are you?'
'Just getting over what happened to Gertrude.'

'Yes, it's terrible. I can't believe it happened. Here, right here. I mean, right there.' She turns to face the cliff edge where poor Gertrude had her misadventure before adding, 'I'm surprised they haven't cordoned more of it off. What if someone else goes over the top?'

I have a vision of Betty Boo taking off with Sheila in tow followed by Sooty, and the three of them disappearing down the cliff.

'Come on, Sheila, I doubt that's going to happen. I don't think it's happened here before and I doubt it will happen again. Gertrude was unwell and probably confused by the storm. The police don't seem too bothered. I suppose they must be satisfied it was an accident, although we need to wait and see what the post-mortem finds.'

'Yes, it was quite a storm. I lost my electrics and had Paul look at them. I wasn't the only one, I think he also had to sort out Tim's lights. Gertrude was probably lost and frightened. It doesn't bear thinking about.' Sheila pauses and looks down at Betty Boo before adding, 'Even so, I wouldn't be surprised if someone gave her a bit of a shove. She did have quite a nasty streak, she put more than a few people's backs up. Especially since she lost Derek.'

I wonder whether she's been speaking with Joyce.

'Why do you say that?' I ask.

'It just crossed my mind.'

'Whose backs?'

'Felicity for one. George, Tim, James, even Mike. She used to have a go at him all the time. He's probably relieved she's not around anymore.'

'Mike's upset. I don't know about the others. Why would they bear a grudge?'

'Oh, just things she used to say to them, the way she used to bait them. I see a lot on my walks, you know.'

'Like what?'

'Oh, that's for me to know and you to find out.'

With that, she gives me a smile, tugs Betty Boo's lead and heads off followed by Sooty. As she goes I peer over the decking balustrade to see who else might be about and spy Felicity tending to daffodils that form a border in front of her lodge. She's just the person I need to speak to.

Felicity

Now the poo lorry has gone, she can get on with deadheading the fading daffodils that form a neat border along the front of her lodge. It had been a good year with an abundance of bright-yellow blooms. But her mind keeps returning to that night. It's muddled, but the more she works with her secateurs, the more she remembers. The wind buffeting the windows and the rain pounding on the roof of her lodge. It had perfectly matched her mood. Pouring herself another glass of wine. Only a little being left in the bottle. Thinking, *where did that go?* then removing an unopened one from the fridge. Sancerre, Peter's favourite. Bought especially for the evening. Their evening. Even though she knew she'd be drinking it on her own. It was what she had wanted. It was right. That night was not one to be spent with anyone else. Was it really thirty-five years? Arriving late at the church, the rain, the umbrella, the walk down the aisle. Heads turning, smiling. She remembers looking through their wedding photo album on the kitchen unit next to the Sancerre. Each picture a distantly happy, recently painful memory. And she remembers the tears creeping out of the corners of her eyes. Feeling them trickle down her face. Then the anger. Thinking of how Peter had not been able to sleep because of the music. How stressed he'd become. The constant late-night music. How it drove him crazy. Drove them both crazy. Then, the heart attack. She remembers hearing the music again in her mind. And she remembers hearing something else. Knocking. Thinking it must be the rain or the wind. But it hadn't stopped. It had just got louder.

Chapter 15

I decide to see if Felicity fancies a walk along the beach to Dunwich for lunch and cross the track to her.

'Morning, Felicity, what a lovely day. How are you?'

She glances up at me and then carries on doing what she's doing.

'Hi, Max, I'm OK now the poo lorry has gone. Just tending the daffs, removing the deadheads. Pretty good show.'

'Yes, you can't beat daffs for a splash of colour.' I pause then ask, 'I suppose you heard about Gertrude?'

She stops deadheading and turns towards me. She looks troubled.

'Yes, James told me. I had to head off early yesterday. I was in Yarmouth nannying my grandchild. I missed it all. Poor Mike, he must be heartbroken.'

'Yes, he's very upset, shocked. We all are. I'm going for a walk up the beach to Dunwich to clear my head. Maybe have a fish and chip lunch at Laura Tea Rooms.'

'Sounds nice.'

'Fancy joining me?'

Felicity stares at her daffodils, ponders a while as though checking a diary in her head and smiles at me.

'It would be lovely, Max, I thought you'd never ask!'

I'm worried she might have the wrong idea. 'It's not a date or anything.'

'I know, I'm teasing. Give me five minutes.'

Laura Tea Rooms, or Laura's as we like to call it, is a wonderful fish and chip café in Dunwich village, a forty-minute walk north along the beach. In my view, it does the best fish and chips in Suffolk. You can either sit outside at trestle tables close to the pebble beach overlooking Dunwich marshes, or inside when the weather is unkind. I hope to be sitting outside today. I also hope that Felicity will tell me about her relationship, or lack of it, with Gertrude. If the walk doesn't do the job, I figure a few glasses of wine afterwards at The Dunwich Boat might.

I return to my lodge to don boots, fleece, walking jacket and rucksack. I also place my binos around my neck. I can't go on a walk without them, especially today with Felicity. I'm meant to be birdwatching not bird-pulling. We walk south along the cliff edge path to the steep Sunrise Park steps that lead down to the beach. They are not for the timid, but we negotiate them successfully. The cliffs give way to shingle interspersed with patches of vegetation including cabbage-like sage-green sea kale and clusters of rare horned poppy with deeply lobed leaves. I love their yellow flowers that decorate the upper beach in June.

We make our way towards the sea, initially slowly as our boots sink deep into the small smooth pebbles, until we reach an expanse of firm, wet sand along the shoreline where walking is less of an effort. The beach is virtually deserted. We head north towards Dunwich with the sea to our right gently easing in and out, spewing its white froth as we pass. A young couple with a small yapping dog repeatedly cast a stick into the water for it to retrieve. An older couple collecting pebbles walk past going south towards the Coastguard Cottages. Two graceful terns with angular wings and forked tails flap above the sea, heads still, eyes intent. They watch for dark shape movement before plunging intermittently to spike their prey.

'It's so beautiful here. With the sun shining and the breeze kind, like today, it's an unspoilt slice of paradise,' I say.

'Yes, it's lovely and with so few people. We're very lucky.'

'My wife Kathy loved it here. She grew up as a girl in Leiston and would bike to the beach with friends after school. I'm from North London. Apart from holidays, our local park was the closest we got to nature. Here you can have it every day, be part of it, breathe it in, feel alive in it.'

'I heard that your wife died.'

'Almost two years ago. Cancer.'

'I'm sorry. You must miss her.'

'Yes, every day. It doesn't seem to get any easier, I suppose I need to give it time. It's what I used to tell my patients. And you? I believe you lost your husband.'

'Peter, he had a heart attack.'

'I'm sorry.'

We fall silent, each aware of the other's loss. It comes to me that if Sunrise Park was not situated on the east coast, it would be much more appropriately named Sunset

Park, as so many of us seem to have lost our partners. I guess for some it's part of the attraction of the place. Being together with others in the same boat, enjoying our solo lives bonded by loss and a common love of nature.

'He'd had heart disease for a while and a previous heart attack. He was always on a short fuse. I thought coming here would relax him; it just made him worse. It didn't help next door winding him up with their incessant late-night music.'

'Gertrude and Derek?'

'Yes, Gertrude and Derek. Nightmare. Whenever we tried to complain, they ignored us. They were as bad as each other.'

'Maybe, but it's terrible what's happened to them. Derek and now Gertrude.'

Felicity doesn't respond. Instead, she changes the subject.

'Look at Southwold; it's gorgeous. I love the ghostly white lighthouse blinking away at us. It's my favourite seaside town, so photogenic. I've been taking lessons to try to capture it.'

'Yes, Southwold was always the kids' favourite. They loved the amusement arcade, quirky pier and crazy golf.'

'How many children do you have?'

'Two, Emma and Greg. Both long flown the nest. Emma's twenty-six, Greg thirty. They live in London.'

'When are their birthdays?'

'Birthdays?'

'Yes, for their star signs.'

'Oh, right. Emma's is September twenty-fourth, Greg's July twenty-fifth.'

'Libra and Leo. Emma's balanced, Greg's dramatic.'

I'm not big on believing in things that don't have a solid evidence base and, to me, astrology falls squarely into this category.

'Not noticeably. Emma's in marketing and loves her amateur dramatics. Greg's an accountant. He's into skiing and supports Spurs. Does that make him dramatic? I guess it might. Astrology's not really my thing.'

'When's yours?'

'May twenty-sixth.'

'Gemini. Curious and playful.'

'I'm not sure about curious, but I'd like to know more about what's meant by playful.'

'You know, having fun, that sort of thing,' she answers, giving me a quizzical look.

'I'm just playing. When's yours?'

'July fifth. Cancer. Intuitive, temperamental, devoted.'

'Devoted? To your children? How many?'

'Two, Tom and Charlotte. They live in Yarmouth. Tom's in sales, Charlotte's an interior designer. One grandchild, Sophie, just two and completely adorable. I try to see her and help Charlotte out whenever I can. I divide my time between here and there, but I don't like to overdo it. Peter would have loved watching her grow up.'

Despite the astrology, I like Felicity. She's bright, thoughtful, around fifty-five with not unattractive blue eyes, a smallish nose and mid-length fair hair. What's not to like? Just the sort of woman I can see getting involved again, but not with me. No one can replace Kathy. I decide to find out about her relationship with the other Sunrise Park inmates.

'How well do you know the other lodge owners?'

'Not well, I tend to keep myself to myself. We chat a bit when they pass my lodge, or if I meet them in the bar or around the site. Mike seems pleasant, George and Julia too. Oh, and James, I know James. I don't really know Tim and Louise. I haven't heard particularly nice things, so I keep my distance. Thankfully, they aren't about much.'

'I wonder if Mike will stay?'

'What, in Dunwich? I don't see why not. He seems to like it here. I can't think of any reason for him to leave.'

'I suppose so, although the memory of Gertrude and how she died might be an issue for him.'

'I hadn't thought of that, I suppose it could be. I know he's blaming himself for letting her wander out in the storm, but I can't see it was his fault. She was always strong-willed and would do what she wanted. Anyway, her mind's been going for a while, she should have been in a home out of harm's way. Still, can't be helped now. I don't like talking about Gertrude. Can we change the subject, please?'

I can take a hint.

'Do you work?'

'No, I'm retired. I was a teacher. Peter was older; when he retired, I did the same so we could spend more time together. We would come here.'

We're closing in on Dunwich and up ahead on the shingle are groups of holidaymakers, a few braving it in costumes and bikinis, some with beach chairs, windbreaks, even Li-Los. Children are playing ball games, building sandcastles and a few are swimming in the cold North Sea. It's what's been missing from the stretch of beach we've just walked along. The area a half mile or so either side of the Sunrise Park steps is often practically deserted. It's part of the charm of the site.

We pass several beached fishing boats with ropes leading into the sea and out to fixed anchors. A couple of anglers are set up on the pebbles trying their luck. We continue, taking care to avoid their lines, before heading up the beach more slowly over deep shingle towards Laura's and then my chance to find out more about Felicity over a bottle of wine at The Boat.

Chapter 16

The outside trestle tables at Laura's are packed with families all tucking into enormous fillets of fried fish accompanied by chips, mushy peas and cups of tea. Water bowls are scattered on the ground providing refreshment for the numerous dogs after their walkies along the coast. It's peak hour for lunch, there's a long queue in line for ordering and it's not moving quickly.

I turn to Felicity and say, 'The queue doesn't look good. How about we try The Boat? Their fish and chips are almost as good, and we can get a bottle of wine. What do you think?'

'Sounds perfect, let's go for it. I've always loved The Boat.'

We walk a couple of hundred yards inland and arrive at an eighteenth-century terracotta roof-tiled pub that sits at the heart of tiny Dunwich village. It was once a thriving port, the second most important in England and rumoured to have had twelve churches all now lost to the sea. We walk through The Boat reception area where the staff nod to Felicity, before claiming a trestle table in the back garden. I don't even bother to look at the menu.

'Fish, chips and a bottle of wine?'

'Plaice for me, please.'

'Red or white? I usually go for the Sauvignon Blanc.'

'Perfect. Their New Zealand's best.'

I head inside to order. When I arrive back, Felicity is standing away from the table talking on her phone. I sit, remove my journal from my rucksack and begin to write a few notes. I find capturing what I do, what I see, what people say, is best fresh just like the fish we're about to be served. Felicity returns and sits opposite me with the tense frowning face of someone who's upset.

'Everything OK?'

'Yes, I'm alright. Making notes in your infamous journal?'

'Infamous journal?'

'Yes, we wonder what you write. Whether it's about us, our secrets, our affairs. It's a bit of a standing joke.'

I look at her, she's smiling but I sense that she's serious.

'I had no idea, I'm sorry.'

'Don't be silly, whatever turns you on. It would be interesting to know what goes in it though.'

I keep my answer vague.

'This and that. What I see, any unusual birds, observations, thoughts, that sort of thing. Nothing special.'

'Am I an unusual bird?' She says with a big smile.

'Maybe.' I smile back.

Felicity adds, 'I like working with words. I used to keep a diary. When the kids came along, it took too much time, so I started playing Scrabble instead.'

'Yes, Scrabble's fun. I used to play with the family. Did you play much with Peter?'

'We often sat out on the decking, sharing a bottle of wine, a bar of chocolate and a bag of letters.'

'What was he like?'

'At Scrabble?'

'As a person.'

'He was clever, highly strung, enthusiastic.' She stops, as though thinking what else to add. 'And kind. He was thoughtful.' She pauses again and then continues, 'We met at teacher training college. He was my first proper boyfriend. He was a teacher, later a head. He was wonderful at it; the children loved him. He was so good with them and with his staff. I was lucky to have him. We had lovely times together, especially here. We enjoyed walks across the heath and by the sea, had meals out, went to concerts, played Scrabble. Life was good… then he had his heart attack.'

Felicity finishes and looks at the table. She's upset. She seems to get upset whenever she talks about Peter. I'm trying to think of a way to change subject when I'm saved by our food arriving. Two giant, oval plates crammed with fried fish, chips and petit pois to which we add salt, vinegar and, in my case, ketchup. I pour us a large glass each of the Sauvignon Blanc and we begin eating in appreciative silence. I watch her; she seems to be savouring every mouthful.

'The fish here's so fresh, it's as good as you get anywhere in the country,' I say.

'Yes, and you can't beat their beer batter.'

It's an open goal. 'You don't need to. It doesn't have any eggs.'

'Very good. You would have got on well with Peter. That's right up his street.'

Back to Peter, it didn't take long. The wine's not taking long either. As I pour what's left into our almost empty glasses, Felicity watches me closely.

'I shouldn't drink so fast; it goes to my head. Since Peter died, it's made me morose. It never used to, we used to get happy together and do silly stuff… you know, dance or… I don't know, fun stuff.'

'Yes, it's the fun stuff, the silly spontaneous stuff, I miss most with Kathy. That and the company. Having someone to share things with.'

'We all need that.'

Felicity takes a gulp of wine, and, with her glass half empty, I have no option but to fetch another bottle. After all, it's part of my interrogation technique. When I arrive back, she's on the phone again and this time the conversation seems more animated. I fill our glasses and seeing me turns her sullen face into a smile. She rings off.

'You sure everything's OK?' I ask.

'Just a few family issues.'

'Nothing too serious, I hope. Families. Greg and Emma are coming to stay for Easter, I can't wait.'

'That's nice. They must be a comfort after losing Kathy.'

'They are. We all need others to help get us through the tough times. Family, friends, neighbours. What's happened to Gertrude has made me think that us lodge dwellers need to stick together. Get to know one another better. Who knows what might happen? When we might need each other for help, support, an ear, a shoulder… tea bags.'

'It's about being thoughtful, being kind. I used to be kind. I used to be caring. Like Peter. He – we – knew everyone. Helped everyone. Losing Peter, I've changed. I've become bitter and selfish.'

'Really?'

'Yes. And it's too late now.'

'What do you mean "too late"? Too late for what?'

Felicity takes another gulp of wine, looks me in the eye and then turns away. She's struggling with something. When she turns back, I see tears well up and spill out of the corners of her eyes. They roll down her cheeks.

'Too late for Gertrude.'

'What are you talking about? Why? What do you mean "too late"?'

'That terrible woman. I killed her.'

'You what?'

'I killed her.'

'You killed her?'

'Well, as good as.'

'Why? What did you do?'

'No, you don't understand, it's what I didn't do.'

'What didn't you do?'

'That night, the storm. I'd had a few glasses of wine. Well, more than a few, I was morose. I was down. Horribly down. It was our anniversary – well, it would have been our anniversary. I had all the photos out. Charlotte was going to be with me, but Sophie wasn't well, and Tom had a work conference. I was on my own. I heard knocking at the door. Well, more of a tapping. I ignored it at first, but it kept on, was getting louder, more insistent. I wondered who it could be so eventually I slipped the chain on and

90

opened up. It was Gertrude. She was like a ghost. Soaking wet, talking rubbish about how I'd killed Derek. How I'd run him over. How it was me who'd been the hit-and-run driver. Me! She went on and on. She was upset and angry. I told her she was being stupid, but she just carried on at me. She wouldn't go away. I closed the door, but she kept knocking and shouting. Eventually, I took off the chain, opened the door and marched her out of my drive. I pushed her away and she headed off. Staggered, really. I didn't think about it at the time, but later, when I found out what had happened to her, I realised she was heading towards the end of the track... towards the cliff edge. I simply didn't think about it. I just went back inside, put myself to bed and went to sleep. It was all my fault. All I had to do was walk her home, keep her safe. All I had to do was the right thing, be nice, be kind, do what Peter would have done. Instead, I sent her away. I got rid of her. She was confused and disorientated. I will never forgive myself, ever. I'm just a horrible person.'

I sit back and take in what Felicity has said. I was hoping my interrogation technique would pay dividends, but I wasn't expecting this. I've had a fair amount of wine so I'm not as clear-headed as I would like to be. I've no idea what to say next. Should I be understanding and tell her, as with Mike, that it wasn't her fault? But what if she's not telling me all that happened? What if it wasn't an accident? What if she marched Gertrude to the cliff edge? What if Felicity had pushed her? I have no idea what to say, no idea at all. She sobs, blows her nose and is quietly distraught. I can't help feeling sorry for her and, after a while, say what seems right, what feels humane.

'You're not horrible. You were upset and you were drunk. You didn't know, couldn't have known, what would happen. It's not your fault.'

She dabs her eyes with a tissue.

'Of course I'd no idea. But she was confused, and she was upset. I just made it worse. I didn't like her, but she didn't deserve that. I abandoned her. The next morning, I woke early and remembered what I'd done. I remembered turning her away. I couldn't bear to be around in case I came across her, so I bolted to Yarmouth. Later, when I heard what had happened, her falling, dying, I was stunned. I had to come back. It's so awful, so horrible. And it's all my fault.'

'It's not your fault, it was a terrible accident.'

'Right. It was a terrible accident, and it was my fault. Max, can we get the bill? I want to go now, please.'

We walk back to Sunrise Park inland through mixed woods with the sea rumbling beneath the cliffs behind the trees to our left. We're subdued and return in awkward silence. I part with her just after entering the site, making an excuse that I need something from the shop. It's probably best for us not to be seen drunk together; the site gossip would be unbearable.

As I enter, Joyce greets me enthusiastically.

'Hello, Max, did I see Felicity with you just now?'

So much for avoiding site gossip. I try to nip it in the bud with some honesty.

'Yes, we just had lunch together at The Boat. Nothing in it though, I promise. I'm not ready for another relationship so soon after losing my wife.'

She smiles at me. 'I understand; others might not.

Around here, gossip spreads like wildfire. You need to be careful.'

'Right. Thanks. Do you have any paracetamol?'

'For the hangover? Good thinking, I like a planner.'

'Something like that. By the way, I've been meaning to ask, I brushed past a lady wearing a red scarf the last time I was in. She seemed familiar. Do you remember her?'

'Red scarf the last time you were in? I can't recall her. Sorry, I don't think it was any of my regulars. She was probably a short-term camper. Old flame then, Max?'

'No, just someone I thought I might have known. Don't worry, it probably wasn't her.'

'I won't. Need anything else?'

'No, that's it.'

'Nothing for Felicity? She's a one and she does like her chocolates.'

'No, nothing for Felicity.'

Joyce gives me a big grin. She never fails to amuse.

Chapter 17

I sleep off the effects of the wine and when I wake, it's early evening. I can't remember the last time I drank a whole bottle of wine at lunch. It did the job though. Felicity, could she be Gertrude's killer? She certainly hated her, was drunk and had the opportunity. Was she lying about marching her to the track and then just leaving her? I want to believe Felicity, I do, but should I? She says she last saw Gertrude heading towards the cliff, confused and alone. If that's true it would mean that unless someone else knew she was wandering around, my theory about Gertrude having been pushed is likely to be wrong. Maybe it is wrong, maybe she lost her bearings and fell. Maybe it was just an unfortunate accident. But backwards? Would she really have accidently fallen backwards? This is getting me nowhere. I decide to see how Mike is coping, cross the drive to his lodge, ring his bell and wait for him to come to the door. When he does, I notice he has red puffy eyes.

'Hi, Mike, I came to see how you are. Is there anything I can do? Anything you need?'

'Maybe some company. Come in, Max. Fancy a coffee?'

'That would be great. I overindulged in Sauvignon Blanc at lunch, I would usually have a decaf but right now I can use the caffeine.'

It's the first time I've been inside Gertrude and Mike's place, so I take a good look around. The Sunrise Park lodges are a mixed bag of makes, shapes, sizes, and ages. Some are more luxurious than others and their specification is a constant topic of conversation. This one is at the top end of the range, being light and airy, with a high ceiling, bootility entrance, a well laid-out kitchen and a good-sized combined living and dining area.

'Nice lodge, Mike. It's a lot like mine.'

'Yes, Gertrude replaced the old one a couple of years ago. Haven't you got three bedrooms?'

'Yes, so Greg and Emma can stay.'

'Wine at lunch? Did you go anywhere special?'

'The Boat at Dunwich. I walked up the beach with Felicity.'

'You were with Felicity? I didn't know you two were close.'

'We're not. She was deadheading her daffodils, and we got chatting. I thought it was about time I got to know her better.'

'How did it go?'

'Good, she's nice.'

'How is she?'

I wonder what to tell him. Whether to let him know what Felicity had told me. He needs to know. I don't want him feeling what happened to Gertrude was all his fault.

'Upset. Like you, she blames herself for what happened.'

'What happened?'

'To Gertrude.'

'Why? What did she have to do with it?'

'It would have been her and Peter's anniversary. She'd had a few drinks. Gertrude showed up wet from the storm, bedraggled and confused. She turned her away.'

'What? Turned her away in the storm? Felicity did? For God's sake, why?'

'Gertrude was shouting the odds about her running down Derek.'

'Oh, that again. Even so, she knew Gertrude was ill, knew she had dementia. I thought Felicity was better than that, much better than that.'

'I guess she blamed Gertrude and Derek for Peter's death. It being her anniversary and drunk, she just didn't have it in her to forgive, or forget.'

'Still, it was mean. In fact, worse than mean, it was vindictive. So, it wasn't just me. I was negligent, she was vindictive. We're both to blame.'

He looks upset and angry, although I also detect some relief that he wasn't the only one to blame. I decide to move the conversation on.

'Mike, have you spoken to the police? Given your statement?'

'Yes, they came earlier. I went through things with them. It seems it's being thought of as an accident. We'll have to wait for the post-mortem, but I don't think they see it as at all suspicious. Confused old lady, out in a storm, wandered off a cliff. Open and shut case.'

'You know, Mike, I'm not so sure.'

'What? What do you mean "not so sure"?'

'Just a feeling. I didn't have much time with her, maybe I'm wrong, so it's probably best to wait for the post-mortem.'

'No, come on. Why not so sure?'

I pause and wonder how much to tell him.

'She was found on her back, face up. Apart from the abrasions, she had no signs of major injury to the front of her head or her hands.'

'That's it?'

I hesitate, then add, 'Her wrists looked fine. She hadn't tried to break her fall with them. I didn't check her back, coccyx, or the back of her head, so I can't be certain, but I reckon that's where the post-mortem will find serious injuries. It all points to her having fallen backwards down the cliff. But why would she fall backwards? I just can't help wondering whether she was pushed.'

'Pushed? You can't be serious. No way. Pushed? Someone pushed Gertrude. Who would want to do that? You're having me on, you are, aren't you?'

'It's just a feeling. We'll have to wait for the post-mortem. Perhaps there's a perfectly reasonable explanation. Perhaps she twisted around somehow, it's not my area of expertise. I could be wrong.'

Mike's eyes are wide, his eyebrows raised and mouth open. He looks genuinely shocked.

'You've got to be kidding me. Of course, you could be wrong. But you're serious, aren't you? You think someone pushed Gertrude over the cliff.'

'Yes. I'm serious.'

'But who would do such a thing? I mean, Gertrude? Are you thinking Felicity? You are? It's why you took her for lunch, isn't it? Felicity, a murderer. You can't be serious.'

'It has crossed my mind, but she doesn't seem the type. Did anyone else have a grudge against Gertrude?'

Mike thinks for a while before responding, 'She wasn't the most popular person on the site. I was surprised; even though she could be mean to me, I never thought of her as unpopular. Feisty, maybe, but not unpopular. Not until I came here.'

'Who did she fall out with?'

'Well, you know about Felicity. Tim, of course, because of the parking. George is another one, she practically accused him and his company of killing Derek.'

'What's his company got to do with it?'

Mike pauses and seems reluctant to answer. He changes his mind. 'He's got a construction company. Derek had a friend who'd picked up an eye injury while working as a subcontractor for them. He let slip they'd recently covered up a series of site accidents when working on one of the Sizewell C preparatory projects. George was worried it would cost his company the bigger, more lucrative building projects out for tender now the new power station is going ahead.'

'But what had it got to do with Gertrude?'

'She and Derek were actively involved in trying to stop Sizewell C. They went on marches, put up posters, attended meetings, that sort of thing. Derek told her about the site accidents and when he was killed in the hit-and-run, she accused George. You know how she was. She couldn't stop herself, would ramble on endlessly about George having killed him. She even tried to report her suspicions to the police, but she had no evidence. Frankly, it was ridiculous, but once she'd made her mind up about something, she never let go. With her dementia, she had no qualms about what she said. She was loud. What Gertrude thought didn't stay hidden for long. George threatened to sue her, but I suspect it was a bluff. The publicity would have been terrible.'

This is getting more confusing by the minute.

'I thought she blamed Felicity for what happened to Derek?'

'She did, and George. She was angry and confused. Would hit out any way she could. At me, at them, at others. She wasn't well, not in the last few months.'

No wonder Gertrude wasn't popular. The more I dig, the more suspects keep coming out of the woodwork. This is getting far too complicated. And what about Mike? He seems to be the only one who stands to gain a legacy from her death. It's in his interest for the post-mortem to go smoothly so he gets his hands on the Halesworth house, the lodge, and some security. I let the thought go.

'The sooner the post-mortem tells us what happened, the better. It would be good to move on. It's not nice being here thinking that one of our site neighbours could have pushed Gertrude over a cliff. Greg and Emma are coming to stay for the weekend, I don't think I want them around knowing that.'

'Exactly, I'm sure it'll be fine. With the police saying they don't think her death was in any way suspicious, I'm sure the post-mortem will conclude the same. Anyway, you'll need to excuse me, I need to get ready. I'm having dinner in Aldeburgh with a friend.'

And with that, he shows me to the door. I can't face seeing anyone else tonight; my brain already has more than enough to process. I make myself an omelette for tea and check the Birdline website to see what unusual local sightings have been reported. There's a purple heron in Southwold, a black kite over Dunwich Heath and, best of all, a white-tailed eagle over Minsmere. I have only ever seen one before. It was the size of a barn door, evil-eyed with an enormous chunky, yellow bill. As soon as it appeared, all the other birds scrambled into the air as one. The fear in them was palpable. It flew slowly, wings alternately flapping then still, floating, majestically crossing the scrape waters looking for an unsuspecting fish, duck, or other tasty morsel. I don't want to miss it, so I make a mental note to visit Minsmere in the morning. I then watch TV, have a bath, update my journal, and turn in early.

I lie in bed thinking. Was it an accident? Was Felicity to blame? Was it Mike? What about George? I don't really know him. Tomorrow, I need to get to know George.

Chapter 18

I wake, pull on tracksuit bottoms, do what I need to in the bathroom, head for the living room, draw back the curtains and let the sun's rays flood the room. I tell Alexa it's time for some Mozart, make myself a cup of decaf, open the patio doors and gaze out at sharp, white light washing over a flat, glistening North Sea. It's lovely.

Leaving my lodge, I walk across to the barrier tape and look down at gentle waves rolling onto a thin strip of sand along the shoreline. It's perfect for a bracing swim to start the day. I change into trunks, sand shoes and beach robe, grab a towel, collect my goggles, lock up and head for the steps that lead down to the beach. I cross the pebbles to the sand, remove my robe and don't waste any time getting into the water. I know it will be cold, very cold, but I'm not one for torturing myself by slowly immersing my body bit by bit. I take a few steps until the sea reaches my knees then dive in, fully embracing the experience. I think of it like how I learnt to manage my panic attacks. I feel the chill, welcome it as a friend, let it wash over me, don't fight it, and tell myself it can't hurt me. I swim a few strokes before fixing goggles over my eyes and heading north. Facing into the wind and tide, I don't make much headway and remain virtually in line with my things on the beach, but I'm soon in a good rhythm.

I let my mind wander, thinking of Kathy, of us swimming here together. She would get me up early if the weather was half decent, almost dragging me to the sea, not wanting to waste a moment of the "deep sense of life" that she said it made her feel. I imagine her with me now. I then think of Emma and Greg and how nice it'll be to see them over Easter. Maybe even have a swim together. After twenty minutes or so, I turn over and float on my back, riding the swell. I lower my goggles, placing them around my neck, and look inland at the sandy cliffs covered in bright green bracken, brambles, small pines and a swathe of vegetation. I scan south towards Minsmere, then north to Dunwich. Someone is walking along the upper beach at the bottom of the cliffs alongside the barrier tape that surrounds the base of the site where Gertrude was found. I try to make out who it is, but they're too far away. I can't even tell if it's a man or a woman. They seem to be looking over the tape searching for something. Just nosy, I expect. I swim back to shore to take a closer view, but when I scan to where the person was walking, there's no sign of them. It was probably one of the campers wondering what the tape is protecting. I head back to my lodge for breakfast.

I have the news on the TV as I prepare my porridge. As always, it's mostly bad but it seems less immediate and less relevant here. That's until there's a piece about Sizewell C. Although it's been given the go-ahead, the protests are continuing, and the environmentalists have not given up hope of the decision being reversed. There's going to be a legal challenge. I have a momentary burst of optimism, but I know it's not realistic. The government will do everything they can to get their precious new power station. I sigh, head outside to eat my breakfast and notice George and Julia sitting at their decking table. George is on his laptop; Julia's reading a magazine. Walking to the balustrade closest to them, I lean over and catch their attention.

'Morning, looks like another nice day.'

Julia looks up at me and smiles. 'Certainly does, Max. How are you?'

'Good thanks. I just had a swim; the water's lovely.'

'Lovely? Don't you mean freezing?'

'No, bracing but lovely.'

She shudders. 'What are your plans over Easter?'

'Emma and Greg are coming to stay.'

'Nice. Our son Alan came last week. We hadn't seen him in a while.'

'They're here for an Ed Sheeran concert.'

'Alan's just started working for an advertising agency in London.'

'Emma's in marketing. Greg's an accountant.'

'They're one of the top agencies. He's doing so well.'

'They both seem happy.'

'And he's got himself a lovely girlfriend.'

It feels like the start of an offspring competition. I change subject.

'I still can't get my head around what happened to Gertrude.'

It does the job.

'Yes, it's awful, such a shock. Poor thing must have been confused in the storm.'

'Probably. It does seem strange though.'

George looks up from his computer and stares at me. 'Morning, Max. Strange? Why strange?'

'Just strange.'

'Intriguing, I would love to find out more, but I need to do some prep for an online meeting. How do you fancy coming over for lunch and a proper catch-up? We're planning to have salade niçoise. Why don't you join us?'

I don't have to think hard about this one. It's exactly what I fancy. 'Sounds good. I'll bring a bottle.'

Julia

Julia couldn't help it. She knew that she should feel sad about Gertrude. She should but she just couldn't. She supposed that it must make her a terrible person. Perhaps she was. But she remembered how Gertrude had always had an eye for George. How sure she was that they used to get together behind her back. She couldn't prove it, but she knew. A woman could tell. Could always tell. The way they had been. So close. So over friendly. How she was always coming around with her big kiss on the lips hello and her, 'I thought you might like to try one of my new recipes.' How he was always helping her out with odd jobs. Jobs "that Derek couldn't possibly manage". A woman knew. She just did. But that was years ago. Then more recently, how it had all blown up between the two of them. How sudden it was. How angry they had become with each other. How George had begun to hate Gertrude, hate Derek. He always said it was over Sizewell. But she hadn't believed him. Still didn't. She was sure it was more. There must have been something else. George used to get so upset when talking about it.

So bitterly upset. Anyway, she was glad that woman had gone. She shouldn't be, she knew she shouldn't be, but she was. She just was.

Chapter 19

I finish my now cold coffee and porridge, head back inside, add a few paragraphs to my journal and check Birdline on my phone. The white-tailed eagle has not been seen since yesterday, but the black kite is still around the heath and the equally unusual purple heron has moved from Southwold to Minsmere. I feel a walk to the RSPB reserve coming on, but I'll need to be back in time for my lunch appointment. I wonder if James is free to join me. I want to find out what Sheila was referring to when she said Gertrude had put his back up. I also want to hear if he's found out anything new, as he's always plugged in to the goings on at Sunrise Park. I don boots, walking jacket, rucksack and binos before locking up and heading next door to see if he's up for a walk. I ring his doorbell and have just a short wait before he pops his head out.

'Yes? Oh, it's you, Max, come in.'

I hover outside his lodge as I don't want to take my boots off for just a brief visit. 'I'm off on a walk. There are reports locally of a black kite and a purple heron. Fancy joining me?'

James raises his eyebrows, it's obvious he's interested.

'Black kite? Purple heron? Where abouts?'

'The black kite's been seen over the heath, the purple heron's at Minsmere.'

'I was planning a walk in that direction. I'm going to The Elver for lunch. I could tag along.'

Now I have a dilemma. Salade niçoise with George and Julia or pub lunch with James? As much as a stone-baked pizza and a pint at The Elver appeals, I figure I can get James to spill the beans on our walk and have George do the same over lunch.

'Sorry, I can't do lunch, I've been invited for salade niçoise at George and Julia's. We can walk across the heath to Minsmere. You can head on to The Elver from there.'

'You can't do lunch? Good... sorry, the walk sounds good. Hang on, give me five minutes to change.'

While waiting for James, I stroll to the cliff edge, and peer down at the beach and out to sea. The tide's out so it would make sense to walk along the shore on the firm sand to Minsmere. We might catch sight of some interesting sea birds and should get a good view of sand martins nesting in the cliffs. When James reappears, he agrees the route and we set off along the cliff edge path, make our way down the steep steps to the beach and head south along the water's edge. We walk side by side; there's just enough firm sand to make it possible without one of us getting caught by the surf that washes onto the beach.

'Any news on the post-mortem?' James asks.

I'm next to the sea so respond while keeping my eyes firmly fixed on the water lapping close to my feet.

'Mike's been told it'll be after Easter. The police have been a couple of times to talk to him. It seems to be straightforward; they're treating it as accidental.'

James picks up a pebble, throws it into the sea and carries on walking. 'I guess so. Confused and disorientated in the storm, she tripped over one of the logs protecting the cliff edge, staggered, then fell. It makes sense.'

'It's possible but the logs are six feet from the edge. And I don't understand how she had so few injuries to the front of her head, wrists and hands. If she'd fallen forwards, they'd have been a mess. From what I saw when I gave her a once-over, there were just scratches from the brambles and a few abrasions. But I only checked her front, the main injuries must have been to her back, her coccyx, possibly the back of her head. That would be most likely to have happened if she'd fallen backwards.'

'Backwards? Why would she fall backwards?'

'Exactly. I can't help wondering whether she may have been pushed.'

I watch closely for his reaction; he doesn't disappoint. He stops walking, grabs my elbow, and fixes me with his eyes.

'What do you mean she may have been pushed? You think Gertrude was pushed? No way. Who would do such a thing?'

'I have no idea. Unprompted, both Joyce and Sheila have said they wouldn't be surprised if someone had given her a bit of a shove. That she had a nasty streak, had put quite a few people's backs up.'

'Really? You shouldn't take notice of them. The site gossips. It makes them feel important. Did they give any names?'

'Sheila mentioned Felicity, George, Tim, Mike… even you.'

'Felicity? Me? She said Gertrude had put my back up? I can't think what she means. I never got on well with her, but there wasn't any ill feeling. I must have a word with Sheila, find out what she's on about.'

I look into his eyes and try to see if he's genuine in not knowing what Sheila was talking about. I guess I need to give him the benefit of the doubt.

'Have you mentioned this to anyone else?' he asks.

'What, about the possibility of Gertrude having been pushed? Just Mike, he was as shocked as you.'

'What, shocked that she may have been pushed or shocked at you for thinking it?'

'Both, I suppose.'

We begin walking again; there's silence between us. James tosses another pebble out to sea.

'If anyone had anything to gain from Gertrude's death, it's Mike. I mean, he inherits the lot. The lodge, the house in Halesworth, the investments. Derek built up a successful photography agency and sold it for a good sum when he retired. The pair of them were reasonably well off.'

I decide not to respond. As we walk along the beach, we keep a look out for birdlife. It's a habit that even Gertrude can't break. Gulls and terns are playing in the gentle breeze over the sea while, inland, sand martins fly in and out of tunnels excavated into the sheer face of the upper reaches of the sandy cliffs. We stop and watch them closely through our binos. They are busy collecting roots and other plant material, bringing them back to line their nests.

'It's good to see them back. Such a lovely, lively little bird. There must be at least fifty,' I observe.

'Noisy though, they always seem to be squabbling,' James responds.

'Nesting, it's a competitive business.'

We start walking again and soon reach Minsmere Reserve, where we head up the beach before continuing south along the perimeter of one of Europe's finest reed beds. We stop still. A large stoat, probably a male, is emerging from a sandy burrow, brown head and back framing his vanilla breast like a choc ice with a bite removed. He sees us and freezes. His head is immobile while his shiny nose twitches and his dark eyes flicker as they assess the situation. We are in a stand-off. I imagine him drawing two pistols on us. Instead, he turns around and skips back into the burrow, followed by his signature black-tipped tail. It's just such an encounter that makes the place so precious.

We scan inland across the reserve for anything unusual. A pair of large waders fly over the reed bed. Curlews, their curved bills pointing to the ground as if being pulled down to earth. To our left, we hear a liquid trill and turn to see a pair of linnets perched upright on a gorse bush, the male with its bright pink forehead and chest, the less showy female more pale and streaky brown. James is watching the birds, but his mind is dwelling on what I've just said about Gertrude.

'Have you told the police about your suspicions? That Gertrude may have fallen backwards, might have been pushed.'

'Not yet, no. I'm no expert. The post-mortem will flag up anything unusual. It will find if she fell forwards or backwards. I can't see why they would take me seriously, I'm not sure I do. It's just something I can't get out of my head. I can't work out from her injuries how else it could have happened.'

'You realise that you're saying we might have a killer amongst us at Sunrise Park. You really need to be careful who you tell this to.'

'Maybe there is a killer amongst us.'

'Come on, Max, listen to yourself, you're getting carried away. I don't believe it for a second. It's like a sick joke.'

We start walking again. I think about what James has just said and wonder if he has a point.

'You're probably right and I'm probably being stupid. But I just can't stop thinking about it. I can get obsessive.'

'I can't stop thinking about it either,' he says, before pausing and then continuing, 'since they found Gertrude, I can't stop thinking about my sister, how she fell, how she died. I keep getting flashbacks.'

'What happened?'

He says nothing for a while. I wait to see if he wants to tell me. When he does, it's as if he's reliving it.

'We were in a fifth-floor apartment in London. We'd not been there long. She was just five. I leant out of the window. It was a long way down. I remember looking at the tops of trees in the park opposite. There was a large bird sitting on one of them. It was jet black. It was probably a crow. I can still see it flapping its wings. When I came back in, I moved away from the window then dared her to do what I'd done. Margaret laughed, pushed past me and leant out. She shouted, "It's so high," toppled, screamed, and disappeared. I couldn't believe it. It took me ages to pluck up the courage to go back to the window. When I did, I looked down and saw her lying on the ground, not moving. She was wearing a light blue polka dot dress and white socks. I'll always remember her dress. She was two years younger than me. I'll never forget it, never forget her.'

It feels like a confession. It's obvious that he still feels guilty. He must have carried that guilt through most of his life. I think of my guilt over Kathy. It seems almost petty.

'I'm so sorry. Did you get counselling?'

'No, I don't suppose anyone did then.'

'I suppose not.' I pause and add, 'It might explain your anxiety.'

'Possibly. I don't like to think about it.'

We walk in silence.

James asks, 'You mentioned about your anxiety having been caused by a patient, a child. What happened? Can you talk about it?'

There are times when I can't bring myself to think about what happened, let alone talk about it. After what James has just told me, this isn't one of them.

'Yes, it's public knowledge.' I pause, brace myself and continue, 'A mother brought a boy in to see me; he was just over a year old. He'd been vomiting, had diarrhoea, was running a fever, high temperature, fast pulse. I diagnosed viral gastroenteritis and told his mum to give him paracetamol, lots of fluids and keep him cool. I advised her to keep an eye on him to make sure he didn't get any worse. If he did, she should contact me. I even gave her my mobile number. She put him down in his cot overnight and in the morning, he was dead. She'd not checked on him. Not once. It was meningococcal meningitis. I'd completely missed it.'

'I'm sure you did your best.'

'My best wasn't good enough. There'd been no rash, no purpura, no neck stiffness. Nothing to suggest it was meningitis. Well, nothing I picked up on. But she depended on me. He depended on me. And I missed it. If I'd just given him antibiotics or referred him, he probably would have been OK. But I didn't and he died. It was my fault. Well, I thought it was my fault. I was cleared of medical negligence, but it got to me. I started to doubt myself. I became anxious each time I had to treat a child, obsessive in making sure I didn't miss anything. I would worry I'd get a diagnosis wrong. I started having nightmares, panic attacks, then constant anxiety. It was horrible. Later, when Kathy became ill, I retired to look after her.'

'Sounds awful.'

'It was. I'll never forgive myself.'

Chapter 20

We walk in silence before reaching the steps and narrow passageway that runs between tall bushes and trees leading to Minsmere Reserve's East Hide. It always gives me a sense of excitement, not knowing what awaits once we get into the two-storey wooden viewing building with its wide window slits looking out over a large expanse of the reserve's saline lagoons. Being here puts the memory of my missed diagnosis to the back of my mind.

The scrape is managed to provide the best conditions for the numerous waders, ducks, gulls and assorted other birds that live, or visit, here. The water level is controlled by sluices, the salinity is monitored, and islands provide nesting sites protected from foxes, stoats, and other ground predators. We enter the hide, head for the upper tier, sit on the bench and peer out. A barrage of sound greets us. Loud-mouthed, harsh-screeching, black-headed gulls and slightly larger Mediterranean gulls lead the chorus, but many other species compete to be heard. Gulls, terns and assorted waders are squabbling, staking out territorial claims, wooing prospective partners ahead of the breeding season. Intermittent fights break out, the noise rising to a crescendo with each cut and thrust. We watch a battlefield fought over by the rulers and potential rulers of a patchwork of prime Minsmere real estate. In a month or so, the battles will become more intense, there will be casualties as they eat the eggs and cannibalise the young of their rivals. It's in their nature. They will do anything to increase the chances of their young surviving.

We spend half an hour watching this glorious spectacle, hardly speaking. Numerous pied, thin-legged avocets with long, upturned bills wade in the shallows looking for crustaceans, worms and other unsuspecting invertebrates. But there's no sign of the purple heron. We leave the hide and walk on to the tidal sluice that sits on the edge of the beach just outside Minsmere Reserve. As we look down into its exposed chambers, water flows in from three sides echoing and resonating to make a satisfyingly deep gurgle. I'm thinking about when the children were young and used to shout out loud to hear their voices come back to them. But James is still thinking about Gertrude.

'I've been mulling over what you said. I can't work out who would have known Gertrude was out wandering about in the storm apart from Mike.'

I decide to be open with him.

'Felicity told me Gertrude knocked on her door that night. She was confused and sharp-tongued. She said she sent her away... well, walked her back to the track. The last she saw of Gertrude was her heading towards the cliff edge.'

'My God, Felicity told you that?'

'Yes, she says she'd been drinking heavily – it would have been her and Peter's anniversary. She hates herself for it. Even so, it doesn't explain Gertrude's injuries or lack of them to her front.'

'No, not unless you think she walked her to the cliff, turned her around and gave her a shove. But who would do that? Certainly not Felicity, I just don't buy it. She hasn't got it in her. Never, not in a million years. It's not in her nature.'

'Who knows what's in our nature? Animals murder their own species all the time. When I was young, I had a hamster. Hammy. He shared a cage with my brother Marcus's hamster, Sammy. Hammy was light brown, Sammy was dark brown, larger, fatter. They spent a lot of time on their running wheel. I always used to boast Hammy was faster. One morning, Mum told me someone had left the cage door open; Sammy was still there but Hammy had escaped. We looked everywhere but couldn't find him. I carried on searching for months but Mum and Dad gave up after just one or two days. I could never work out why. I cried myself to sleep many times over Hammy. Years later, at a family meal, Mum asked whether I remembered when Marcus's hamster ate mine. I was shocked. To be fair, it was as much that Sammy had eaten my Hammy as my parents had lied to me. Hamsters are cannibals; many species are cannibals. Pigs, hedgehogs, spiders, even rabbits are known to eat their own species. Ant colonies fight vicious wars. Male lions slaughter all the cubs when they takeover a new pride. Our closest relatives are among the worst. Chimpanzees kill each other at the same rate as we do. It's often to make sure their own young survive. They will do anything for their families, anything. Murder is in their nature, it's in all of ours.'

'Really, Felicity? Why would she need to protect her kids from Gertrude? And I assume it's lucky Gertrude ended up halfway down the cliff or Felicity would have gorged on her body.'

I realise he's joking, but I check for a smile anyway.

'You take my point, it's in us all. Yes, it's buried deep. Most of us control the urge, but in the right circumstances, who knows what we're capable of?'

'Maybe, but not Felicity.'

We walk on along the coast towards Sizewell, keeping our ears alert for the sound of anything unusual. I have heard, and seen, woodlark and nightingale here. But not today. Today, we hear another sound. It's coming from the beach in front of the Sizewell power stations. As we get closer, we see a long line of protesters holding aloft placards and chanting what sounds like, 'EDF off.'

'Mike is with them,' James says, pointing him out. 'Look, he's holding a placard: "I don't want to be beside the C side".'

We approach our neighbour.

'Mike, nice slogan. What are you doing here?' James asks.

Mike does a double take, smiles, then waves his placard.

'Gertrude would never have forgiven me if I'd missed this. She and Derek were part of the Stop Sizewell C group that organised it. We've walked from Leiston; it's done me good. There's over three hundred of us. I wanted to be here for her. It seems right.'

'She'd be proud,' I say, scanning around and noticing several photographers. 'Looks like you're getting good media coverage.'

'Yes, we've had press, TV, radio. The decision may have been made, but it's not too late to reverse it.'

The chanting dies down, and instead we hear a small group with placards shouting, 'Jobs not snobs.' They are goading the Stop Sizewell C protesters. What look like security staff in orange jackets are trying to keep the two sides apart. As I watch, I see the human barrier breached, the two opposing groups clash, and punches are thrown. Several uniformed police officers appear and some of the troublemakers are removed. Then I see another face that I recognise. Tim is manhandling a few of the anti-Sizewell protesters away from the pro group. It's like he and his team are defending them. And it's obvious that he's seen me. He gives me what I can only describe as a prolonged glare, then returns to his work in hand with what seems like increased vigour. He's not one for taking prisoners.

'This is getting nasty,' James says, touching my arm. 'We need to get going, and anyway, I've got a lunch appointment.'

I look around at the protest scene, think about staying, but then remember my salade niçoise with George and Julia. As we leave, I pat Mike on the back.

'Have fun and go easy on the "jobs not snobs" brigade.'

George

George pulls into Sizewell car park. He's been tipped off about the march. From his high vantage point, he can watch what's going on. Protesters. Hundreds of them. With their sandals, denims, beards and socialist ideologies. He notes their placards. He notes their faces. Angry faces. Some young, some old. *I'll give them "Sizewell C, not for me"*, he thinks. *They have no idea. Saving the planet when locals don't have jobs. Climate change, green energy. As if what we do makes any difference. India, China, Brazil, they're the ones that need to change. Anyway, nuclear is green. Morons.* Then he sees three faces he recognises. Mike, James and Max. *What are they doing here? Mike's just lost his sister. What's he doing here? These people really are crazy.* But he wasn't going to let a few protesters ruin things. He needed Sizewell C. The contracts were almost in the bag. The wheels had been oiled and the leg work had been done. He just needed the projects to be signed off. A few bloody protesters. Holding things up, slowing things down. Consultations, reviews, hearings, appeals. He needed them to just get on with it. It was simple. The country needed the power, his company needed the work. Why couldn't they just get on with it? Bloody activists. *Oh well, I better get back for lunch with Max. I wonder what he'll have to say for himself.*

Chapter 21

We retrace our steps north along the coast back to Minsmere, then cut inland through the reserve and arrive at a junction that forks off to Island Mere. This is where we part company. James continues through the reed beds to the quiet, narrow road that leads to Eastbridge and The Elver pub. I watch him go, wondering how he will react to my suspicion about Gertrude's death. It's good to have someone else in the know but what if it's him? What if he's the murderer? I feel a tightening of my stomach and realise I'm biting my lip. I just don't know who I can trust.

Taking the wooden ramp to Island Mere hide, I breathe in the damp earth smell of untamed reed bed that hints at wilderness, adventure and respite from the chores, responsibilities and repetition of everyday life. I join several other birders on the top shelf of the double-decker viewing hut who already have their binoculars and telescopes trained on the mere. There's a brief turning of heads as I arrive, before they all get back to the serious business of bird spotting. A murmur goes up from the hide inhabitants as a marsh harrier comes into sight, flapping lazily over the reed bed. It's a male with something in its talons, probably a small bird or mammal. Another harrier joins him; it's larger, darker, chocolate-brown with a cream forehead. The female. The two engage in an arial dance, the male rising high in the sky followed by his mate before he passes the meal to her. Another collective murmur breaks out. A chestnut-streaked thickset heron has broken cover to our left and is slowly skulking through the shallow waters. Bittern. I watch transfixed before being distracted by the unmistakable nasal pings of a black-moustached bearded tit flying low over the reeds. It's a remarkable bird. I once read that they rise high in the sky in large flocks in the autumn as a way of assessing their numbers and determining how many need to migrate away from their reed bed to preserve an optimum population.

I spend a further half hour in the hide in the hope of seeing the purple heron but there's no sign of it. I reluctantly make my way out of the reserve, taking the path over the heath that leads back to my lodge and lunch with George and Julia. I've only walked a short distance when I notice a woman heading towards me. She has a familiar face.

'Felicity, I thought it was you. Have you recovered from our lunch? It took me a while.'

'Fancy seeing you here, Max. I'm fine. Sorry if I got a bit morose. Please don't tell anyone what I said about Gertrude; it wasn't my finest hour.'

Sadly, she's too late with her request. Do I fess up or keep quiet and hope she never finds out? I opt for the latter and add a sprinkling of guilt to my touch of anxiety.

'Where are you off to?'

'Oh, just taking a walk. Enjoying the sun, clearing my head. You know. You?'

'I've been with James seeing what birds are about. There was a report of a purple heron and a black kite. I'm now heading back to the lodge.'

'James? You've been with James? Any luck?'

'Not with them, but I've just seen marsh harrier, a bittern and bearded tit.'

'I'm not a bird person, but it sounds successful. Maybe see you later, I must get a move on.'

'OK, enjoy your walk.'

We part with me wondering why, if she's just clearing her head, she's in such a hurry.

Chapter 22

I consider whether George and Julia are red wine, white wine or Prosecco people. As it's salade niçoise, I go for a New Zealand Sauvignon Blanc. Even if it's not their cup of tea, it's mine, so at least one of us will be happy. I head next door and make my way up the steps leading to their decking where George is putting plates, cutlery and glasses onto a round, wooden table. He's short, stocky, with a close-cropped, almost shaven, bull-like head and thick stubby hands. A bruiser, someone to have on your side in a fight. Julia is busy inside; she's the same height as George but leaner with grey-blue eyes and a more open, less intimidating manner.

'Hi, George, how was your morning?'

He gives me a lukewarm smile and shakes my hand.

'I've had a couple of useful online meetings, and I tackled a few jobs around the lodge. There's always something. One of the bedroom window locks was broken; I managed to mend it, then I fixed a dripping tap. But the kitchen skylight won't open, I can't seem to sort it.'

'Have you called Harvey? He's pretty good at that stuff.'

'Yes, he's coming later. I try to do what I can, but it's nice to have a decent handyman on tap.'

'I've had a problem with my outside lights; Paul's been fixing it. Where we live in Surrey, getting an electrician is almost impossible. I… I mean where I live.'

'Yes, the benefits of a Sunrise Park lodge.'

Julia shouts "hi" from inside and then appears with a bowl of olives that she exchanges for my bottle of wine.

'Thanks, Max, my favourite and nicely chilled. Have you had a good morning?'

'I've been with James, we walked to Minsmere checking what birds are around.'

'Anything unusual?'

'No, but some nice sightings. We were hoping to catch sight of the purple heron that's been seen. I've not had one here before.'

'Right. I assume it's like a grey heron but purple?'

'Well, sort of. It's darker, slimmer, thinner bill with a black stripe down a longer neck.'

'I'll take your word for it. I assume you didn't see it?'

'No, it's secretive, it could still be there.'

'Does that count? Can you add it to your list, as you were in the same general area as the bird?'

I get the impression Julia's not a birder. I feel the need to justify myself.

'I'm not a twitcher. I don't travel all over the country for a bird I've not seen before to add it to my list. I just love watching them and identifying them. It's satisfying, gives me a focus, takes me out of myself.'

'A bit like George and his trains.'

'You a trainspotter, George?'

'Used to be, not really got the time now,' he answers, downing an olive. 'It's not something I can do in Dunwich with there being no trains. Of course, when they build Sizewell C, they're likely to reopen the Leiston branch from Saxmundham. Another benefit of the project.'

I'm not sure that being able to trainspot is a great reason for building a nuclear power station, but I've just arrived, so I let it go. George pours us each a glass of wine and we sit around the table chatting while nibbling on the olives. I hadn't clocked George as the trainspotting type but there's no accounting for taste. The mere mention of the subject has set him off.

'There used to be a railway running through Saxmundham, Leiston, Thorpeness and as far as Aldeburgh. Beeching wanted to close the whole of the East Suffolk line, but the locals fought to keep it open. The Aldeburgh branch survived until the mid-sixties. There's a group of us trying to get it reopened.' He stops, pauses then adds, 'It's not looking promising.'

The disused track is now a path running between Aldeburgh and Thorpeness flanked by RSPB North Warren with lagoons and marshland hosting thousands of ducks, swans and geese in winter, and breeding bitterns, marsh harriers, woodlarks and nightingales in spring. Reopening the Aldeburgh train line would create havoc.

'I can't see it reopening, George. Apart from anything else, the RSPB would never let it happen. It would destroy an internationally important bird habitat.'

'I know, just like Sizewell C. That's going ahead so why not reopen the Aldeburgh train line? Think of the boost to tourism, local jobs and the area.'

George and I are on a collision course; this could get heated. Julia, with impeccable timing, disappears inside just as I rise to George's bait.

'The area is precious, so many species will suffer, many of them rare, some endangered. I don't think Sizewell C should go ahead, let alone reopening the Aldeburgh train line. Sorry, George, the area doesn't need a railway or jobs that badly.'

'Are you seriously against Sizewell C when the country needs energy? Come on. For a few birds? You're crazy. You, Mike, James, the lot of you.'

'What's wrong with renewables? Look at the wind farm just off the coast here. It's cheap and clean. And it's safe. No long-term issue with dangerous waste. What about solar?'

Julia chooses the moment to reappear with three huge bowls of salade niçoise copiously decorated with large, pitted olives.

'Now, now, guys. Calm down. Let's eat. And please can we talk about something else? There's no point giving yourselves indigestion.'

'Thanks, Julia, it looks amazing. Are the olives from Dale Farm shop?'

'Of course. Nothing but the best.'

We eat, drink and chat while looking out over the sea.

'How long have you had your lodge?' I ask.

'Almost twenty years,' Julia answers. 'The site's changed a lot. When we first arrived, it was almost all caravans and tents. The lodges have been added over time.'

'You must be some of the longest serving inmates?'

'Probably, let me think. Sheila's been around as long as we have. Derek and Gertrude were here when we arrived; they bought their lodge before us and upgraded it a few years ago.'

'Were you friendly with them?'

'We were at first, but we fell out.'

'Fell out?'

George joins in. 'Gertrude came on to me. Julia never forgave her. It didn't help when Sizewell C was proposed. Derek and Gertrude were against it. Like you, Max. But they were angry, bitter, wouldn't talk to me when they found out I was all for it. They couldn't see the wood for the trees.'

I can't help noting the irony of George's expression.

'Sizewell's hundred-year-old Coronation Wood was felled in preparation for the project. Planning approval for the new power station hadn't even been granted. Gone is a valuable habitat for birds, bats, butterflies and insects; gone is a noise barrier to the power stations. Well, we can't see that wood anymore.'

'It's a wood, Max, get over it.'

'It's not the just the woods. It's the marshes, the heathland, the wildlife. All being eaten away bit by bit. I worry for our children. I worry for us all. Nature keeps us sane.'

George and I sit in silence working out whether to leave it there or go for the full falling out. Julia takes the opportunity to fill our glasses with wine as if topping up the water bottles of two boxers between rounds. It's like she's saying, 'Here you go guys, knock yourselves out.'

But George changes the subject.

'Max, this morning when we were chatting, you said Gertrude's fall seemed strange. What did you mean?'

I partly regret having said it, but now that George has picked up on it, I either need to lie or let them know my suspicion.

'I think she may have fallen backwards.'

'Backwards?'

'The police asked me to check her over when they brought her up the cliff. From her injuries, I think that she must have fallen backwards. I just can't see how it would happen, unless—'

George beats me to it. 'Unless she was pushed? You think that Gertrude was pushed. Really? You think so?'

'I can't help wondering.'

'Have you told the police?'

'Not yet. I thought I'd wait for the results of the post-mortem. It's next week, so I guess we'll find out then.'

'Do you have any other evidence?'

'Not really. I've spoken to some of the others on the site. It's complicated.'

'Complicated? How's it complicated? Old lady with dementia falls down a cliff.' He pauses and then adds, 'I suppose it will all be down in your journal. I imagine that would make a good read.'

'The journal's personal. It's just notes about nature, things I observe, what people say. It's of no interest to anyone else.'

'Come on, Max. What else do you know?'

'Nothing really. Just things people have said.'

'Like what? What things?'

'Like who might have wanted to give Gertrude a shove.'

'And who might have wanted to give her a shove?'

'Pretty much everyone.'

'You're crazy. I'm sure the inquest will find it was an accident. Confused old lady in a storm who went too close to the edge, turned around, lost her balance and toppled over. You need to stop your imagination running riot like this, it can't be good for you. You're obsessing.'

Ouch. I decide to change the subject, and we chat about various less contentious issues including the weather, holidays, Brexit and Covid. I can't help myself though and, when I feel George has calmed down and the time is right, I bring our conversation back to Gertrude.

'Julia, you mentioned the other day that Gertrude was a bit of a flirt, that she came on to George and to others. Who else did she come on to?'

Julia smiles. 'You're not just obsessing, are you? You're investigating.' She pauses before adding, 'There were rumours about her and Simon. You know, The Six Bells manager. He was a fair bit younger than her; it created quite a stir.'

'No one's mentioned it. Was it serious?'

'Not sure. They did used to spend a lot of time together, but I've no idea if it went any further. It was a long while ago. Why would you want to know?'

'Oh, just curious.'

I make a mental note to follow it up with Joyce before

131

bringing the conversation back to finding out more about Julia and George.

'What made you decide to have a lodge here?'

'What, here in the "killings fields"?' George responds. 'We live in Bury St Edmunds. I own a local company, and we like spending time by the sea. It's a lovely place to come for some peace and quiet.'

'What sort of company?'

'Construction, we do jobs all over the east coast.'

'How's business?'

'Is this part of the investigation?'

'Just neighbourly interest.'

'Right. It's up and down. Brexit and Covid haven't helped. The cost of materials has rocketed, lead times have gone crazy, subbies are hard to get as they've gone back to Eastern Europe. Lots of projects have been put on hold. It's difficult. Sizewell C can't kick off soon enough.'

'Any idea when that will be?'

'They're already talking about the advance contracts. Stuff like worker facilities, rail improvements, the bypass. It's going to be a lifesaver for us all.'

'I imagine they'll pay well. Leiston could become a boomtown.'

'Yes, for a time, when Sizewell B was being built, it was like the Wild West during the gold rush. Can't wait.'

I visualise brothels, drunken brawls and gun fights. I see images of aged RSPB and National Trust volunteers trying to cope with them.

'I worry about the effect it will have on the area – how it could impact small, quiet villages like Eastbridge and

Theberton, what will happen to Minsmere and Dunwich Heath.'

'It'll be fine; and anyway, it will only be temporary. Once it's built, everyone will leave apart from a few bodies left behind to run the thing. It will be as though it had never happened.'

'Try telling that to the woodland, marshes and wildlife that's been decimated in the meantime.'

'That's just NIMBY, Max.'

'It's not NIMBY. It's caring for our planet, caring for future generations and not thinking that because we can do something, we should do it. It's not NIMBY, it's just not being selfishly short-sighted.'

The conversation keeps coming back to our area of disagreement. It's like an itch that won't go away and needs to be scratched. Julia, having had enough, raises a less contentious subject.

'You were saying earlier, Max, that your kids are with you for Easter?'

'Yes, Emma and Greg are joining me tomorrow and staying the weekend. They're going to an Ed Sheeran concert in Ipswich on Monday night.'

'That'll be nice for you, and for them. They must miss their mum.'

'We all do. They've supported me. I can't imagine how I would have got through it without them. They helped me care for Kathy. I was used to doing it for other people, but with Kathy… I went to pieces. I'm so much better now thanks to them and being here. The lodge, the sea, the heath, the marshes, the birds. They've helped me so much.'

We fall silent. George gives Julia a look as though he's saying, 'OK, let's wind it up there.' Julia immediately picks up on it.

'Max, it's been lovely. We need to sort a few things out around the lodge before Harvey turns up.' She pauses and then adds, almost as a reflex, 'We should do it more often.'

George gives her a disapproving look. I take the hint, say my farewells and head off. I've got much of the information I wanted from George, and a better feel for why he fell out with Gertrude and Derek. I also now know how badly his construction company needs the Sizewell C contracts. I can't help thinking that he could easily be behind what happened to Gertrude. The lunch has confirmed my view of him, and it's not good.

Chapter 23

I settle into my recliner to see off the effects of the Sauvignon Blanc. After a brief nap, I spend the rest of the afternoon online shopping before writing notes in my journal and reviewing my thoughts on who might have shoved Gertrude "out of the way". I have several suspects with reason to help her over the cliff but no one who stands out as most likely. I need to think like a detective. Means, motive, opportunity. Everyone seems to have had the means, quite a few had a motive, but who had the opportunity? I narrow this down to just Mike and Felicity. As far as I'm aware, they were the only ones who could have known she was wandering around in the storm. I draw up a list of the main suspects and what I know so far.

Mike: He didn't always get on with Gertrude, his business has failed, and he probably inherits her lodge, house and investments. He has motive, but why now? I suppose she may have needed to sell her house and lodge to finance moving into a home. He could have deliberately let her out of her room and led her to the cliff, but then what was she doing knocking on Felicity's door? Unless he had the idea after she'd been to Felicity's. He's in the frame, but he does seem to have cared for her and he did – does – seem upset about losing her.

Felicity: She blames Gertrude and Derek for her husband's heart attack. She admits that a disorientated Gertrude called on her and accused her of killing Derek on the evening she fell. Felicity was drunk, upset and blames herself for not helping Gertrude. What if Felicity had had enough? What if her grief for Peter on what would have been their anniversary, combined with alcohol and the accusations over Derek, created a potent mix in her mind that sent her over the edge, or, rather, caused her to lead Gertrude over the edge? But has she got it in her? She seems caring, open and honest. And why would she have told me Gertrude called on her that night? If she'd said nothing, no one would have known.

George: His company needs the work from Sizewell C projects. Gertrude and Derek were actively opposing the new power station, but so were lots of people. I can't see him taking out the entire anti-Sizewell brigade. More importantly, Gertrude was accusing him of killing Derek to keep him quiet about the accidents on his construction sites. What if she was right? What if he suspected that Gertrude was going to draw attention to the accidents? But how would George have known Gertrude was outside in the storm?

And what about my other neighbours? I don't know where to start with them. Gertrude certainly knew how to make enemies. It seems her dementia meant she didn't know when to keep her mouth shut. She'd say whatever came into her mind without evidence or justification, even if it did upset others.

I'm not sure I'm cut out for this kind of work. It was easier as a GP, investigating the underlying cause of a patient's symptoms. I had to ask the right questions and make educated guesses from their responses, but I also had help from a barrage of tests including examination, bloods, urines, X-rays and the rest. And if I still couldn't work it out, I always had my trusty hospital colleagues to refer them to. Yes, I sometimes got it wrong. Missing Seb's meningitis and Kathy's lymphoma. But this seems so much harder, more complicated. I could take my concerns to the local constabulary but I've no hard evidence; they'd probably think I'm crazy. No, I need to wait to see the results of the post-mortem.

I press on, thinking about who else might have given Gertrude a helping hand over the cliff. Sheila mentioned she knew Gertrude had managed to put Tim and James's backs up. I need to find out why. I need to hang around the decking to catch her as she, Betty Boo and Sooty pass by the lodge on their late-afternoon walkies.

I mix myself a "hair of the dog" gin and tonic before calling Sally to make sure it's OK for us to visit her over the weekend. We have a good catch-up and arrange for me, Greg and Emma to visit her for afternoon tea in Leiston on Easter Sunday. She would otherwise be on her own, so it works out well for her. It also works out well for us, as she is famed for her amazing chocolate cake, and I've given her plenty of time to get baking.

I put on a fleece and sit outside making more notes in my journal while waiting for Betty Boo to lead Sheila to me. I listen to the rich echoing flute of a blackbird that leads the Sunrise Park early evening chorus. A great tit beats out the rhythm with doggedly repeated variations of "teacher, teacher, teacher" and a mournful robin provides perky backing vocals. It's not long before I see Betty Boo arriving with Sheila and Sooty in tow. I greet them and speak to Betty Boo first. I'm counting on Sheila stopping so I can say nice things to her pride and joy on a lead.

'Hello, Betty Boo, how are you today? Has Mummy been looking after you? Have you been good for Mummy?' I realise it's a bit soft, but it does the job.

Sheila walks over to the decking balustrade, looks up at me and bends down to pet her darling Betty Boo.

'You have been a good girl, haven't you? Now, no sitting, you can do that when we get home. Say hello to the nice doctor.'

'Retired doctor, Sheila. I was hoping to see you. I wanted to ask you about what you said. About not being surprised if someone had given Gertrude a bit of a shove, that she'd put a few people's backs up.'

'Oh that. Well, I've been thinking about it more since this morning. I got a bit carried away. I'm not sure anyone would have gone as far as to give her a push. She was often disorientated and, with the storm, could easily have been confused. She could have panicked and tripped over one of the logs by the edge of the cliff.'

'You mentioned about her putting James's back up. What was that about?'

'No idea. I've seen them arguing a few times over the last few weeks. They were really going at it. One of them wasn't happy about something.'

'Any idea what?'

'No. Maybe ask Joyce,' Sheila says with a grin.

We all make fun of our resident shopkeeper, but she does have her uses.

'And Tim?'

'I wouldn't ask Tim.'

'No, Tim and Gertrude. You said they didn't get on.'

'Well, Tim's not nice; he's drunk and rude most of the time. Gertrude was never one to let things go. There was the parking issue, and he works at Sizewell. She hated the power stations. She and Derek fought to stop Sizewell C. When Tim had a go at her, she would give as good as she got. He never liked it.'

'Did Tim and Derek argue?'

'All the time, worse than Tim and Gertrude. They detested each other. I never saw them come to blows, but it wouldn't have surprised me. Anyway, why all the questions? Do you really think she could have been pushed?'

'It's not impossible. As you say, she had made a few enemies, but it's hard to think that one of them could shove a poor, defenceless old lady over a cliff. Arguing with her, even being rude to her, but giving her a shove?'

'It's a funny world, Max. Who knows what might have happened? Anyway, we must be on our way. We need to be back before it gets dark. Come on Betty Boo, come on Sooty.'

I watch them head towards the clifftop path and then update my journal with what Sheila has just said. I conclude that I need to find out what Gertrude and James were arguing about, and I need to find out what Tim was up to on the evening Gertrude fell. I think I'll head to The Six Bells for dinner on my own tonight, I need to do a bit more digging.

Tim

Tim downs the remains of his whisky and sets off for The Six Bells. As he does, he hears gulls overhead. He hates their mournful, resonant, high-pitched cries. He loves it here at the lodge, but the birds. He hates the birds. The magpies, the crows and especially the gulls. Noisy pests, covering his decking with poop. Taking stuff out of the bins. Waking him up in the morning. Pests. Always getting under his skin. Just like Joyce. And as he walks, the anger rises within him. Soon, his mind is seething. He'll pop into the shop and give that mouthy bag what for. He thinks about what Gertrude had said. More gossip spread by Joyce. He had to stop her. He couldn't risk Louise finding out. Christ, he couldn't risk that. He knew the cat was well out of the cat flap, but he had to make sure it stayed in the shop. Joyce's shop. He smiles as the metaphor comes to life in his mind. It doesn't work if the flap is to the outside, so he pictures it between the shop and Joyce's apartment upstairs. And Max, anti-Sizewell Max with his spouting on about Gertrude having been pushed. All the speculation fertilising the rampant grapevine. More people sticking their noses in. Talking about him. Pointing their fingers. He needed Joyce to stop, he needed Max to stop. Above all, he needed a drink.

Chapter 24

I set off just after 7pm up the track to the site pub. It's a glorious early evening. The sun is low, the sky glows pink, and the air is still. The perfect theatre for the penetrating song of a thrush whose repeated phrases, some soft, others harsh, accompany me on my journey.

Inside The Six Bells, "Stormy Monday" is playing. I've always liked John Mayall & the Bluesbreakers. I nod to Simon, who is sitting at his usual table, in recognition of his great taste in music. Our shared passion for sixties and early seventies rock is a bond between us and one of the reasons I like coming here. Julia and George are sitting at a table for two in the corner. I say "hi" before approaching the bar, where Paul and Harvey are at the far end drinking with Tim. Becky is talking to them from behind the counter. I catch her eye and order a pint of the local Ghostship bitter. Tim immediately comes over for a chat.

He's above average height with solid features and a pot belly sagging proudly under his "May Contain Alcohol" T-shirt. His brown eyes are slightly bloodshot, glassy. It's obvious that he's already had more than a few.

'Max. I hear you've been asking around about Gertrude. Poor lady, it was a terrible accident. I wasn't her biggest fan, but I wouldn't wish that on anyone. I can't see what all the fuss is about though.' He then moves closer into my personal space. 'Why all the questions? What's Gertrude got to do with you?'

I back away slightly so it feels less confrontational.

'Nice to see you too, Tim. I didn't know her well, but she was always pleasant to me. I was the one who spotted her halfway down the cliff and the police asked me to take a quick look at her to confirm that she was dead, see if there was anything unusual. I just can't work out how she managed to fall the way she did.'

'And what does that mean?' he says, moving closer again.

This time, I stand my ground.

'Backwards, she probably fell backwards.'

Tim looks at me and his mouth breaks into a forced smile which could be almost classed as a smirk. He seems to be weighing me up, judging me – and not favourably.

'She probably fell backwards. Right. How do you work that out?'

'She had scratches but little injury to the front of her head, her face, hands, or wrists. It seems strange.'

'She could have toppled over backwards, or she could have twisted when she fell.'

'She could have, but it seems unlikely.'

'But not impossible. Have you mentioned this to the police?'

'Not yet. I'm waiting to see what the post-mortem finds. They suspect accidental death, which, to be fair, is reasonable in view of her age, dementia and the storm.'

'Exactly, exactly,' he says, backing away from me.

'I'll make sure the police know everything I've found out. I won't let them gloss over it just because she was old and confused.'

'And what have you found out then?' Tim says, moving in closer again.

I back away. I can't help feeling we are like partners in a slow step dance.

'Bits and pieces, nothing concrete. How well did you know her?'

'We hardly ever spoke.' He pauses then adds, 'Funnily enough, she came to my door the night she went missing.'

'Gertrude came to your door that night? What time?'

'I don't know, maybe around nine. She was in a state with the storm. She kept knocking on my door and, when I opened it, she started talking rubbish. Calling me names and accusing me of stuff. My lights had gone out and she seemed confused in the dark. I sent her away.'

'Do you know where she went?'

'No idea. Home, I assumed. I guess not now. I suppose I should have helped her, but she'd annoyed me. I'd had a few and wasn't feeling very helpful. I couldn't have known she would walk out over the cliff, could I?'

'Especially not backwards,' I immediately retort and regret it at once.

'Don't be a dick, Max. I feel bad enough about it already. Frankly, you can go screw yourself.'

'Kind of you but I must get something to eat. I had a salad for lunch and I'm starving,' I retort as he turns away.

Our conversation over, I order the BBQ chicken wings followed by a burger, then settle myself at a table tucked away in the corner of the eating area to mull over what Tim has said. So, he also knew Gertrude was out in the storm and he's saying he hardly ever spoke to her. I can't see how it fits with what Sheila said about having seen them arguing. I assume it was about his car blocking Gertrude's view of the sea, or maybe about Sizewell, but it could have been about anything. I need to find out why they were arguing, and I need to find out what "stuff" she was accusing him of.

My phone rings: it's Emma. I respond at once.

'Hi, love, how are you?'

'Good thanks, Dad, looking forward to spending Easter with you. What do you need us to bring?'

'Just yourselves, maybe an Easter egg. I'll go to Dale Farm shop in the morning for supplies. I thought I'd book an Aldeburgh restaurant for tomorrow night, we can eat in on Sunday, maybe have a roast, and you have the concert on Monday.'

'Sounds great. Let's try to fit in some crabbing at Southwold like we used to do with Mum. She loved it. Maybe fish and chips at the Riverside. And we need to visit Nana and Grandad's bench at the Coastguards.'

'Perfect. Can't wait.'

We chat some more before Becky brings my starter and I ring off. It'll be hard spending Easter without Kathy but knowing Greg and Emma will be here makes it much less daunting.

'They look good, as always,' I say to Becky while admiring my BBQ chicken wings.

Unusually for Becky, she's not smiling. She moves close to me and leans down confidentially.

'I couldn't help overhearing you and Tim. In fact, I think the whole place must have heard the pair of you. He's not the nicest person when he's had a few but he's not all bad.' She then pauses, before asking, 'Do you really think Gertrude falling like that was strange?'

'I don't know, it just doesn't seem right. I guess we'll find out more from the post-mortem.'

'Yes, I suppose so. Don't mind Tim though, he's alright when you get to know him.'

Chapter 25

Becky heads back to the bar and I tuck into my chicken wings. They are piled high and smeared in a thick, sticky, addictively delicious sauce. Within seconds, my hands and face are a mess. I manage six wings and four napkins before admitting defeat. I take a gulp of my pint before looking up to check what's happening. Mike has just entered the pub, and I watch as he scans the bar and restaurant. He notices Julia and George sat together and says hello. He then sees me on my own and comes across.

'OK if I join you, Max?'

'Of course. I've just finished BBQ wings, I've a burger coming.'

'I can tell. The wings, I mean. Your face is covered in sauce. Have you considered using a napkin?'

'Four so far, what I need is a wet wipe. How are you doing?'

Mike sits down opposite. 'OK, I guess. I can't get used to Gertrude not being around. I tried to sort some of her stuff out earlier but didn't know what to do with it. I suppose I need to bag it up and take it to one of the charity shops in Leiston. I just don't feel ready. Not yet.'

'Give yourself time, there's no hurry.'

'Yes, I suppose so. I can't even bring myself to throw away the stuff I don't like. She's left me with a cupboard full of Marmite, apricot jam, dark chocolate, muesli and granary bread. I'll never eat them. I don't suppose you want any of it?'

'I wouldn't say no.'

Becky arrives with my burger. Mike orders the same and I add a couple of pints of Ghostship and two whisky chasers. It's Friday night. I finish my pint and look across at Mike.

'Are you on your own over Easter?'

It's only after I've asked the question that I realise how insensitive it is. Mike seems to be OK with it though.

'Yes. I was supposed to be joined by an old university friend. I bought us tickets for a concert at Snape on Monday night, but he called earlier to say he can't make it. His mother's had a stroke. I don't suppose you want to join me for Beethoven's *Sixth*? Simon Rattle's conducting the LSO.'

'Wonderful. Yes, please. I love the *Pastoral*. Rural life, birds singing, streams flowing, the storm, the calm after. Greg and Emma are staying for the weekend, but they'll be at an Ed Sheeran concert in Ipswich on Monday night. So, yes please. But only if you let me pay for the ticket.'

'No, it's my treat; you've been so supportive. You can buy the interval drinks.'

'How about I book a restaurant, and we eat before the concert?'

'I've already booked Mainsail in Aldeburgh for 6pm; the concert starts at 7.45pm.'

'Sounds good, but you must let me pay for the meal.'

Mike shrugs, agrees and then asks when Emma and Greg are arriving.

'Tomorrow mid-afternoon. It'll be lovely, I'm really looking forward to having them here. We've planned walks, crabbing at Southwold, and arranged to see Kathy's sister in Leiston on Sunday. Easter without Kathy is going to be hard, but the kids will keep me busy. They'll make it bearable.'

'My family's all gone now,' Mike says. 'Mum had a brother who died just after she did, Dad was an only child. Neither Gertrude nor I had children. It's sad really. My ex, Alicia, didn't want them – well, not with me. Of course, she then goes and has two with her new partner. He seems nice enough, it's not his fault his wife's a bitch.'

I like Mike and I feel for his situation. I even toy with inviting him to our roast dinner on Easter Sunday, but not for long. I'm seeing him on Monday, and I don't want to spend too much of my Easter with him, not when Greg and Emma are going to be here. I want them all to myself. We sit in silence for a while, neither knowing what to say, before we resort to the comfort of chatting about the latest reports on Birdline (lesser yellowlegs on the scrape at Minsmere, no sign of the purple heron, glossy ibis now at Eastbridge).

When we've finished eating, we polish off our pints and down our whisky chasers before Becky arrives to clear away the plates. Mike heads for the toilet, I head for the bar where I secure us each another pint of Ghostship.

Tim is still there and even louder than before. He's been making good use of the time while we've been eating. Emboldened by the alcohol, I decide to tackle him again about Gertrude and move towards him.

'Hey, Tim, you told me earlier that Gertrude was talking rubbish and accusing you of stuff on the night she fell. What was that all about?'

He looks at me with disdain, drunken disdain.

'None of your business.'

I half expected his response but I'm in no mood to leave it there.

'Come on, what could she have said that was so bad that you can't share it?'

Tim looks at me and shrugs.

'Oh, alright. If you must know, it was the usual: my car blocking her view of the sea. Crazy, she was, always on about it. Her and Derek gave me serious grief. If I want to park outside my lodge, I bloody well will. They tried to get us thrown off the park over it. She was a mad woman. Derek was just as bad. I shouldn't say it, but I didn't shed any tears when he was run over.'

'Hit-and-run, wasn't it? They still haven't found out who did it.'

'No, I don't think so. I'd like to shake his hand though.'

'That's harsh,' I say taking a good swig of beer.

'Maybe.'

'Interesting that what happened to Derek was just months before what happened to Gertrude. I wonder if they're connected?'

'What do you mean by that? Come on? You must be joking. I know what you're thinking. You're as crazy as she was. It wouldn't surprise me if you've written all sorts of crap in that journal of yours. I hate people like you, making up lies, spreading rumours based on nothing. Some amateur sleuth putting two and two together and coming up with something ridiculous. It was an accident. I know it, you know it, we all know it. She was a sick old woman. She was scared, confused and on her own in a storm. She fell over the cliff. Backwards, forwards, what does it matter? She fell. End of. All these accusations, all this he says this, she says that. It's all because of you. Stop it. Just piss off, Max. You've had a few too many Ghostships; you're seeing things that aren't there. You're as crazy as she was. You're a nutter.'

That seems to have flushed out the real Tim. I'm even more riled now. I respond, but only after another slug of beer.

'From what I can see, you're the nutter. Turning away a frightened old lady who needed help. Sending a sick, confused, defenceless old lady out into a storm close by a dangerous cliff. How could you? You may as well have killed her. You're the nutter. Probably worse.'

'If you weren't such an old man, I'd make you pay for that,' he responds, moving closer to me, then prodding my chest.

Tim is loud and everyone's heads are turned in our direction. Becky comes across to calm things down.

She gives Tim a close, hard stare and says, 'Come on, easy, you've had enough.' She then glances at me and adds, 'You too, Max, let's play nice.'

I'm angry, very angry. I can't believe he's called me "such an old man". I'm tempted to strike the first blow, but Mike has arrived back from the toilet in time to catch the last few exchanges and he drags me away.

'Wow, Max, you're a bit of a tiger when you've had a few.'

'Well, he's such an arsehole. It wouldn't surprise me if he had something to do with what happened to both Derek and Gertrude.'

'What, over a sea view? Really?'

'Well, maybe there's something else we don't know about.'

'Perhaps, but it does feel like you're clutching at straws. Maybe Derek was run over by some cowardly jerk who'd had a few too many and couldn't admit to what he'd done. Maybe Gertrude just fell off the cliff. Maybe you need to be careful what you say to people and leave investigating to the police.'

'You're probably right. It's possible I'm being a bit obsessive, but I can't let it go.'

'Obsessive?'

I wouldn't normally explain so readily but after the spat with Tim and oiled by the drink, I think, *to hell with it.*

'Yes, I get anxiety, it makes me obsessive. I turn things over and over. I won't – can't – let them go. I've been like it for a while.'

'What set that off?'

'I misdiagnosed a patient. A child. He died. There was a hearing; I was cleared. It was horrible. I was a nervous wreck. Guilt, anxiety, panic attacks, the works.' I stop, take a sip of my pint and continue. 'Then I missed Kathy's signs of cancer. She lost weight. I told myself she was on a diet, being good. We both had night sweats, I put it down to stress. She was often tired, but so was I. We were getting old. She had itchy skin, we put it down to an allergy. It was lymphoma.' Another sip. 'The signs were there but I missed them. Years of being a GP and I fucking missed my own wife's lymphoma. By the time she was diagnosed, the cancer had spread to her liver. It was terminal. I should have picked it up. I failed her. My anxiety came back, the panic attacks returned, and I retired from practice to look after her. My anxiety settled but it never really left. Things worry me more than they should. I get bees in my bonnet. I've learnt to manage it with CBT, nature walks, relaxation, music. If it gets too bad, I've got tablets. And booze.' Another sip.

'I'm sorry, Max, I had no idea.'

'I shouldn't have said anything; it's the drink.'

I sense it's time to call it a day. Mike and I bid farewell to Julia and George, who are making a night of it, and head back to our lodges. It's dark and as we walk; we hear footsteps on the gravel behind us. I stop, then turn around. Nothing. We walk on, the footsteps behind continue. I turn around again, light up the path with the torch on my phone, and a muntjac deer stops in its tracks, startled. It stares into the light for a few seconds before running off through the bushes. My heart is pounding, my set-to with Tim has got to me more than I thought. I let myself into my lodge, turn on the electric heater to boost the temperature, make myself a decaf and resort to my journal.

It's been an eventful day, but I don't feel much further forward in working out what happened to Gertrude. If anything, it seems to be getting more complicated. One thing I am sure of, though: her death is suspicious. She may or may not have been pushed, but either way, I'm going to get to the bottom of what happened. Maybe I am being obsessive and maybe I'm right to be.

Chapter 26

I get to sleep quickly but wake after a couple of hours needing a drink of water and a pee. Getting back to sleep isn't easy, so I end up making a shopping list for the weekend on my phone. I then search online to find out more about what happened to Derek. I come across a report in the *Leiston Gazette*. It confirms what Mike has told me that it was a hit-and-run on the road to Aldeburgh with no witnesses. It was thought he was killed instantly. There's another, more recent piece also in *The Gazette* that says the incident is still under investigation and that there are no leads. There's also an appeal from the police for anyone with information to come forward. I lie awake wondering whether Derek's hit-and-run was accidental. What if it was deliberate? What if it's connected in some way to what happened to Gertrude? What if I'm right and she was pushed? What if someone had a grudge against the pair of them? What if one of my neighbours is a murderer?

Emma and Greg are coming tomorrow; I can't stop them now. A serial killer staying in one of the lodges could be just a flimsy wall away from where they'll be sleeping.

Where I'm sleeping. I get up and close the bedroom window and think hard whether all the other windows are shut. I can't be certain, so I check them all. I make sure they're closed, make sure they're locked.

When I return to bed, I need to take my mind from thinking about what may have happened to Derek and Gertrude. I need to stop myself going down an anxiety wormhole and ending up in a full-blown panic attack. I try to clear my thoughts and focus on my breathing and relaxing my body. I let go from my toes to the top of my head. I tell my Alexa to play the saintly, medieval, monophonic music of Hildegard von Bingen. Her gently soaring spiritual melodies always manage to calm me down. I breathe slowly while relaxing my muscles and easing the tension in my body bit by bit. It takes me a while to get my mind to fully settle, though thankfully it eventually works. But I'm restless through the remainder of the night and, at one point, wake shaken from a vivid dream. I'm in a building, possibly a school or a warehouse. I can't get out, the doors are locked. I keep trying them, but they won't open. I run up and down several flights of stairs looking for a way out but can't find one. I'm trapped. Eventually, I descend to a basement that's in darkness apart from a small crack of light that comes through a door in the far wall. This one opens. I rush up metal stairs into the street where a group of people are outside. They're waiting for me. Two faces turn in my direction, one of them is Kathy, the other is Gertrude. She's wearing a red scarf. They beckon me to go with them. As I do I feel a sense of relief, a sense of freedom.

When I open my eyes in the morning, it's dark. My

curtains are closed and, unusually, the bedroom window is also closed. I recall my thoughts of the previous night. I'm still tired and there's a familiar feeling in the pit of my stomach. I hope that my focus on what may have happened to Gertrude, my confrontation with Tim last night and looking into Derek's hit-and-run have not set off another prolonged period of anxiety. Not again. I don't think I could go through it again. Not without Kathy. I think about Gertrude. Maybe she threw herself off the cliff or let herself be blown backwards by a gust of wind. Why not? Derek was gone, her dementia was getting worse, she was increasingly angry and confused. Maybe she just gave up? I can understand that. She wouldn't be the first.

This is senseless. I need to snap out of it. Forcing myself to get up, I head for the living room, open the curtains and am greeted by another sunny morning. I play Wishbone Ash's "Blowin' Free" with the volume right up. The signature opening riff pulls me in. I close my eyes, feel the shuffle then wait for the pause before the stomp. One, two, three… my head moves with the beat. In no time, I'm head banging, in the moment, the pain gone, feeling the music rushing through me. Like when I was sixteen, like when it was all before me. When life was something to be looked forward to, exciting, an adventure. It does the job and when it's over, I sit in my recliner, content, feeling my heart rate return to normal.

It's time for some relaxing music and I opt for Eric Satie's *Gymnopédies* to accompany me as I breakfast overlooking a calm North Sea. My mind is settled. If the weather holds, it'll be a lovely Easter with the kids. Like when we used to rent a lodge and spend time here together as a family. Kathy loved it; we all loved it. They were such good times. I scan out to sea and note a raft of common scoters floating on the water just far enough out to tempt me back into the lodge to take a better look at them through my telescope. The light is good and there might be a velvet scoter amongst them. There are around fifty or so of these dark, long-tailed, round-headed sea ducks bobbing one behind the other. The almost black males contrast nicely with the lighter-brown females and their paler faces. Every so often, one dives under the water to be followed by others until only a small number remain up top. They then reappear either where they submerged or a short distance away. As I watch, a group leaves the raft, flying away south in a long, straggling line parallel to the shore. I'm engrossed and feeling calm. Thank you, Eric. Thank you, scoters.

The drive to Dale Farm is just a few miles and takes me though the small, pretty village of Westleton with its large, central green renowned for annual dwile flonking and barrel rolling competitions. I can get all the basics at the site, but the farm shop has a wonderful butcher and lots of enticing treats. I select a nice piece of sirloin for roasting before filling my trolley with essentials that include hot cross buns, Suffolk cheeses, local chutney, pork pies, luxury biscuits and other assorted comfort foods. As I'm about to leave, I realise I haven't bought the Easter eggs. I select a large chocolate rabbit for Greg and an equally large duck for Emma. I also buy a selection of mini eggs for the traditional Easter Sunday egg hunt. Kathy would be upset if we let that one slide.

Chapter 27

I'm all done and back at the site within an hour. I park by the side of my lodge, remove the bags of shopping from the boot of my car and climb the steps to the decking. It's obvious something's wrong as soon as I get to the front door. It's open, not wide open, but open. The lock is broken; it's been forced. My heart begins to pound, my stomach knots and I bite my lip wondering if someone's still inside. I hope it's the kids having arrived early, but I know it's not. They would have used a key. I put my head around the door and enter slowly, tentatively. I think about calling out and letting the intruder know I'm here, but I can't. My mouth is too dry, my throat too tight. I tread slowly, carefully, listening for sounds and watching for movement. When I enter the living room, it's a mess, with drawers pulled out, cupboard doors open, and books strewn across the floor. But it seems whoever did this has gone. I'm alone; just me biting my lip.

I can't get my head around why anyone would want to break into my lodge. I don't have anything particularly valuable. As I think this, I realise my laptop is missing from where it had been charging on the coffee table. I note my telescope remains in the corner of the room, still looking out to sea. Then my mind races to my binos, my treasured last present from Kathy. I check and breathe a sigh of relief to see them hanging on the hook where I keep them. I look around to see what else might be missing, but there's nothing obvious. The TV is fixed to the wall, so I get why it's not gone, but why leave my expensive telescope? I need to call the police, but I'm unsure if I should call 999 for an emergency or 101 for a non-emergency. I call 101. I don't think it's particularly urgent, and anyway, I can't see what they'll be able to do about it now.

The last time I reported a break-in, I was at medical school. The police took hours to come, asked lots of questions about what had been taken, dusted the place for fingerprints and homed in on an ashtray containing a roll your own cigarette butt of one of my housemates. Having smelt the butt, the officer asked us who had been smoking cannabis. It all got quite heavy, but we persuaded him that, being medical students, we wouldn't be so stupid. We'd have been thrown out. Fortunately, he pretended to believe us. I asked him about the chances of getting our stuff returned and he said we could buy it back at the local pub on a Wednesday evening. I have a suspicion I won't be getting the same advice this time. I can't see me buying my laptop back at The Six Bells.

The lady taking my call is, in fact, extremely helpful, letting me know that, even though it's not an emergency, the police will be with me in under half an hour. There are advantages to being in Suffolk, where crime is amongst the lowest in the country and response times correspondingly prompt. I plonk myself down in my recliner, trying to take in what's happened. I'm upset, I'm angry and I'm aware of a metallic taste from chewing my lip. I need to do something, so I put the shopping away, but decide not to tidy up until after the police have been. I make myself a comforting mug of tea, sit out on the decking and draw in a long, deep breath. I consider more Satie, even Hildegard, but settle for Einaudi. Thankfully, my therapeutic Alexa's still here. The sun is shining; a cool breeze blows off the sea; the raft of scoter is nowhere to be seen but towards the horizon, a large container ship is working its way north. Long-tailed, great, and blue tits feed on the nuts in the bird feeders, while, behind me, a wood pigeon coos soothingly. It's a lovely, tranquil scene, the opposite of what's inside my lodge, the opposite of what's inside my head. My CBT training kicks in. Thank goodness no one was here when it happened, Greg and Emma hadn't arrived, no one was hurt. So, my computer's been taken. It's backed up in the cloud, it's insured and, anyway, I needed a new one.

In under an hour, a police car arrives and out steps the police officer memorably called Cliff with a colleague I don't recognise.

'Dr Middleton. Good to see you again.'

'Not really. Wasn't good last time and not so good today. Where's Roger?'

'This is Jim, he's the crime scene investigator. What's happened?'

'Break-in. The front door's been forced, the place is a mess.'

'Anything missing?'

'As far as I can make out, just my laptop.'

'Very common. There's been a spate of it in the area. Kids, there's a gang of them that pinch computers and IT equipment and then sell them for a fraction of what they're worth. If I had a pound for every laptop stolen around here, I'd be a rich man.'

'Not as rich as them.'

'True. I'll need you to make a statement. Jim will be dusting for prints, taking a few photos, the usual.'

I think it's not so usual for me. Cliff asks me to run through what happened, checks whether I can remember anything that might help and notes down details of my missing laptop. We share a pot of tea and some oat biscuits during which I take the opportunity to find out what's happening about Gertrude.

'Any news about when the post-mortem's taking place?'

'Gertrude? Next week, after Easter. It should be a formality. You know, I can't believe I'd never been to Sunrise Park until a few days ago, now I'm a regular. It's a nice place. I might check out a lodge for myself. The wife and kids would love it.'

'You don't think it's a bit risky, what with residents falling down cliffs, burglaries and the like? I've been meaning to contact you about the way Gertrude died.'

'The way Gertrude died? Why's that?'

'I examined her when she was brought up the cliff, but it was only later I realised her injuries seemed to point to her having fallen backwards. I can't work out why that would be.' I look at him to see his reaction and then add, 'Unless she was pushed.'

Cliff gives me a funny look, then gets me to sign and date my statement.

'That's a serious allegation. Don't you think we need to wait for the post-mortem before such speculation? I know you're a GP, but my advice is to leave it to the experts.'

'Ex-GP.'

'Exactly.'

Jim says he'll be another fifteen minutes, so Cliff takes the opportunity to look around my lodge. In theory, he's examining the crime scene and searching for clues; in practice, I suspect he's checking out the layout, fixtures and fittings of my Sunrise Park home. He arrives back in the living room, has a quick word with Jim and then turns to me.

'Nice place, very nice place. I like the layout. It's light and the decor's great. We're all done; we need to go. Thanks for the tea and biscuits. If you think of anything else missing, anyone reports that they saw anything suspicious or a lodge comes up for sale, let me know.'

'What are the chances of getting my laptop back?'

Cliff gives me another funny look, taps Jim on the shoulder and they leave.

Chapter 28

Shortly after they've gone, there's a knock and I find Mike peering in through my front door, looking concerned.

'Max, what's happened? Are you OK?'

'Break-in. They forced the door.'

'I can see, I'm sorry. What did they take?'

'From what I can make out, just my laptop.'

'Bloody kids, they sell them for next to nothing to buy drugs.'

'That's just what Cliff said, although not the drugs bit. Hopefully my laptop is funding something a bit more worthwhile.'

'I thought I recognised Cliff.'

'Yes, he's thinking of buying a lodge here.'

'It would cut down on his work mileage.' He smiles, looks at me for a reaction then adds, 'Is there anything I can do?'

'No, I can manage. I just need to get things sorted before the kids arrive.'

'OK, I'll leave you to it, but shout if I can help.'

It's good to know that we now have a Sunrise Park mutual support network. After Mike leaves, I look around again at the mess. It's depressing. My things have been rummaged through, the carpet has muddy footprints that I'm pretty sure aren't mine, and there's glass on the floor from a broken photo frame. It's one of my favourites, with me sitting with my arm around Kathy on the family bench at the Coastguards. I let out a sigh and begin to clear up. It takes a while, but eventually everything is back to normal – well, outwardly normal.

I need to calm down, I need the therapy of working though what's happened. I need to write up my journal. I thought I'd left it on my bedside cupboard, but it's not there and I don't recall coming across it when I cleared up. I wrote an entry in it when I was in bed last night so it should be around. I check down the back of the bedside cupboard, but there's no sign of it. I look under the bed; nothing. I search the lodge checking bookshelves, my rucksack, drawers, everywhere. I double check, still nothing. My stomach tightens and my heart rate ramps up again as it dawns on me where it is. This wasn't kids pinching a laptop to fund drugs. Of course it wasn't. This was no opportunist burglary. Whoever did this must have known what they were after, and it wasn't just my laptop. It was my journal.

My mind tries to process things. The more I think about it, the more questions I have. Who would want to steal it? Why? What could they have been after? Was it something I've written? Was it to do with Gertrude? Or Derek? But how would they know what was in it? They couldn't. Maybe they just needed to find out what I know?

But what could I know that they would be so scared of? And what if I'd been here? What if the kids had been here? Would they have attacked us? My brain keeps firing off questions that ricochet around my mind. I'm losing control. I recognise the signs. I've been here before. Constantly tense, always on edge. I need to ease my mind out of it, break the vicious spiral. I need to walk. I need to be surrounded by calming heather, soothed by the sight of the sea, comforted by birdsong. I need to get away from my lodge, from my thoughts, from the ceaseless questions battering my brain. I pull on my fleece, lace up my boots and stride, almost run, to my sanctuary. To Dunwich Heath. To nature.

I walk through the site, out across Minsmere Road and, as if on autopilot, follow the path towards the heath. I walk fast, not thinking, not observing, just walking. The movement calms me; my mind slows. I reach a clearing, stand still with clenched fists and arms outstretched, take a deep breath, and quietly scream.

'Oh God what's the point. I can't do this. I just can't. Not on my own, not again, not without Kathy.'

There's a bench on my left facing out across the heath to the sea. I sit on it and stare mindlessly in front of me. After a while, I put my head in my hands and begin to shake uncontrollably. I well up. Tears begin to fall. I think of Kathy, Seb, Gertrude, my journal, my fears for Greg and Emma. I sit gulping in deep breaths, sobbing, feeling hopelessly sorry for myself.

When it subsides, I'm exhausted, no longer thinking, completely drained. Slowly, the world comes back into focus. Around me are the greens, purple-browns, and yellows of the wide-open coastal heathland. Golden gorse bushes bathe in the light with their scent of coconut reminding me of sun lotion and beach holidays abroad. High above, I hear the frantic but somehow soothing trills and whistles of a skylark. I look up to see white speckled clouds dotting an azure sky. In front of me, a deep-blue sea sparkles in bright sunlight as it stretches away to the horizon. Come on, Max, pull yourself together. For Emma and Greg, for Kathy, for me.

I close my eyes and allow myself to be comforted by what surrounds me. The sounds and smells of nature. After a while, I notice its balm settling my mind. I feel comforted, I feel calm. I realise that the switch to a constant state of gut-wrenching fear is no longer on. I haven't gone back there, at least not for now. Instead, I sense a different feeling. Relief. I'm going to be OK. I'm going to be alright.

It's then that I remember I've left the lodge unlocked, that the front door will be open. I need to get back and I need to get ready for Greg and Emma. When I arrive at the lodge, I check the door lock; it will have to be replaced. I give site handyman Harvey a call. He's Emma's age, always reliable and always pleasant. I take a deep breath and make the call.

'Harvey, it's Max Middleton.'

'Hi, Max, what can I do you for?'

'I've had a break-in. The front door has been forced. I urgently need a new lock.'

'A break-in? That's rum. Did they get much?'

'Just my laptop, I think.'

'Bloody kids, they get on my wick.'

'How quickly can you get it fixed? Emma and Greg are due this afternoon. We're planning to go out for dinner. I wouldn't want to leave without the place being secure.'

'It's Easter Saturday, I'll have to get one from Leiston and they've been in short supply due to the number of recent burglaries. It could be expensive, and it could be tricky to get it done in time. When's Emma arriving?'

I recall Harvey doing a job for me when Emma was last staying. They seemed to get on well; in fact, I sensed a bit of a spark. It could prove useful.

'Mid-afternoon, maybe around 3pm. I know she'd be keen to see you.'

'How many keys will you need?'

'Just two: one for me, one for the key safe.'

'OK, I'll do what I can. See you around 3pm.'

Typical handyman. He tells me how difficult it'll be to sort out and then, after a little thought, works out how to get it done anyway. I suspect, on this occasion, Emma arriving has something to do with it.

I make myself a cup of tea and have another search for my journal. Maybe I've missed it, maybe there's somewhere I haven't looked. Of course, I don't find it, but I need to make sense of what's happening. I need to write. I take out an unused notebook from my desk draw, remove the seal, open it and start again on yesterday's entry.

After a while, I take a break and think about lunch. I'm not hungry but I manage to force down a pork pie. I then prepare the beds, sort out towels and do all the things Kathy would normally have done when we used to rent a lodge here. I also do what she would normally have wanted me to do... book The Lifeboat restaurant in

Aldeburgh for dinner. Jobs done, I ease myself into my recliner, put my head back and close my eyes. The decking doors are open. I consider closing them, but I'm enjoying the gentle breeze that enters the room. I hear the rhythmic breaking of waves on the shore, and the sun's rays warm my face and relax my mind, as a hot water bottle soothes an aching stomach. It's not long before I nod off.

Harvey

Harvey drives to the site wondering what job George wanted him to do this time. Things had worked out well. He needed to fix Max's door and could kill two birds with one stone. His site job was fine, but he needed the extra work George gave him. It was the only way to keep his head above water. His luck would change soon. His latest betting contact in Newmarket would see to that. His tips had been better. It was only a matter of time before he had a big win. Then he could get away. Leave it all behind. Find somewhere else, somewhere bigger, better. Somewhere he could be someone. Meanwhile, doing jobs for George would pay off the debt. It was such a mess. He didn't like George; he was a rum 'un. He didn't like doing jobs for him, but he had no choice. After all, George had bailed him out. He would have to do what he had to do. Anyway, now he could see Emma. She was nice; she seemed to like him. And she lived in London. It would be good to get to know her better. Maybe take her out. Harvey smiled to himself as he thought, *that's three birds with one stone.*

Chapter 29

I'm woken by a gentle tap on the shoulder and the sound of Greg and Emma talking softly in the room. It takes me a while to understand what's happening. I open my eyes, slowly get up, and we share huge, tight hugs. Well, Emma and I do, Greg's a bit more reserved. Emma, being her mother's daughter, immediately tells me off.

'Hi, Dad. It looks like you were having a nice rest, but you shouldn't leave all the doors open. Especially the front door, who knows who might take advantage. Even here in Suffolk, you need to be more careful.'

'Hello to you too, Emma. I'll explain about the door, let's get you settled in first.'

I help bring in their bags, show them to their rooms then put the kettle on.

'How was the journey?'

'Fine. M25 was a bit busy,' Greg answers. It's his specialist subject. 'A12 was good but there was a long queue at the A14 roundabout, so we took the short cut through Belstead. You know the one, narrow, winding, blind corners, no passing places. In all, we took just over two hours. Not bad for Easter Saturday.'

I take a good, hard look at him. He seems well. His mother's light-blue eyes are clear, golden-brown wavy hair shining, his face relaxed.

Emma doesn't let Greg's journey review pass without comment. 'Just over two hours, yes, but only because you drove like Lewis Hamilton. I wouldn't be surprised if you picked up a few time penalties and a speeding fine somewhere along the way.'

Greg smiles and takes it as a compliment. 'I was breaking in my new convertible. It's a lovely car, it handles so well. You must come for a ride in it, Dad. It's going to be sunny all weekend, we can have the top down.'

'I saw it outside. It looks nice.'

'Nice? It's lovely. You like it, don't you, Em?'

'Of course. I'm sure you'll be very happy together.'

Greg loves his cars, while for Emma, a car is just a way of getting from one place to another. She takes after me. Having a ride in an open top does sound fun though. Cold, but fun. The doorbell rings again. It's Harvey with toolbox in hand. He's a local lad with sensible brown eyes that peer out from a clean-shaven, kindly face. He's known for being dependable and reliable. He's also a good handyman.

'Hi, Max. How's things?'

'Alright, considering everything that's happened. Greg and Emma have just arrived.'

'Hi, Emma, Greg. I guess your dad's told you about all that's been going on around here?'

Emma smiles at Harvey. 'Gertrude?'

'Yes, Gertrude, and now the break-in.'

Emma looks at me, her eyebrows raised, her mouth

open. 'Dad, what break-in? When? Why haven't you told us?'

'I've not had a chance. I had a break-in this morning. It was nothing serious, no one was hurt. I was out shopping. It's why the front door was open.'

'Did they take much?'

'My laptop.'

'What, nothing else? Not your sound system, telescope, binos?'

'Everyone's saying it's local kids; there's a gang that pinches laptops.'

Emma's shocked. 'My God, Suffolk isn't what it used to be.'

'True. Never mind; I'm OK, it's insured, and I needed a new computer.'

Greg's not so relaxed. 'Did they take your iPhone, the one we got you for Christmas?'

'No, thankfully I had it with me.'

'That's something.'

'Yes, it's lucky; I recently got frustrated having to unlock it all the time, so I've turned the auto lock off.'

'That's not very clever. If they'd got your iPhone, they'd have had free rein. You might want a rethink.'

'Maybe.'

'Have you programmed in our contact numbers?'

'Yes, even I managed to do that.'

Harvey, needing to get on with the door, cuts in. 'You're lucky, we managed to get you a new lock. I should be able to sort it in no time.'

'Thanks, do you want a cup of tea when you've finished? I'm about to make one.'

'Great, white no sugar.'

We sit outside around the decking table. Emma smiles as she checks me out, making sure I haven't lost, or gained, any weight. I take a good look at her. My girl. We've always been close. She appears well, her short, blonde hair giving her a Debbie Harry look. Not that she's probably ever heard of Blondie. She's trim, possibly too trim, and casual in a loose white top, denim jeans and trainers. I check if she's added to her facial jewellery and am pleased to see just the familiar earlobe piercings and her small, left-sided nose stud. She seems happy. It's not always been so.

I listen with pleasure to Emma's bright, lively voice as she exclaims, while looking out to sea, 'Every time I sit here, I'm surprised how nice it is. It's gorgeous.' She pauses then turns to me. 'So, how are you, Dad?'

'I'm OK, not bad.'

'Really?'

'I'm OK, especially now you and Greg are here.'

'But when you're on your own, how are you really?'

Emma and I have always been honest with each other. Well, that's what I like to think. When she was young, I used to read her a chapter of *Harry Potter* every night and first, by way of warming up, we would have a catch-up. How was your day? What have you been up to? That sort of thing. Once, I told her I was sad because Greg was going to be away for a week on a school trip. It was his first time away from home; I was going to miss him. Her reply was, 'Well, he is, so get over it.' That's my Emma. I owe her some straight-talking, I owe her the truth. I look out to sea and then back at Emma.

'It's tough. I feel sad, lonely. I miss your mum. I miss her all the time, every day. I can't get used to her not being here.'

'It's OK, Dad. You need to grieve for her, you need to give it more time. They say it gets easier.'

'I used to tell my patients exactly that. Maybe it does, maybe it will. Eventually.'

Emma and Greg have just arrived; it's too soon for this. I just want to spend time relaxing with them. I gaze out to sea checking the birdlife, scanning for anything interesting.

'Look, there on the water, a raft of common scoter. There must be a hundred or so of them. We get a lot these days, occasionally there's a velvet scoter with them. They're slightly larger with a white wing patch.'

Emma's not fooled. 'Are you trying to change the subject, Dad?'

'Maybe. We'll have lots of time to catch up. Let's just enjoy being together and taking in the view.'

'You mean the scoters?'

'Yes, the scoters.'

Greg is not one for taking time easing into difficult conversations. He points to the large taped off gap between the trees on the edge of the cliff and wants to know about the elephant in the room, or, in this case, down the cliff face.

'Is that where Gertrude fell?'

Emma gives him a hard look but I'm happy to discuss it. After all it's pretty much all I've been thinking about for the past few days.

'Yes, I had to hold on to the laurel tree on the right to see her. She was halfway down the cliff covered by a

175

bush. All I saw at first was something red. I knew she was missing and when I looked through my binos I couldn't make out much. But I had a feeling it could be her.'

'What's that birding term you use? The general impression word, isn't it GISS or something?' Greg says, smiling at me.

Emma immediately tells him off. 'That's so out of order, Greg. I can't believe you would joke about something like this. My God, Greg.'

'Sorry, but it's Dad, it's what he does when he spots birds.'

What Greg says makes sense. 'He's right, Emma. It was a kind of GISS thing. The red could have been anything, I just had a feeling. It seemed right. Much like birding.'

Emma nods. 'I'm surprised more of the area hasn't been cordoned off… incident scene or whatever it's called.'

'It was initially. Once they'd recovered the body, they just left the barrier tape along the cliff edge.'

'Do they know what happened?'

'Not really. They think she wandered over the edge in the storm. She was old, had dementia, was probably disorientated, and most likely confused. If they thought it was anything else apart from a tragic accident, I'm sure they would have kept the whole area cordoned off. At least until after the post-mortem.'

'On the phone, you said it was probably an accident. Why probably?'

I wonder how much to say but figure that, as we will be together for a while, I may as well tell them what I've been thinking.

'I examined her when they brought her up. She had no injuries to the front of her head, her face, wrists, or hands. Just a few scratches. It was as if she'd fallen backwards. But why would anyone fall backwards over a cliff edge? I can't help thinking she might have been pushed.'

Greg and Emma look at me, both wide-eyed and clearly stunned. There's a long pause before Emma responds.

'You can't be serious, Dad. Pushed. You mean, like, murdered?'

'The more I talk to the other lodge owners, the more I think it's possible. There are a lot of people here who didn't get on with her; she was difficult.'

'She was old, sick, confused and harmless. I can't believe anyone would do that to her. Not shove her over a cliff, not on purpose.'

Greg, being Greg, sees an opportunity to have a dig at his sister. 'How do you shove someone over a cliff not on purpose then, Em?'

Emma stares daggers. I ignore him.

'Maybe, but I'm going to find out what happened, one way or another.'

Emma's face breaks into a smile as she continues to look at her brother.

'Wow, Greg, one moment Dad's a GP, the next he's a detective like Grandad.'

Harvey pops his head through the patio doors. 'All done. Any chance of that cup of tea?' I nod and Harvey continues, 'I have two keys, one for you and one for the key safe. Do you want me to put it there? What's the code?'

I don't want anyone but Emma and Greg knowing the code. 'It's OK, I'll do it.'

I then take the two keys and replace the one in the key safe with a new one before making Harvey a mug of tea. He cradles it as he stands facing Emma with the sparkling, sunlit sea behind her.

'Hi, Emma. Lovely view,' he says, looking directly at her.

None of us are sure whether the view he's referring to is of her or the sea. There was a time when Emma would have been hugely embarrassed, but she's a big girl now.

'Thanks, Harvey,' she says, flashing him a smile.

Now it's Harvey who's embarrassed.

'No, I mean the sea. It's a lovely view of the sea. Are you here for long?'

'We're here until Tuesday. We're seeing Dad over Easter, our aunt on Sunday and Ed Sheeran on Monday.'

'Are you good friends with Ed?'

'Funny. He's playing Ipswich.'

'The way they're playing, even on his own he should have a chance.'

Emma grimaces. Harvey feels the need to justify himself.

'Just teasing. I saw he was headlining. It looks like a great line-up.'

'Yes, The Darkness, Passenger, Lewis Capaldi. Should be amazing.'

'The Darkness are from around here, like Ed.' He pauses and then asks, 'How are you keeping?'

'Good thanks. Lowestoft.'

'Lowestoft?'

'Yes, The Darkness are from Lowestoft.'

'Right.' Harvey pauses and looks at Emma as though gathering his thoughts. 'Anyway, do you fancy a drink sometime?'

Emma turns to me, then Greg. She's clearly tempted by the offer. I won't stand in her way; it's always good to be in with the site handyman.

'Thanks, but we've only just arrived,' she replies. 'I need to see what our plans are. I've got your number. I'll give you a call when I know what's happening.'

Harvey finishes his tea and heads off, leaving me and Greg wondering whether to rib Emma about him or let it go. I decide to let it go, but Greg is unable to help himself.

'He's keen. They could probably sense the vibe all the way up the coast in Southwold. Anyway, I thought you already had a boyfriend. Your dentist? Or is he just a fill-in? A bridge?'

Emma gives Greg her daggers stare.

'Ha, ha, very funny. I'm twenty-six, I need to keep my options open. Anyway, Harvey's sweet.'

I make a mental note to ask about "her dentist", before trying to ease her embarrassment.

'And he's a very good handyman.'

'Thanks, Dad. I'll keep it in mind. Can we change the subject? How are the plans for the weekend coming on?'

'I've booked The Lifeboat in Aldeburgh for 8pm tonight, I thought we could go crabbing in Southwold tomorrow morning like you asked, lunch at the Riverside Inn, visit Aunt Sally in the afternoon and eat here tomorrow night. I've bought a joint of sirloin. You could always meet Harvey for a drink after at The Six Bells.'

Emma nods. 'Sounds great. What about Nana and Grandad's bench? We need to sit on their bench, we can't come here and not do that. Mum would never forgive us.'

'Of course. It's where we scattered your mum's ashes so it's her bench too. I wanted to talk to you about updating the plaque to include her. I thought we could go for a walk there now. We've plenty of time before we drive to Aldeburgh for dinner. Maybe we can agree the wording.'

Chapter 30

The tide is out so we opt to head south along the shore to the Coastguards. We follow the cliff edge path that leads to the site steps down to the beach, passing spreads of nodding bluebells, clumps of bright-yellow daffodils and scatterings of delicate, pink, ragged robin. Several butterflies flit from plant to plant. I point them out to Greg and Emma.

'Large white, the wings have broad black tips. The ones with the two spots and the streak are females. There's a small white, smaller obviously, less black on the wing tips. And that's an orange-tip, it's one of the first to appear each year.'

'On that bush, what's the dark one?' Emma asks.

'It's a peacock, very common. In the summer we get lots of them. They love the buddleia. And that's a red admiral, they're just as common here.'

I'm encouraged by Emma's interest, hoping that, by getting her to name the butterflies, flowers, and birds, she will start to notice and appreciate them. I've tried to get her and Greg to do this since they were little, but it's never taken hold. Nature has been such a comfort to me since I lost Kathy, who knows when they might need to draw on it. We continue along the path to the site steps, descend to the base of the cliff and head directly across the wide expanse of pebbles to the water's edge. Emma and I watch Greg skim stones before joining in. I point out a pair of terns repeatedly diving into the water and a cormorant making its way south offshore. A couple of standing-up paddle boarders are tentatively propelling themselves forward on their floating platforms. The sea may be gentle, but they aren't making it look easy. I suspect it isn't.

Greg turns and points to a rectangular patch of vegetation marked out by barrier tape that runs along the base of the cliff and up either side.

'I assume that's where they found Gertrude.'

'Yes, about halfway down the cliff. In those bushes.'

Greg wanders over to take a closer look, then returns to where we're standing.

'I'm surprised there's no sign of anything apart from the flimsy tape. It's like the police have just left things for later.'

'They probably have. They're waiting for the result of the post-mortem. I guess they think it was an accident so there's no need to do more.'

'Do you really think she was pushed?' Greg asks.

'Maybe, but I'd rather not talk about it. Not now. You've just arrived. I want to forget about all that and just spend time with the two of you, catching up, enjoying your company.'

The tide being out means that we can walk along

the edge of the sea where there is wet sand that is firmer underfoot than the pebbles. We're heading towards the bright white dome of Sizewell B that is lit from the west by the late-afternoon sun.

'What's the latest on the new power station, Dad?' Emma asks.

'Sizewell C? It's going ahead, the government's committed to it.'

'How do you feel about that?'

'Don't get me started. It doesn't make sense for the environment, doesn't make sense for the economy. It could be catastrophic for this whole area. Minsmere is sensitive; so many species depend on it. Some of them rare. It's an internationally important habitat. Anyway, renewables are so much more cost-effective.' I stop walking, point out to sea, and add, 'Look there, hundreds of offshore wind turbines. They're cheap, effective and clean. They're the future. Not dangerous, environmentally damaging, expensive nuclear power.'

We continue walking, our eyes focused on Sizewell and its two, soon to be three, power stations.

'Won't it create lots of local jobs?' Greg asks.

'Very few once the thing is up and running. Maybe short term, but most of the workers will come from outside the area. They will all have to be housed, many of them will be sited close to Eastbridge. Think of the impact the whole thing will have on those poor people. A tiny quiet village swamped by thousands of workers who will stay ten years before buggering off, leaving hardly any legacy at all apart from a pile of beer cans and a stack of used condoms.'

'Wow, sweet image, Dad,' Emma says. 'I imagine some will say you're being a bit NIMBY.'

'I am, but my backyard just happens to be a site of international importance for wildlife.'

'Just playing devil's advocate. I'm with you. Wrong solution, wrong time, wrong place.'

'Exactly. But there are lots of locals who support it. They need the work. George in the lodge next to ours, the one closest to the sea, he has a construction company. Things are slow and they're relying on the contracts Sizewell C will generate.'

'There will always be pros and cons,' Greg responds. 'The politicians need to weigh them up and decide for all of us. It's democracy.'

'Yes, and our job is to make sure their decisions are based on fact, on reality. On what's right for the majority, not on vested interests or, worse, lies.'

Greg stops walking. 'Lies? What lies?'

'Oh, people twisting the facts to their own end, hiding information, covering things up. It happens all the time when large contracts are involved.'

'With Sizewell C?'

'Maybe.'

'How do you know?'

'Just what I've heard. What I've been told. It's probably nothing. You know me, I take three and three and come up with an improbable number.'

The sand we walk on is covered with small stones of varying shapes and sizes. Hidden among them is the occasional shell or piece of sea-smoothed glass. Emma has been gathering some as we walk and it's a good way for her to change the subject. She holds one up. It's oval, medium-sized, dark orange and very smooth.

'Look at this one, do you think it's amber?'

I take it and press it against my forehead. 'It's cold. If it was amber, it would be warm. It's also quite heavy. Sorry, it's just a pretty stone, amber would be lighter. There used to be a lot of it around here but it's very rare now. What else have you got?'

Emma shows me her collection of stones and smooth sea glass. I pick out a large, mottled-grey stone with a good-size hole running through the centre.

'Nice lucky stone. We can add it to the string of them I've got hanging from a tree at the back of the lodge. I've been collecting them since you last came. Around here, people call them hag stones. They're considered protective when worn or strung together. They keep us safe.'

Greg reflects, 'Pity Gertrude wasn't wearing one.'

We pass a large tree lying horizontally, lifeless, on the pebbles. It's halfway up the beach with its branches shiny cream polished where the bark has been stripped off by the elements. Its roots are twisted, gnarled and tangled. We take a closer look. It's like the skeleton of some washed-up sea creature. It makes me think of death. Of Kathy, and of Gertrude.

After walking for about a mile, we reach the start of Minsmere and follow the steep sandy path that leads to the top of Dunwich Heath cliffs and Kathy's parents' bench. There's no one sitting on it, so Greg and I ease ourselves down and appreciate the view out to sea, along the coast and across the reed beds of the flagship RSPB reserve. Emma reads aloud the inscription on the brass plate to the side of the bench. We know the words well.

'For Olive and Eric Westleton, who loved this place.'

I think of them spending their time together at the Coastguards, enjoying the scenery, soaking up the sights and sounds of the birdlife. I then remember scattering Kathy's ashes here.

'What do you think we should put for your mum?'

We sit in silence. The three of us waiting for inspiration. In the background, we hear the cry of gulls. A wedge-shaped skein of geese honk as they pass overhead.

'How about keeping it simple?' Emma says. 'For Olive, Eric and their daughter Kathy. They loved this place.'

I like it.

'Sounds perfect. What do you think, Greg?'

'I'll go with what you both think.'

'OK. No need to make a final decision now, but it works for me.'

We sit taking in the view. Clouds pass overhead, their cotton wool shapes and fine, wispy trails drifting through a static blue sky. Immediately in front of us is dry, sandy heathland covered in bracken, heather and gorse. It gives way to Minsmere's wonderful wetlands that stretch as far as Sizewell. We watch a marsh harrier majestically glide over the reed beds. Inland, in the distance, red deer are drinking from a pool of water surrounded by ancient forest. Close by, a whitethroat blasts out its vigorous, scratchy, high-pitched warble. It reminds me of the noise we used to make with our ink pens to annoy the teachers at school.

'There are few places in England that compare to this part of the Suffolk Coast. It's flat without the awe of the Lake District, the ruggedness of the moors, or the prettiness of the Cotswolds. But it has a beauty of its own. To me, it feels wild, but safe. It's like a cosy blanket wrapped around me, giving a sense of belonging, a sense of being part of something more. I'm not a religious person, but if I was, this would be my church.'

'And nature your God, the birds your angels and Sizewell your devil,' Greg adds.

I look to the south where the sun illuminates the shiny white dome of Sizewell B. A constant reminder of the impact of man. I feel the threat of Sizewell C hanging in the air. It's a menace to this special place, a place that's home to so many rare plants and animals, but only for as long as we decide it to be so. It's a beautiful scene. I feel it deep inside me. I think of Kathy, of us here together as a family and how we used to be when the kids were growing up. I feel sad for what we had and ache to have those times back. Then I think how lucky I am to have such wonderful memories.

'When you were both very young, maybe four or five, we would come here, and you would want to play hide and seek. Your mum would take you off to hide behind one of the bushes and I would count aloud to twenty. Then I'd come and look for you. I always knew where you were as I could hear you whispering to each other, giggling, and saying "shush". I would creep behind a different bush and shout, "got you" and then "no". You would laugh and I would do it again. When I got to the right bush, you would jump out and shout "surprise". I would look at you, look at your mum and think I was the luckiest man alive. I didn't want it to end, but it did. I never really noticed. Not until your mum died. You need to capture your memories. Before you know it, the present is gone but you control the memories it makes. Collect them, preserve them, cherish them like stones from the beach. I'm lucky, you and Kathy have given me all the precious stones I need. Thank you for coming this weekend; it's made all the difference.'

Emma gives me a hug. 'Aw, Dad. We love you too, don't we, Greg.'

The words help. I feel less sad, less alone. I sit for a while staring at the view and feeling a warm glow before getting up, clapping my hands together and saying, 'Fancy a cup of tea and some scones from the Coastguards? My treat.'

Chapter 31

We walk the hundred yards or so from the bench across a broad grass clearing at the top of the cliffs to sit at one of the café's wooden trestle tables. I head indoors to the tearoom and reappear with three cream teas. Emma greets me with a smile, hands out the plates and knives, distributes the scones, jam and cream, then pours the teas. She has taken over where Kathy left off. When we're settled, she looks at me with her serious face.

'We've been having a chat. We're worried about you, Dad. What you were saying earlier about missing Mum. You seem lonely. Is there anything we can do? Do you want us to spend more time here with you? Do you want to come and live with one of us?'

I realise they are being thoughtful, caring, but I can't help feeling I'm a burden.

'No, Emma, I'm fine. I am. I just need time. I love spending my days here; and anyway, you have your own lives to lead. Just visit me when you can. I'm fine, really.'

'Have you made many friends here? Fellow birders, medics, Spurs fans?' Greg asks.

'One or two. I've got to know some of them better in the past few days after what happened to Gertrude. Mike and James seem nice – they're keen birders. A few are less friendly but that's to be expected. I can't say there are any other Spurs fans. That's also to be expected.'

I think back to when I followed Spurs as a North London schoolboy. Going to all the home games with my mates. How I later enjoyed having season tickets, taking Greg and Emma. Then I wince as I think how unpredictable they were – still are. Always there or thereabouts, but rarely winning anything. It's too late now to switch to a more consistent team; being a Spurs fan is a lifelong sentence.

'Haven't we got a game today?' I ask.

'Yes, away at West Ham, it's a 5.30pm kick-off. Any chance of watching it on TV when we get back?' Greg answers.

'Of course, it should be a good game.'

'Could be a tough one, we're so unpredictable and they're on a good run. We need to win to stay in with a chance of qualifying for the Champions League next season. I'm not confident.'

'It's Spurs. I'm never confident.'

We enjoy our cream teas before setting off back to the lodge across the heath. A linnet gives us a burst of its sweet melody from the top of a gorse bush to send us on our way. As we walk on, I point to sand martins and swallows catching insects overhead.

'Will the swallows have come from Africa?' Emma asks.

'Probably. Some will have flown around eight thousand miles practically non-stop. They need to be where the insects are, which is here in our spring and summer, Africa in our autumn and winter.'

The sun is weaker now but still showing. The breeze coming off the sea to our right is picking up, the air increasingly fresh and bracing. I hear the caws of crows and then the deeper, more guttural croak of a raven. Looking up, I see its large black form passing lazily overhead with its distinctive, wedge-shaped tail.

'Raven, there in the sky heading away from us. Beautiful. The crows are seeing it off. Not so common around here. It's associated with Apollo the Greek god of prophecy. A messenger symbolising bad luck.'

'Let's hope it's a West Ham supporter,' Greg says.

A robin crosses the path in front of us.

'That fellow's thought to symbolise hope, revival, good things to come.'

'Let's hope it's a Spurs fan,' Greg responds. 'With our lack of recent trophies, I wonder whether we should replace our cockerel mascot with a sweet little robin.'

It's not what I'm thinking. 'Robins are incredibly aggressive. Their red breast is a threat to other males. Apparently, ten per cent of robin deaths are inflicted by rivals. They peck at their necks until they sever the spinal cord. They'll do the same to other species, especially if their young are threatened.'

Greg smiles. 'Sounds perfect – Spurs need to show more aggression.'

As we enter the woods on the last leg of our return journey, we hear loud churrs, squeaks and squeals. It's as if a large bird is being attacked. It's coming from close by in a tree. Greg asks what it is. I take a good look through my binos and catch sight of the culprit.

'Have a guess, one turn each, no looking. I'll buy the meal tonight if either of you get it right.'

We stop walking, the harsh churring continues and I wait for them to guess. They confer then Emma leads the way.

'Too loud for a small bird, it must be a crow or a magpie. Something like that.'

Greg doesn't agree. 'Too obvious, what about a jay?'

Emma looks at her brother. 'Oh, good one. How about a jackdaw or a bird of prey? Maybe a kestrel or sparrowhawk?'

I'm genuinely impressed that they've taken in more from our walks over the years than I'd thought. It's time to get going, though, so I hurry them up.

'Come on, we've got a match to get back for. You need to take a guess.'

Greg goes first. 'I'm going for jay. It's large enough and uncommon, the kind of bird you would set a quiz for. Emma?'

'I'm going for something more obvious. Magpie.'

'Sorry but you're both wrong. It's an agitated grey squirrel. Look, it's there, halfway up the tree on the large branch with its tail fluffed up. It will have young already at this time of year, it could be something's threatening them. A concerned parent sticking up for its family.'

Greg looks puzzled. He doesn't believe me. 'No way, it sounds like a bird.'

The squirrel comes to my rescue almost immediately,

moving closer to let us watch it belt out its anguished-sounding alarm call.

'It can be dangerous for the parent as it draws any predator away from the young onto itself. It's just one of the jobs of raising a family.'

Greg replies, 'OK, you win but I already thought you were buying dinner tonight.'

'Don't worry, I am.'

As we start walking again, a great tit blurts out its repetitive see-saw call. We watch as it works its way around a low tree. Emma identifies it straight away.

'Great tit, even I know that one. Tell us something about them, Dad.'

'They've been known to enter hollow trees and bludgeon roosting bats to death before dragging them back to the nest for a tasty family takeaway.'

Emma's not impressed. 'Gross, too much information.'

'The smaller bird there, the blue tit, it's just as committed to raising its young. They time their breeding season to coincide with the peak season for their favourite caterpillars. Parents can fly up to a hundred miles each, collecting them before their chicks fledge.'

Even Greg's impressed by this. 'Wow, that's commitment.'

'Producing and raising young is the be all and end all for every species.'

Greg's not so sure. 'Maybe, but not us, not man. Not now. Most of us just want to have a good time.'

'Possibly, even so, who knows how far we'll go to protect our offspring. See them successfully fledged.'

We soon arrive back at Sunrise Park where Greg and

Emma head off to the lodge while I pop into the shop to pick up a newspaper. Joyce welcomes me in.

'What do you want, Max?'

I can't work out whether this is a "what do you want?" as in "what is it this time?" or whether it's "what do you want?" as in "what can I get you?". I feel I'm not so much a sales opportunity as an annoying interruption.

'Have you got a *Telegraph*?'

'Why do you want that? Why not get *The Sun* like everyone else?'

I can't help but be drawn in by her charm.

'It's got the best sports coverage, best crossword, and I like Matt's cartoons. The articles are a bit right wing; I don't usually read those.'

'Well, I don't have one.'

'What do you have?'

'*The Sun*.'

'OK, I'll take *The Sun*.'

Joyce sighs and hands me a copy. 'Anything else? James was in buying more chocolates and flowers just now and Tim has just stocked up on his usual. It's Easter, I'm closed tomorrow, what else do you need?'

'His usual?'

'You know, his something for the weekend.'

'Sorry, do you mean what I think you mean?'

'Yes, condoms for his fancy woman.'

'What fancy woman?'

'I shouldn't really say, he doesn't like people talking about it. It's an open secret on the site but he doesn't want his wife to find out. He gets angry.'

'Come on, you can't tease me like this. Who is it?'

'Oh, alright. If you ask me nicely.'

'Please.'

'Go on then, you forced me. Becky, the waitress. But it didn't come from me. He's old enough to be her dad; in fact, around here, her grandad.'

I'm totally taken aback. Tim and Becky! She seems so nice. No wonder she was sticking up for him in the bar last night. I honestly hadn't seen that coming. It prompts me to follow up on my conversation with Sheila.

'Talking of fancy women, do you know anything about Simon and Gertrude?'

'Simon and Gertrude? What about Simon and Gertrude? Oh, I get it. That was years ago when they were friends, good friends, but I don't think it was anything more. She and Derek were going through a rough patch; she needed an ear. No hanky-panky that I know of. Why? What makes you ask? What do you know that I don't?'

'Oh, just curious.'

'Curious. You're a dark horse, Max. I'm going to have to keep an eye on you.'

I pay for the information by handing over cash for the unwanted *Sun* newspaper and set off back to my lodge. On my way, I catch a glimpse of a tiny goldcrest flashing bright-white wing bars and yellow forehead stripe as it flits through the branches of a large conifer. Incessant movement, wings whirring, almost hummingbird-like. Lovely. My head, though, is still whirring from what I've just been told. Tim and Becky! Who would have thought it?

Chapter 32

As I approach my lodge, I see a figure on the patio by the front door. It puts me on edge. After the walk and spending time with the kids, I've put the break-in to the back of my mind. I don't think I could cope with another incident. Two burglaries on the same day would just about finish me off. But it's Paul, my handy electrician.

'You alright, Max? Just making sure the switch is OK.'

'Great. Thanks.'

'I see Harvey's put a new lock on the door.'

'Yes, he did a good job as always. I'll make us a brew while you finish off.'

I go inside, put the kettle on and ask Alexa to play Cat Stevens. I'm soon humming along to the simple but gloriously uplifting "Moonshadow". It was one of Kathy's favourites. She chose it when planning her funeral. I picture her face when she told me that it made her feel alive, in the moment. She'd read Cat Stevens wrote it after seeing the shadow of the moon for the first time when on holiday away from the streetlights of London. The revelation made him leap and hop around with joy. Kathy said that she wanted us to remember her like that. Happy.

Paul comes inside, having finished checking the switch.

'It's fine. Let's hope it doesn't happen again.' He smiles and says, '"Moonshadow". Jean loved it. We loved it. We used to sing along to it together. It was our happy song. She would play it a lot towards the end. She said, like Cat Stevens, she was comforted by having been found by the "faithful light". We played it at her funeral. One of the few songs that still makes me feel happy… and sad.'

I think about telling him that we had it at Kathy's funeral, but it somehow doesn't feel right. We listen together, both lost in our memories. I feel a silent bond. When I hand him his cup of tea, he stares into it, cradles it lovingly, blows on it, then takes a sip. I wonder where Emma and Greg have got to.

'Have you seen Greg and Emma, my grown-up family? They should have got back here from our walk by now.'

'No, I'd only just arrived when you showed up. I met them when they were here a few weeks ago. Nice kids.'

'They're a comfort to me after losing Kathy. How are your girls?'

'OK, but Karen's been playing up at school and Kylie's gone quiet. She's become withdrawn. After losing their mum, what can you expect?'

'Give them time. They'll need time and support. It must be tough for the pair of them.'

'It is, very. They need me, but I can't always be there. I do worry how they'll turn out. I thought losing Jean was the worst thing that could happen, but watching the effect on them, it's just as bad. Anyway, I better get going. Thanks for the cuppa.'

'Thanks for sorting the switch.'

I see Paul out and check the front door as he goes. It's fine. The new lock's a bit stiff but everything's as it should be. Just as I'm about to go back inside, Greg and Emma emerge from the summerhouse that sits in the corner of my lodge plot.

'I was wondering where you two had got to.'

'We didn't want to interrupt you. We weren't sure whether to tell you, we didn't want to upset you. When we got back, we found something by the front door. This.'

Greg hands me a very dead, jet-black crow. I stare down at the large bird, then check it over. It has injuries to its left eye, a fractured left wing, fractured left leg and several shotgun pellets in its body. Hopefully it died instantly without too much suffering.

'It's been shot. Probably kids or a local farmer. I wonder what it's doing by my door?'

'And this was with it,' Greg says, handing me a note. It reads, 'Jobs not snobs.'

It's like I've been punched in the guts. Someone's put it here. Why would anyone do that? I understand that feelings on Sizewell are running high, but this. A dead crow. My God. I stare one last time at the lifeless body, shake my head, put it in the bin and we go inside. Emma offers to make another pot of tea and breaks open a packet of comforting chocolate biscuits. There's silence as we struggle to process what's happened. Greg turns on the TV. The match kicks off but I'm not really concentrating. My mind is elsewhere, attempting to figure out who might have put the crow there. I try reasoning that it's a sick joke, someone having fun. Maybe it's connected with the burglary. A crow. I recall that, spiritually, it signifies rebirth and the ability to adapt. But many cultures have it as an omen of bad fortune or upcoming tragedy. Irish mythology has it as the companion of Morrigan, the goddess of war and death. My mind races. Is it a threat? Maybe someone is warning me off opposing Sizewell C. Maybe, it's connected with what happened to Derek and Gertrude. I'm biting my lip again.

I try to watch the football, let it distract my thoughts from the crow. It looks like it's finishing in a draw, then Harry "one of our own" Kane curls the ball into the top corner of the West Ham net. Greg celebrates loudly and cheers again as VAR confirms the goal. When the final whistle blows, I join him in celebrating. I'm a bit over the top but it's a release from the tension. Spurs therapy. If only we could win more often. If only all this would stop.

Chapter 33

Once the match is over, we change and head off to Aldeburgh for dinner at The Lifeboat. The family has eaten there many times over the years; it's always excellent. The atmosphere is low key, the decor understated and the food, while not Michelin star-quality, is consistently good. Kathy always insisted we ate there whenever we came to Suffolk; it would seem wrong not to do so tonight. The trip takes about thirty minutes, initially along narrow roads flanked by heathland, then passing through Westleton village, skirting around the centre of much larger, more industrial Leiston before entering the pretty, medieval, seaside town of Aldeburgh. We find a parking space outside the restaurant, which is no mean achievement, and arrive promptly for our 8pm booking. Downstairs is full and we are shown upstairs to a cosy corner table. I look around to see if there's anyone I know. I once met an old school friend here who was on a yachting holiday. It's that sort of place. Greg and Emma study the menu; I don't need to. I'm highly predictable and will be going for my usual fish soup followed by sea bass washed down with a bottle of Sauvignon Blanc.

Greg puts the menu down and looks at me.

'Dad, who do you think put the crow there?'

'I imagine one of the pro-Sizewell C brigade. No idea who though.'

'But why?'

'Sizewell's divisive. People get worked up.'

'Yes, but that's sick. And you know what you were saying earlier about Gertrude having been pushed, that there are a lot of people at the site who didn't get on with her, that she was difficult. She was against Sizewell C. Could the same person have done that?'

It's not a discussion I want the rest of the diners to hear. I lean forward confidingly.

'I didn't say she was pushed. I said, I thought she might have been pushed.'

Greg, following my lead, also leans forward and speaks softly. 'OK, but who by?'

I question how much to tell him, think about saying nothing, then decide it can't do any harm to share what I know with him and Emma.

'There are a few candidates. I'll give you top line, but you mustn't say anything to anyone. It could start all sorts of rumours and bad feeling. You must promise. Both of you.'

The two of them promise and I fill them in as best I can. I tell them about Mike, who stands to inherit Gertrude's house and lodge; Felicity and her unforgiving grudge; aggressive Tim, who works at Sizewell; and George, whose construction company depends on contracts from the new power station. I then tell them how almost everyone is convinced Gertrude's fall was an accident. How they think I'm crazy. Greg and Emma listen intently. When I eventually draw breath, Emma smiles broadly before offering her own theory.

'Maybe it's all four of them together like in Agatha Christie's *Death on the Nile*.'

'You mean *Murder on the Orient Express*,' Greg corrects her.

'Thanks, Greg, handy correction. "Death in Denial" seems more apt, though, for this little mystery,' Emma fires back.

I can't let that go.

'Come on, guys, this is serious, this is real. It's Gertrude's death we're talking about. Someone living just yards from me could be a murderer. This isn't Agatha sanitised Christie.'

Greg presses on. 'We do get that, Dad. It can't be nice thinking that one of your neighbours or one of your friends could be a killer. But which one do you think it is?'

Typical Greg, he's not one to give up. Although I don't want to speculate, it's only the kids, and what harm can it do to think aloud.

'If I had to put money on one of them, I'd say Tim. They argued, she would have a go at him about his parking. He saw her on the night she fell, admits he was drunk and has never liked her. He's a nasty piece of work. He could have given her a nudge on the spur of the moment. The opportunity presented itself and he went for it.'

'You need to tell the police,' Greg says.

'I'm not ready. I've no evidence; and anyway, they haven't carried out the post-mortem. I need to wait, see what they find. Now, please can we enjoy the meal and not talk about Gertrude… or Sizewell.'

Our starters arrive and while we eat, we have a family catch up. Greg has recently split from his girlfriend. She was attractive, intelligent, fun, but clingy. He insists it was never serious. Emma's new dentist boyfriend sounds nice. He's a few years older than her, has his own flat in North London, likes amateur dramatics and plays the violin. She wants to know if he sounds too boring. He's kind, generous, witty, and fun to be with. She usually goes for the more edgy types, but if he makes her happy, I'm only going to say one thing.

My fish soup with garlic rouille and croutons is as good as always. I finish my glass of wine and need to go for a pee before the main course arrives. I descend the stairs to the ground floor and as I'm about to enter the hall leading to the gents, I catch sight of James sitting at a corner table. When I come out, I walk over to him to say hello. He's surprised to see me, but not as surprised as I am. With him is Felicity.

'Hello, James… Felicity.'

'Hi, Max. We weren't expecting to see you here,' a flustered faced James responds.

'Likewise. I'm upstairs with Greg and Emma. Are you regulars?'

'I come here a lot. It's our first… first time together.'

'Together?'

'Yes, together.'

'Does that mean what I think it does?'

James looks at Felicity, she nods, and he draws a deep breath.

'Yes, we were going to tell everyone but, with all that's been happening, we decided to keep it under wraps for a while. We're together, we're a couple. We have been for months.'

I'm shocked.

'No way. You're joking. I didn't see that coming.' I realise this hasn't come across as very supportive, so quickly add, 'I'm happy for you both. Really happy. Really, I am.' There's a pregnant pause. I continue, 'Oh, I get it, James, our walk when you headed off for lunch at The Elver. Felicity, when we met, you were heading there as well. And Joyce, the chocolates, the flowers. It all makes sense.'

Felicity looks up at me. 'You don't think it's too soon?'

'Too soon?'

'I mean, after Peter?'

'That's not for me to say. If it's right for you that's all that matters. You need to do what makes you happy. We only get one go at life. We need to make the most of it. Don't risk looking back thinking what might have been, look forward, think what could be. Go with your instinct. Only you know what feels right.'

'It does feel right.'

'Then, that's your answer. Sorry to leave you but I need to get back for my sea bass. I'll see you back at the site.'

James nods and, in a hushed voice, says, 'Please keep it under wraps for now, you know what people are like about this sort of thing.'

I leave them to work out how to take things forward and ascend the stairs gathering my thoughts. James and

Felicity are a couple. Do I tell the kids? I didn't make any promises. I've shared everything else with them. I arrive back at the table where our main courses have just arrived.

'Guess who's sitting downstairs having dinner together?'

'Brad Pitt and Angelina Jolie?' Emma immediately answers, shooting me a big smile.

'Very funny. Have a proper guess, they're from the site?'

'It's not one of those quizzes where we get a guess each and if we get it right, you buy dinner, and if we get it wrong, you buy dinner anyway?'

'No. Well, yes, I suppose it is. But when I tell you who it is, you must keep it a secret.'

'Is it one of those "patient confidentiality must keep it secret" secrets, or more the "only tell family and friends in a crowded restaurant" type secret?'

'If you don't want to know, I won't tell you.'

'Just kidding. Greg and I promise to keep it a secret, don't we, Greg? Just tell us, Dad, put us out of our suspense.'

'James and Felicity. James who's next door to me and Felicity who's over the track next to Mike.'

Emma's impressed. 'Wow, that will have the site gossips talking. Joyce will have a field day, probably already has. Why do they want it kept secret?'

'I guess they're not ready for others to find out, it's only a couple of years since Felicity's husband Peter died.'

Greg leans forward. 'The Felicity who hates Gertrude? The Felicity who thought Derek had as good as killed her husband? The Felicity who says she turned Gertrude away on the night she was supposed to have fallen? The Felicity who might have helped Gertrude over the cliff edge?'

'Well, yes, that Felicity.'

'Does that make James a suspect too? By association?'

'I suppose so, but James is OK. I don't believe for a second he would – he could – do anything like that. In fact, I don't believe Felicity could either.'

'But you don't know, do you?'

Emma breaks in, 'The food is excellent by the way. You should try it, Dad.'

Chapter 34

We arrive back at the lodge and, although it's getting late, decide to play Scrabble outside on the decking. It's what we regularly used to do on family holidays. Greg turns on the patio heater and we wrap ourselves in thick, woollen blankets. I open a bottle of merlot, unwrap a bar of chocolate and ask Alexa to play Nick Drake. We used to listen to him in the car on long journeys, the kids often falling asleep to his soft, gently soothing voice. The neighbours can't possibly complain. All that's missing now is Kathy. I set up for the four of us. Greg and Emma give me a strange look. I remove one of the word trays and we draw a letter to see who goes first. It feels just like old times. I'm usually highly competitive. I've always been unhappy if I don't score at least twenty-five points in a go and will sometimes push the two-minute time limit to find the optimum word. Tonight, though, I don't feel the need. I'm just enjoying sitting with Greg and Emma listening to Nick, hearing the sea break on the shore beneath the cliffs and spending time together as a family.

I break off a slab of chocolate and suck on it hard until it melts. It takes me back to family caravan holidays in the South of France when we would sit outside late into the night playing games, listening to the cicadas, and swatting away mosquitoes. Long evenings with all the family sat around a small camping table listening to Joni Mitchell, Neil Young and Cat Stevens. The four of us together. Happy. After a while, Greg raises his eyebrows and looks at me.

'Are you OK, Dad? You've been quick with your goes, put down two words scoring under twenty and not once said how bad your letters are.'

'I'm just enjoying the evening.'

'Yes, but with Scrabble that means winning. You're not.'

When I play a game, whether it's Scrabble or cards or any board game, I have always had an overwhelming need to win. If I can't or don't, I can become sullen and withdrawn. I tell myself it's just a game and doesn't matter. I tell myself to simply enjoy playing. I tell myself it's a nice way to pass the time. But each time, I revert to type. I can't stand not winning. I feel I'm a failure. But not tonight.

'Maybe I've mellowed.'

'Gone soft, you mean.'

'Maybe, losing your mum has put a different perspective on things. It's not about winning; it's about being here with the two of you. Just being happy.'

I look across the table at Emma, she looks back and smiles at me with her crinkly eyes. Eyes just like Kathy's.

'Yes, you do seem different, Dad, more philosophical. I can't say it's not good. Maybe you need to chill like this more often, drop the Gertrude thing. Just enjoy being here.'

It's my turn and, as luck would have it, I've picked up an "S" and a blank. It's set me up for "jealous", and a high-scoring, seven-letter word. As I lay it down, I look at Greg. He's wincing. Then I look at Emma and think about what she's just said.

'I probably do need to chill more, this is fun. But I'm not going to drop the Gertrude thing. I realise everyone thinks I'm crazy, but I need to find out what happened. I've come this far. I'm not going to let it go now. It's important to me. Especially since the misdiagnosis and then failing your mum.'

'How many times, Dad: you didn't fail Mum, you supported her,' Emma responds sharply.

'I failed her. I'll never forgive myself. Not picking up the signs, missing her lymphoma. I was blind. Worse. Stupid and blind. It cost your mum her life.'

'It didn't. Of course it didn't. We've been through this so many times. If you'd picked up on her lymphoma, you'd have made sure it was treated. You didn't because the signs weren't clear. Just like with Seb. It wasn't your fault. Neither was your fault.'

'I think a lot about Seb. His mum trusted me. I let her down. She never directly accused me of failing him, but I could see what she thought. It was in her eyes.'

'That was you. You imagined it. It was you and your guilt. But you had nothing to feel guilty about.'

'You know I contacted her to see if it was OK for me to attend the funeral. She wanted me to stay away. I wrote to her, she never replied.'

'But you did your best.'

'Maybe, but it wasn't good enough. My best wasn't good enough.'

'Come on, Dad, think how many patients you managed. How many you diagnosed and treated. Thousands? How many times did you miss something? How often did you get it wrong? A handful? No one's perfect, not even you. Stop beating yourself up. Stop crucifying yourself. You've no reason.'

'No reason? Your mum? Seb?'

'Stop it, Dad. Even if you did get them wrong, it wasn't on purpose. You didn't mean to. It wasn't your fault. They weren't your fault. Your patients loved you. Mum loved you. We love you. We need you to be strong.'

'Yes but—'

'Enough. Stop it. Stop it, please. We're here to spend Easter together as a family. It's what Mum would have wanted. Don't ruin it. Please, don't ruin it.'

Emma's right. Of course she's right. I need to let it all go. The guilt, the anger, the selfishness. I've been trying. At first burying it, covering it up. Then facing it. CBT. Getting the feelings out, analysing them, putting them into perspective. Now I live with it. I'm fine when out walking across the heath, spotting birds, spending time in nature. But every so often the ground just falls away. Sometimes for what seems like no reason, more often when something unexpectedly reminds me of Kathy. A tissue lying on the ground fallen from a loose sleeve. The smell of her favourite caramel popcorn. Schubert's *Impromptus* on the radio. Unfinished knitting. Emma's eyes. I know I need to think of the positives. Be thankful for what we had, not dwell on what I've lost. Be happy with everything I've got. I love Greg and Emma so much. They give me such strength. But sometimes it's just so hard.

Chapter 35

I wake several times through the night, my mind troubled and restless. Eventually I get to sleep only to be woken early by the mellow, flute-like song of a blackbird. It's my cue to head for the living room and step outside. I'm greeted by the dawn sun shining low across the sea, its intense, yellow streak illuminating a tangerine sky. I hear the familiar sound of waves gently breaking as they meet the shore beneath the cliffs. It's going to be a lovely day and I'm going to try not to think about Gertrude, the break in, or the dead crow. It's Easter Sunday.

There's no sign of the kids so it's a good time to set up the Easter egg hunt. I hide half of the mini eggs around the living room, then walk towards the sea placing some in trees and others under bushes away from the cliff edge. That should keep them busy for a while. I make myself a cup of decaf, sit out with it on the decking and watch the sunrise reflecting across the water. Inevitably, I think of Kathy. It's only my second Easter without her in forty years. I sit remembering moments from the time we shared together. It moves me to ask Alexa to play Simon and Garfunkel's "Kathy's Song". It was our song. If I'm feeling sad or lonely, I play it and feel her with me. Don't ask me how or why, but it helps get me through these moments.

As I sit, I sense hands being placed on my shoulders, and feel a kiss on the top of my head. Emma is up early. She's been woken by the music and joins me at the table.

'Are you OK, Dad? I love this song; it reminds me of Mum.'

'Morning, Emma. Yes, we loved it. Played it over and over when we first met. It helped bring us together, that and our mutual love of Leonard Cohen.'

'Leonard Cohen?'

'It was a phase we were going through.'

I decide my private moment with Kathy and our song is over so instead ask Alexa to play Leonard Cohen. We hear the wonderful guitar intro leading into "So Long Marianne", before Leonard invites his little darling over to the window. Greg then arrives, sits with us, and asks what could possibly possess us to play Leonard Cohen this early in the morning. I have no excuse and tell Alexa to stop. Emma's not happy.

'Come on, Dad, put it back on. Leonard Cohen's a perfect way to start Easter Sunday.'

Greg's not backing down without a fight. 'Let's be a bit more upbeat. Let's compromise. How about some Lou Reed? Alexa, play "Sunday Morning" by The Velvet Underground.'

I'm not happy about my Alexa being hijacked, but within seconds, the three of us are singing along to "Sunday Morning". Greg is right: it's perfect. I wonder how it's possible to switch from sadness to happiness in such a short space of time. When Lou has finished, Emma disappears inside before returning with two Easter eggs that she hands to us.

'Here you go. Happy Easter, Dad. I got you a duck. Greg, I got you a rabbit. They seemed appropriate, what with you being a quack and Greg being mad.'

I feel Emma's in need of another natural history lesson.

'Thanks, Emma, but it's hares. Mad March hares.'

'Same thing.'

'Not really.'

I see Emma shrug as I nip into the lodge to fetch the chocolate rabbit from Dale Farm for Greg and the duck for Emma.

'I got you both the same.'

Emma watches me return. 'Easter eggs?'

'No, literally the same. What are the chances? Happy Easter.'

'Great minds,' Emma says. 'Here, Greg, I'll swap my duck for your bunny. You can have one of each.'

Greg takes Emma's duck and looks at his two chocolate gifts.

'Thanks, Emma. Thanks, Dad. I'm sorry, I didn't have time to get you eggs but I did bring a box of chocolates. I thought we could have them after dinner.'

I recognise the box I took to his place when I was there at Christmas. I accept it with a smile, and we discuss our plans for the day. We agree to a full English breakfast followed by the Easter egg hunt, crabbing at Southwold and then lunch at the Riverside Inn in Southwold. This is all before our mid-afternoon visit to Kathy's sister Sally in Leiston. It's going to be a full day, but the weather's fine and we want to make the most of it.

We eat breakfast outside, bathed in the morning sun. It couldn't be more perfect. Well, it could. Greg tells Alexa to play "Perfect Day", and the three of us sit happily soaking up the music, the view and each other's company. It's moments like this I try to capture. Memories to use when things get tough. My precious stones.

'I once read that life shouldn't be measured by the number of breaths we take but by the moments that take our breath away. It's corny but true. The perfect days, the perfect moments. For me, it's the first time I set eyes on your mum. It's when she lifted her veil and smiled at me just before we got married. It's your first cries when you were born. It's your graduation ceremonies. Oh, and it's Ricky Villa rounding the City defence to score the winner in the 1981 Cup Final.'

'Dad, you're such a romantic,' Emma says.

'I can't believe you didn't mention Lucas Moura's second half hat trick against Ajax that got us into the Champions League Final!' Greg adds.

'I wasn't there, Greg, or it would have been top of my list.'

I sense that the time is right for the children's Easter egg hunt. We do it every year. Always ten eggs and always Greg wins. Last year, it was his six to Emma's four. They rapidly manage to find the eggs scattered around the lodge but take longer with those outside. Emma finds an egg hidden in a tree. Greg finds one of the eggs under the bushes. He then delves further into the vegetation and emerges with an object which he holds aloft.

'I've found a torch.'

Greg has a big smile on his face, like a fisherman who's just landed a whopper. He examines his catch.

'It's a serious torch. Zoomable, rechargeable, adjustable focus. It even looks to be waterproof. It's in decent condition, it must have been lost recently. I'll hand it in to the site office and see if anyone's reported it missing. Hopefully, no one will claim it. I could use a good torch.'

While Greg and I are looking at the torch, Emma finds the last two eggs and the hunt ends in a five-all draw. She's delighted and celebrates by dancing around Greg chanting the not entirely accurate "loser, loser". He, in turn, shines the powerful torchlight in her eyes. Even in daylight, it's very bright. Someone will be missing it.

Chapter 36

It's mid-morning when we head off for the twenty-minute trip up the coast to the typically English seaside town of Southwold. Greg drives us in his new convertible with the top down. I sit in the front, enjoying the breeze on my face and the sun on my head. It's a new experience. I love the sense of freedom, the wide expanse of sky and the frequent bursts of birdsong. I also savour the passing aromas, particularly when we drive past a large pig farm. They somehow make the journey more real.

We used to come to Southwold a lot when the kids were young to enjoy the short, quirky pier, sandy beach, and colourful beach hut-lined promenade. Today we head for the harbour on the north side of the murky, fast flowing River Blyth where the unmade dirt and pebble track tests the tyres and suspension of Greg's new pride and joy. The tiny village of Walberswick sits across the river to the south, connected by a rowboat ferry. Greg parks just outside the Riverside Inn on the quayside and we select the most suitable of many small jetties for our crabbing competition. I take a close look at the boats moored alongside the wooden platforms, many of them fishing vessels out of Lowestoft: *Laura K*, *Avril Rose*, *Emma H*, *Gemma P*. Lining the jetties are large plastic containers, buckets full of fishing gear, ropes, floats, nets, grappling hooks and lobster traps. Tyres have been wrapped around thick, yellow lichen-encrusted posts to cushion the clumsy coming alongside of the more sensitive leisure vessels. In the shallow waters lie dark green fronds of bladderwrack where redshanks and oystercatchers wade in search of worms, crabs and other tasty morsels. On the bank, arrow-like wader footprints criss-cross the mud, and the occasional crab risks predation by scurrying from one hiding place to another.

I've brought three lines with weights to which we tie bacon as bait. Kathy won the last time we came, catching fourteen crabs in the sixty minutes allowed. We collect a bucket of river water as temporary home for our crabs, and I signal for battle to commence. Greg whoops as one immediately takes his bait. It's medium-sized and holds on to the bacon with a vice-like grip before being extricated and dropped in the bucket. Emma then catches a tiddler. I've not even seen a crab close to my bait. I move station and quickly have two crabs grabbing at my bacon. I pull the line in slowly and manage to land one but the other jumps off. Our bucket gradually fills with crabs of all sizes jostling for position with their razor-sharp pincers. I call time after an hour. I've caught ten, Greg twelve and Emma fourteen. She wins with the same total as Kathy last time. Buzzing, she does a little jig and looks to the sky as she sings.

'Championee, championee, ole, ole, ole. Are you watching, Mum? This is for you.'

It makes me both happy and sad.

'Well done, Emma. I imagine your mum's smiling on you.'

'Yes, it's one for the girls.'

'Come on, let's put the crabs back, drop the stuff off in the car and take a walk by the river before lunch.'

We head east along the quayside towards the sea, passing an old, rusty cannon that stands guard in front of the whitewashed Riverside Inn with its 1953 flood level marked halfway up the building. Kathy's dad used to talk about how Southwold had been a virtual island for two days and how several local residents had been lost in the waters. Laughter bursts out from drinkers sitting out in the sun by the river. A skein of honking geese pass over in the sky to the north, encouraging me to look across Southwold's flat town moor and golf course. I notice a trio of women golfers walking up one of the fairways. I do a double take: one of them is wearing a scarf. A red scarf. I shudder. I can't help thinking of Ann. I know it's not her, but I can't help staring. I'm brought around by Emma's voice.

'Come on, Dad. You and your birdwatching.'

'Greylags,' I mutter.

We walk past busy yards full of cranes, hoists, ropes, wire rigging, and boats of all sizes propped up in dry dock on stone blocks, wooden rests and metal scaffolds. We're accompanied by the sound of power washers, lathes and welding gear as work continues even on Easter Sunday. Numerous small black fishing huts and lockups sit on raised platforms against the possibility of an overflowing river, all padlocked in fear of mischief.

'Plaice, skate, lemon sole, mackerel, lobster, crab, prawns, cockles and whelks all landed daily, subject to seasonal availability,' I read aloud from a chalkboard sign outside one of the longshore fishing huts.

'Mum used to hate the cockles and whelks,' Emma responds.

We pass long, outdoor trestle tables full of diners eating fish and chips. It's time to return to the Riverside Inn for lunch. We retrace our steps, and I order three pints of Ghostship to go with our fish and chips, which we tuck into outside overlooking the river. If it wasn't for the golfer and her scarf, it would have been the perfect Easter Sunday morning.

Chapter 37

It's 3pm by the time we've had lunch, walked briefly around Southwold town centre, spent a few pounds at the amusement arcade on the pier and driven to Leiston. We pull up in a quiet residential street with cars parked either side of the narrow road in time for our chocolate cake catch-up with Kathy's sister Sally. Greg manages to squeeze us into a spot almost opposite her terrace house. We walk through her compact front garden, ring the doorbell and are welcomed by Sally with hugs all round. I've not seen her since Kathy's funeral. I've spoken with her on the phone, but feel guilty I haven't found the time, or, more truthfully, the courage, to visit. Although Sally was quite a bit older, the two sisters were close and looked similar. I couldn't face being with her and not Kathy. It's easier now the kids are with me. Well, I thought it would be. Our hug sets me off. It sets us both off.

We remove our shoes and Sally takes us through to her living room, which reminds me of the ones you find in new-build show homes. It's pastel perfect. Even the pictures have the look that seems to be trying as hard as possible not to offend, not to provoke or make you think. As sisters, she and Kathy may have been close, but their tastes were very different. Kathy liked a rustic feel. Warm, organic, with deep, earthy colours. She liked art with character, usually modern, often abstract. She liked wood sculptures, pottery, artefacts from around the world. She liked her home to reflect her personality. Open, vibrant, sometimes controversial. Sally disappears and returns with a tray on which sit a pot of tea, four cups and an enormous, much anticipated, can't-wait-to-eat-it chocolate cake. The three of us plant ourselves in a line on the sofa, Sally puts the tray on a coffee table in front of us and then sits in an armchair opposite.

'Wow, that looks amazing,' I say.

'My pleasure, you always were one for my chocolate cake,' she answers, before adding, 'as Mum used to say, "Receiving fills the belly, giving fills the soul". How have you been keeping, Max?' Sally asks as she cuts the cake.

'Trying to come to terms with losing Kathy. I'm sorry I haven't been to see you; it's been difficult.'

'I understand. I do. I'm still struggling with it. I miss her.'

Sally is silent, looks to the floor. It's obvious she's thinking about her sister. She raises her head again, pours the tea, before handing out napkins and slices of chocolate cake. I take a bite out of mine. It's very good. Sally looks at me, then Greg and Emma.

'It must be nice, the three of you being together for Easter.'

'Yes, it's lovely, really nice.' I pause then add, 'As is the cake.'

'How are things at the lodge? I hear you're spending a lot of time there?'

'Yes, it works well for me. It's smaller than the house in Surrey, I don't rattle around on my own so much. I've less to look after, fewer reminders of Kathy. I like to remember her, of course I do, but at the house, it's too much. I think of her all the time. Here, I've got the sea, walks, Dunwich Heath, the birds. They take me out of myself. I don't dwell on things so much.'

'Are you planning to sell?'

'Sell?'

'The house?'

'Probably. I haven't been able to face it. Most of the time it just sits unoccupied. Keeping it doesn't make any sense.'

The doorbell rings. Sally gets up, opens the front door and we hear her welcome in her late husband's older brother, Bill. Sally's husband, Graham, had a heart attack and died about five years ago. He and Bill owned the local builders merchant yard and trade supplies shop. Bill still runs the empire and Sally retains a share in the business. We shake hands as he enters the room, not sure whether to hug or not. We go for an awkward mini hug. I've not seen him since Graham's funeral.

'Bill, good to see you. How are you keeping?'

'Good thanks, Max. You?'

'I'm OK.'

'Sally told me you were coming, I wanted to pop in and say hello.'

Emma and Greg give him a hug. The room is silent. It feels awkward. Sally pours Bill a cup of tea and hands him a slice of cake. He receives it with a knowing smile.

223

'How's Orla?' I ask.

'As good as can be expected.'

'How's the care home working out?'

'It's fine. They're good with dementia. I visit most days. They're always friendly. Orla loves her singing, they all do. She sings songs she remembers from her childhood in Ireland. She doesn't really recognise me anymore though.'

'I'm sorry. At least she seems happy; it's not always the case.'

The silence returns, a radiator gurgles, a dog barks.

'I heard a woman died falling down the cliff at Sunrise Park,' Bill says.

I'm surprised the news has reached him. The jungle drums haven't wasted much time. My slice of cake hovers in front of my mouth. I didn't want to think about Gertrude today, but Bill's put me on the spot.

'Yes, Gertrude, my neighbour, she had the lodge opposite.'

'Opposite? I'm sorry. Did you know her well?'

I put the slice of cake down and take a sip of tea instead.

'Not really. We used to say hello, wave to each other from our decking. Like Orla, she had dementia.'

'Oh, I see. Must be a shock though. What happened?'

'It was in the bad storm the other night. The police think that she was probably confused, wandered out of her lodge and fell down the cliff.'

'Accident then.'

'I'm not so sure.'

'Why not?'

'Her injuries were more like she'd fallen backwards. I can't work out how she would have done that.'

Sally joins the conversation. 'That's the first time I've heard of anyone falling down the cliff there. The site always looked safe enough. Aren't there dead tree trunks lying across the path blocking the edge? We knew a couple who had a lodge at the park. Their decking had a great view of the sea. It was a lovely spot. Graham and I used to go for lunch.'

'Who was that?' I ask.

'George and Julia. George used Graham and Bill for his building supplies. He liked to keep them sweet. He got good prices and used the yard here in Leiston to store his materials.'

'I know them. Their lodge is next to mine, we recently had lunch.'

'How funny. Please say hello from me when you see them. Julia was OK, I wasn't so keen on George. He was a bit smug... opinionated.'

'I know what you mean.'

'I don't think he treated Julia very well and, from what Graham used to tell me, he didn't treat his workers much better.'

'He's not so bad. He's still one of our best customers,' Bill says. 'I see him sometimes. We go shooting, help the local farmers control the pests. He's a good shot.'

Greg looks across at me. I know what he's thinking. There's an awkward silence broken only by the sound of teacups being lifted to mouths.

'How's the business going?' I ask.

'It ticks along. We're expecting things to pick up once

the Sizewell C work starts coming in. The contractors are all licking their lips; we should get our share.'

Emma joins in. 'You're not a big fan of Sizewell C, are you, Dad.'

Bill looks at her and then me. 'Some are, some aren't. It depends on your viewpoint. If you're into the scenery, nature and the wildlife, you'll be against it. If you're after clean energy and building contracts, it's a different matter. Divided the town, it has.'

'Dad's worried about how it would affect Minsmere.'

I decide to keep quiet on the matter; it's not Bill I need to convince. I finish my slice of cake and run my tongue around my teeth to remove the leftover sticky bits. Sally, wanting to change the subject, looks directly at Greg and Emma.

'And how are you youngsters keeping?'

Greg and Emma fill her and Bill in on their news while I check my phone. There are a few messages, including one from James wanting to know if I can do 1pm lunch with him and Felicity tomorrow at his lodge. It's when the kids will be heading off for their Ed Sheeran concert so I text back, *Yes, that would be lovely.* It should certainly be enlightening.

We have more tea, a second slice of cake and chat for over an hour before Bill has to go. We see him out, chat some more then sense it's time to for us to leave. There are parting hugs with Sally before we walk through her front garden, step between two parked cars, glance in both directions and begin to cross the road to Greg's convertible. As I do so, a large, dark car pulls out from the kerb a short distance away and accelerates in my direction. It heads straight for me. I freeze. My legs won't work; they're cemented to the road. It approaches fast, but I can't do anything. I prepare to be hit, but instead find myself propelled through the air before landing heavily on the pavement opposite. Next to me, also on the ground, is Greg. As the car speeds off, I try to make out the number plate, but it's gone too fast. I can't be sure, but what I think I've seen is a black Land Rover with a silver tow ball. I catch my breath and look across at Greg.

'Are you OK?'

'I think so. You?'

'In one piece. I banged my side when I landed. I'm probably going to have a juicy bruise or two. I should be OK. What the hell was that about? He came out of nowhere. He was driving like a maniac.'

Emma has watched it all from Sally's front garden.

'My God, what just happened? He was crazy. You could have been killed. You too, Greg. Very brave. What you did was practically suicidal.'

Greg picks himself up and rubs his right knee.

'Rugby, one of the benefits of a private education. Arguably the best tackle I've ever made. Did you get the number plate?'

'No, it all happened too fast.'

I'm shaken; we could have both been killed. I look back towards Sally's house.

'We need something sweet for the shock.'

I tell Sally what's happened and in no time we're self-medicating with more tea and chocolate cake. We sit in silence, recovering and trying to work out what's just happened.

'Did you see who did it?' Sally asks.

We shake our heads.

'What kind of car was it?'

'Large and dark, we think it was a Land Rover. It came out of nowhere and accelerated in our direction. Like it was aiming for Dad,' Greg answers.

Sally furrows her brow.

'It's normally such a quiet street. We get little traffic apart from those who live here. Rarely anything going too fast.'

'Whoever did it was either crazy or knew what he was doing. Probably both,' Greg responds.

'He?' Sally asks.

Greg looks sheepish. 'Point taken. Or she, or they.'

'It seems Leiston's a hotspot for it,' Sally says. 'We had a hit-and-run in the town just over a year ago; a woman was badly injured. She died later. And a man was killed in another just up the road several months back.'

'Derek, Derek Talbot? Gertrude's husband?' I ask.

'Yes, that's him, photographer. He was Gertrude's husband? Gertrude who fell down the cliff. Really, he was her husband?'

'Yes, it does seem strange. Talk about lightning striking more than once.'

Sally now has a huge frown across her forehead. 'You haven't made any enemies around here, have you, Max?'

'I may have upset a few people with my views on Sizewell C and I've been questioning how Gertrude fell off the cliff. I suppose I could have put a few backs up.'

'Typical Max. You're just like Dad, you won't let things go. You're always probing, asking questions, turning over every stone. You should have been a detective like him.'

'I was happy as a GP, thanks. Well, most of the time.'

'I know. You were a good GP. It's just that I see a lot of my dad in you.'

'Maybe, but I bet he didn't fail his victims the way I failed Kathy.'

I feel bad as soon as I've said it. Emma immediately shoots me a hard look.

'Dad, how many times? Stop it, just stop it.' She then looks at Sally and says, 'He didn't fail Mum, he looked after her. He cared for her. He loved her.'

Chapter 38

Upset and shaken, we drive back to Dunwich in silence. I don't say anything to the kids, but the shock has got to me. I need to rest. When we arrive at the lodge, I tell Greg and Emma I was planning to cook a roast dinner. I also tell them I'm not feeling well, I need to have a lie down. Emma immediately becomes Kathy, takes control and starts to prepare the meal. I disappear off to my bedroom.

I undress, get into bed, pull the duvet up to my neck and think about what Sally had said. Whether I'd made any enemies. It mirrored what I'd been thinking. That it was deliberate. That the driver was trying to hit me. But, why? It doesn't make any sense. Maybe there's a connection with what happened to Derek and Gertrude, the break in, the dead crow. I'm not a great believer in outrageous coincidences. I like to look at the facts, assess the data and draw conclusions strictly from concrete empirical evidence. In this case, I can only think that two and two equates to there being a deranged person on the loose. Not just on the loose, but in Leiston, possibly Dunwich. And I'm lined up to be their next victim.

My breathing is shallow, my heart pounding and my stomach turning. I feel nauseous. I sense the start of a familiar trembling. I need to nip this in the bud. I get out of bed to open the window, letting in air and the calming sound of the sea. I lie back down and concentrate on relaxing my body, letting go of the tension. I work slowly from my toes to my head, and then in the opposite direction. Each time I get so far, then tense up. It's not working, my mind is in overdrive. The window is open. What if the killer enters? Come on, relax. But I need the air; more than ever, I need the air. And I need to hear the sea, the soothing rhythm of the sea. Relax. But the patio doors are open. What about Emma and Greg? Could the killer come for them? Relax. The tension's not going away. If anything, it's getting worse. I recognise the signs and know what's coming. I've been here before. I'll never forget those moments. Moments of sheer terror. When I thought I was dying. When I would lose command of my body and be overcome by spasms. Terrible uncontrollable spasms. I feel it happening again, but now I know what to do. I need to resist fighting the panic, go with it, welcome it in. If I fight it, I've lost. If I fight it, it'll keep coming back. I could be condemning myself to months, even years, of panic attack torture. I try not to resist. I know it can't hurt me. It's just my sympathetic system going into overdrive. A vicious spiral I mustn't feed. I use all my will power and let the spasms wash over me. I focus on them, not trying to stop them. I'm curious. Welcome back, old friend, how are you? Where have you been? Let me feel you, examine

231

you, get to know you again. Come on, bring it on, do your worst. I'm ready.

Several waves of panic wash through me; the second is the worst, coming just a few minutes after the first. The third is less severe. Within thirty minutes, it's over. I'm tired, exhausted, but it's over. In the past, the waves could go on for more than an hour. Those were the bad days, the days before I knew what to do. When I thought, despite my medical training, that there was no way out of my torture. When I thought I might die. Then I read a self-help book and learnt how to manage the attacks. Not as a doctor, but as a patient. Combined with antidepressants, it probably saved my life. Not from the panic attacks, but from what they and my anxiety made me want to do to myself.

I wonder whether to take a tablet now but decide against it. The panic could be a one-off and it would be good to keep my big gun in reserve. Knowing there's something to fall back on has often been enough to help me remain calm. I tell Alexa to play Hildegard von Bingen and try my relaxation exercise again. Toes to head, head to toes. I concentrate on my breathing and feeling my chest gently rising, gently falling.

I close my eyes and imagine my safe place. I'm walking across Dunwich Heath. The sun is shining, the birds are singing, the purple heather is in bloom. I come to a clearing away from the path that is surrounded by shady trees and bright-yellow, coconut-scented gorse. I lie down in sweet-smelling soft grass and close my eyes. The air is warm, a gentle breeze brushes my face, and I hear the familiar "running up to bowl" cadence of a chaffinch.

Close by is the reassuring summer buzz of a bumble bee. In the distance, the sea gently rumbles as it breaks on the shore beneath the cliffs, and, high above, a skylark performs its liquid warble. I'm relaxed and without a care. I'm in my safe place breathing slowly in and out, in and out, in and out. Soon, I fall into the blessed release of sleep.

I'm under the sea trying to reach the surface. Someone's holding my feet and each time I try to swim up, I'm pulled back down. Kathy is above the water calling to me, beckoning me. I can't reach her. I try, I just can't. I struggle, kick my legs and eventually wriggle my feet loose. I rise a short way up only to be caught once more and pulled back down. Each time I think I've escaped, I'm caught. I give up and turn around to face my attacker. To tackle them head on. I know they're there, but the water is murky. I can't make them out. Then I see a black shape. A crow. It's wearing a crimson scarf and moving towards me. I turn to swim away, swallow water, choke and wake up sweating.

Hildegard has finished. My hard-won state of calm has gone and been replaced by a vague sense of terror from my confused dream. I lie in bed trying to make sense of it. As a GP, I would sometimes be asked by patients to help interpret their dreams, but I always refused. It wasn't my area. Some I referred for therapy and for some it seemed to help. I recall reading that dreams of being trapped then escaping can represent trying to get away from something happening in real life. It would make sense; there's a lot for me to want to get away from. Then there's a knock on my door. It's Greg; dinner is ready.

Chapter 39

I try to put the dream to the back of my mind and settle myself before joining Greg and Emma. When I do, I'm hit by the intensely nostalgic smell of Sunday lunch with all the family. It's instant relief. I think of me with a gin and tonic, Kathy with a white wine, a crossword half finished, Emma and Greg playing with the cats, football on the TV. They have prepared the works. Beautifully browned sirloin of beef, crispy golden potatoes, minted peas, buttered baby carrots, even enormous, fluffy Yorkshire puddings.

'Wow, it all looks and smells great. Your mum taught you well.'

'A joint effort. Literally,' Emma says. She pauses, smiles, and adds, 'I did the cooking. Greg did the prep and laid the table.'

'Thanks. You can come again.'

'How are you feeling?'

'Shaken. Better than I did, but still shaken.'

'Not surprising. Hopefully nothing broken. Will you need a check-up?'

'I've given myself a comprehensive going over.

Everything's fine. I'll be sore in the morning but it's nothing ibuprofen can't take care of. How about you, Greg?'

'I'm OK, nothing my body hasn't gone through playing rugby.'

'Do you often play rugby on the road?'

'I'm fine, just a few grazes. Have you thought about what happened?'

Emma jumps in before I can answer. 'Dad, are you OK to carve? The meat has rested long enough. I'm starving.'

I sharpen the carving knife, snip off the butcher string and begin to cut thin strips of perfectly cooked, softly pink-in-the-middle, medium-rare roast beef. I was worried I may not have an appetite, but the look and smell of the joint have my juices well and truly flowing. I answer Greg's question as I carve.

'Yes, I've thought about it and the more I've thought about it, the more I can't help thinking it was deliberate. That the driver was trying to hit me. That there's a connection between what happened to Derek, Gertrude and now me. It's as though there's a mad person loose, and I'm next on their hit list.'

Greg hands me warmed plates to place the slices of beef on, then puts them on the table, and we sit helping ourselves to the trimmings.

'Looks great, I'm ready for this,' he says, picking up his knife and fork, before adding, 'Dad, you do realise someone's probably trying to warn you off, that maybe they don't want you asking questions about Gertrude and Derek? And the crow. Maybe it's something to do with

Sizewell. You need to back off and leave it to the police. Who knows what they might do next.'

I know Greg's trying to protect me, but I can't – won't – give up because someone might be threatening me.

'Do you remember when you were young and used to play in goal for Rovers? You would dive headfirst to take the ball off the feet of the opposition strikers. The number of times you were kicked in the face or the body, but you didn't care. It scared me silly. You were so brave, so fearless, probably stupid. Whatever you did, you always threw yourself in, never worrying about the risk or the consequences. Well, I'm like you. There's no way I'm going to back off, no one's going to intimidate me into giving up. I'm going to find out what really happened to Gertrude, whatever the cost. Even if I do get kicked in the head.'

'Then you need to speak to the police and tell them what you know.'

'I will, but I'd rather wait until after the post-mortem. I've already told them about my concern over Gertrude's fall and they weren't interested. I can't see that a dead crow, or nearly being hit by a car, will change that. What will change things is if the post-mortem finds something suspicious. If it doesn't, I'll challenge it.'

'Then you need to be careful.'

'Greg's right, Dad, you need to be careful,' Emma says. 'We can keep an eye out for you, but please promise us you won't do anything silly. You won't put yourself at risk.'

'Of course, but I can't expect you two to babysit me.'

'We can try.'

I don't want them to worry about me and need to reassure them.

'What time are you heading off for the concert tomorrow?'

'It starts at 2pm, we plan to leave around 1pm. Why?' Greg answers.

'I've been invited for lunch at 1pm with James and Felicity, so it works out well. They can babysit me. We can go for a walk in the morning, and you can keep an eye on me then.'

'What about tomorrow night?' Emma asks.

'Mike has invited me to a concert at Snape; we're eating in Aldeburgh first.'

'Anything good?'

'Not seen the menu.'

'Dad.'

'Beethoven's *Sixth*, you know, the *Pastoral*. One of my favourites.'

'OK, just so long as you're with someone.'

Our roast dinner is as good as it smells, and we enjoy seconds before Emma clears away the plates and follows it up with a large tarte Tatin. We spend the evening enjoying the food and wine, chatting, laughing, simply being together. They are great company and take my mind from thinking too much about what's been happening. I feel very lucky. They more than justify the sleepless nights, worry and sacrifice that went into raising them. It makes me feel that Kathy and I had a purpose, and our purpose has been realised.

Chapter 40

I sleep only fitfully. After a few hours, I give up and lie in bed awake, going over what's happened. I need to make sense of things. I find my journal and write up yesterday's entry. I'm not sure I've ever experienced a day with such highs and lows. With my thoughts captured and my mind tidied, I try to get back to sleep. It's hard. I worry I might wake with another panic attack. Previously, once I started having them, they would keep returning. I'd get them every night. It took months before they stopped. I dreaded the evening arriving, was frightened to get into bed, scared to go to sleep. The insomnia made things worse, creating a vicious spiral. It felt like an endless tunnel. It took over a year of tablets, CBT and nature walks to fully get through it. But now, having come out the other side, I know I can manage it. With the help of Alexa and Hildegard, I eventually get back to sleep.

I wake to sunlight streaming through partially open curtains. I'm immediately grateful I've managed to sleep for so long, not had another panic attack and not had any more vivid dreams. It's a good sign. Yesterday was a setback but an understandable one. Who wouldn't be traumatised by a close shave with death from an attempted hit-and-run?

I put the kettle on and, while waiting for it to boil, check my telescope to see what's out at sea. The view is hazy but close in there's an assortment of birds sitting on the water that I scan for anything unusual. Having satisfied myself there's nothing special, I make an instant decaf and head outside. The sun and the view warm me through. It's as if my mental battery is being recharged. A robin busily hogs the bird feeder while a female chaffinch, brown with dainty white wing bars, struts back and forth on the ground picking at discarded fallen seeds. I'm there on my own for almost an hour before Emma joins me.

'How are you this morning, Dad?'

'I'm OK, it took a while but in the end I had a decent night's sleep. I'm not too sore, I think I got lucky.'

'Yes, with a little help from Greg. But you do need to let the police know.'

'I will, I will. It's a lovely day, are you up for another walk along the beach to say hi to your mum at the Coastguards?'

'Yes, sounds good. Should I wake Greg?'

'Let's give him half an hour, he needs his beauty sleep. We can make breakfast. The works?'

'Seems wrong not to.'

The two of us busy ourselves in the kitchen before Greg emerges and we eat our hearty full English on the decking. Once we've cleared away, we gather our rucksacks, put on our walking boots and head out south along the sandy cliff edge path before descending the wooden steps to the shingle beach below. Ahead of us is the wide expanse of shimmering North Sea whose waves are breaking gently and spewing bubbly, white surf onto the shore. Behind us, inland, are the steep cliffs covered in short trees, bushes, and scrub all jostling for their share of the sun. To our right and left are long stretches of almost deserted beach curving away into the distance.

We head south making slow progress walking over sinking pebbles, their underfoot crunch giving way in places to the softer, more mellow squelch of sand. A couple is walking along the shoreline ahead of us holding hands. They weave their way around pebble mounds and occasional overly enthusiastic wave incursions. We pass a man lying on his back with his eyes closed. He's sunning himself, flanked by his water bottle and rucksack, with his feet planted on the pebbles, his knees, face and sun cap pointing to the sky. An enormous herring gull struts back and forth, seemingly confused, as a deck chair attendant on a beach where someone has removed all the furniture.

My journal is in my rucksack and every so often I stop to record things that grab my attention. It slows us down, but I enjoy describing what's around me and capturing the thoughts it triggers. I share passages with the kids, who add their own descriptions. It's something I started doing when I first suffered from anxiety and read that writing and mindfulness could help. They did. They somehow slowed my brain, stopped the incessant whirr. I learnt to spend time focusing on the here and now, not the future. Not on what might happen, but on what is happening. What's in front of me.

'It's so lovely here, it calms me, makes everything right. Do you remember the William Blake poem 'Auguries of Innocence'? I used to recite it to you.'

'Yes. I loved it. I still do,' Emma responds. 'It inspired me to discover poetry. I'll never forget it:

To see a World in a Grain of Sand
And a Heaven in a Wild Flower
Hold Infinity in the palm of your hand
And Eternity in an hour.'

'That's it, Emma. That's what I feel when I walk along the shore here or over the heath. As though I'm part of something much bigger, so much more enduring. Eternity. It puts things in perspective, makes my worries, my anxieties, seem almost irrelevant. Unimportant. I'm not religious, but it feels spiritual.'

Emma looks at me with a slight frown, the slight frown that has always accompanied her wanting to discuss something serious.

'I'm scared of dying, I always have been. The idea of nothing, I can't get used to it. I lie in bed wondering what it would be like and how many years I have left. I sometimes work out how many weeks, days, even hours. I don't understand why old people aren't more scared of death.'

'Old people like me?'

'You're not old, Dad. Old people with just a few years left.'

'I have no idea how long I might have left, but I'm not frightened of dying. I used to be when I was your age, but not now.'

'Why not now?'

'I don't really know. I've often thought about it. I reckon as you get older, your brain prepares you. Your memories become a much larger part of your life; you have less future to lose. Your parents and friends pass away; you get used to seeing them go. You realise that if they can go through it, so can you. And you get tired, your body starts to break down, life holds less appeal. Death might seem terrifying to you now, but by the time you get to my age, it will seem natural, the way of things. Even something to look forward to.'

Emma is silent for a while and then holds my hand.

'Mum? Has losing Mum made life less important?'

'Maybe, or maybe it's just growing older. Don't get me wrong, I love life. Assuming I'm healthy, I want to live for long as I can. Anyway, there's things I still want to do. Like meet my grandchildren!'

She squeezes my hand, looks at me and smiles.

'No pressure then.'

As on our last walk, we reach the boundary with Minsmere and head inland up the steep sandy path to the family bench. Two people are already sat on it. I shouldn't let it upset me as it's not owned by us, but I always feel a sense of annoyance when it happens. I let it go. As we get close, I recognise Julia… and George. I wonder whether to mention the crow. I'm very tempted. I'm increasingly thinking it was him, but I don't want to ruin our walk.

'George, Julia, fancy seeing you two. These are my children, Greg and Emma.'

Julia stands up, George follows suit and looks at the two of them.

'Nice to meet you, your dad's told us a lot about you.'

'All good, I hope,' says Emma.

'I had lunch with George and Julia on their decking just a couple of days ago,' I say to Emma and Greg, before turning to George and Julia. 'Funnily enough, you came up in conversation when we were at my sister-in-law's yesterday. Sally, Sally Smith. She lives in Leiston. Her husband Graham owned the local builders merchant yard and trade supplies shop. She said you know each other.'

George raises his eyebrows. 'Sally and Graham, I remember them well. I used to do a lot of business with him.' He pauses then adds, 'It's very sad. We were at Graham's funeral, it's the last time we saw Sally. How is she?'

'She's good. I imagine you now deal with Graham's brother Bill.'

'Yes, he's very helpful.'

'She said to pass on her best wishes.'

There's a brief silence while we all look out at the view. I feel the urge to comment.

'I love it here, it's awe-inspiring. Kathy and I dedicated this bench to her parents, they used to come here a lot. They would picnic looking across Minsmere, over the reed beds and out to sea. We scattered Kathy's ashes here.'

'This bench. Really?' Julia says. 'I can understand why, it's a lovely place. Such a glorious view.'

Not to be outdone, George adds a helpful rider. 'And set off nicely by the bright white dome of Sizewell B. I was just trying to work out where Sizewell C will sit.'

He's deliberately, mercilessly, homed in on my soft underbelly. Not wanting to be drawn into another Sizewell C argument, I change subject.

'You haven't lost a flashlight torch by any chance? It's zoomable, rechargeable, with an adjustable focus. I think its waterproof. We found it yesterday under a bush by the cliff edge. Well, Greg found it during an Easter egg hunt.'

George is immediately interested. 'Sounds like a serious bit of kit; they're not cheap. I'd be happy to take it off your hands.'

George is the last person I'd want to donate it to.

'Let me see if I can find the original owner. As you say, it can't be cheap and they're probably missing it.'

'We need to head off now, maybe see you later,' George says, looking disappointed.

We watch as they walk away across the heath towards Sunrise Park before taking their place on the bench and looking out over Minsmere Reserve. A large expanse of golden-brown reed beds dotted with shiny freshwater pools are enclosed by the two Sizewell power stations to the south, dense forest to the west and the North Sea stretching to the horizon in the east. Walkers, some with enthusiastically playful dogs and others with binoculars and telescopes, make their way leisurely along the shore accompanied by the frantic cries of gulls guarding tiny territories on the Minsmere scrape or squabbling over catches out at sea. A family is paddling along the shoreline. Emma watches them for a while.

'We've not been in for a dip yet. Come on, guys, let's get our feet wet. We probably won't have another chance before we go home tomorrow.'

Greg is up for it, but I give it a miss. I'm happy to remain on the bench. I want to spend more time enjoying the view, taking it in, thinking of Kathy. As I do, I'm inspired to write an entry in my notebook. It's just such moments I like to capture.

The two of them return with their clothes soaking wet. They've been having more than a paddle. I finish off my journal entry and we set off across the heath back towards the lodge. The sandy path is flanked by prickly gorse bushes smothered in an explosion of vibrant, bean-like flowers. Yellow, the colour of spring, the colour of the sun. The perfect antidote to all that's been happening over the past few days.

Chapter 41

When we arrive back at the lodge, Greg and Emma change out of their wet clothes ahead of their appointment with Ed Sheeran. I make us a pot of tea and cut us a piece each of what is left of the tarte Tatin. It will keep us going. We sit on the decking looking out to sea. Emma points out a motor yacht powering south towards Aldeburgh full of people having fun on a day out.

'Dad, do you remember when we were on holiday in Mauritius? I must have been eight or nine and we were due to go on a boat trip to a coral island. Mum was ill but you took us anyway.'

My mind draws on a memory of a distant family holiday. It's not one I'm likely to forget.

'Yes, I regretted it almost immediately. When I booked, they said it would be a lovely, relaxing catamaran trip with calm sea, beautiful scenery and a nice buffet lunch. Halfway out, we got hit by a storm. It was a nightmare. You were both terrified and cried for your mum. How could I forget it?'

'You freaked out,' Emma continues. 'You weren't used

to looking after us without her. At first, you had no idea how to handle it. You got frustrated. Told us to stop whining. I was so scared. Then you figured out what to do. You made us pretend it was a fairground ride. We sat in a row, put our hands in the air and screamed each time we went up and over a big wave. It wasn't scary anymore; it was fun. You calmed us down, looked after us. We needed you and you were there. You were great, I've never forgotten it.'

'I still worry about you, wonder if you're both OK. I know you're grown up, but I can't help it. Life's not a fairground ride. With your mum gone, it's my job to keep you safe, watch out for you. You're the most important thing in my life. You do know that, don't you?'

'We do, but maybe now it's our turn to watch out for you,' Greg says.

'You do realise, if anything should happen to me, you will need to look after Emma? You'll be all she has.'

'I know, Dad, but she's a big girl now, she can look after herself. Anyway, she's got her dentist. And Harvey.'

'I mean it, I'm relying on you.'

'Nothing's going to happen to you and even if it did, of course I'd be there for Em.'

Our eyes exchange a look that seals a contract of understanding.

'But it's Greg you want to be concerned about. Don't worry, Dad, I'll look after him,' Emma says.

We sit in silence, enjoying the view and listening to the sound of the sea. Greg looks at the time on his phone, turns to me and touches me on the shoulder.

'We need to set off in ten minutes. Do you mind if I take the torch? The last time I went to a concert there, I found a great parking spot but it's down a side road that's not well lit.'

'Why not use your phone like everyone else?' Emma says.

'Yeah, but I want to try out the torch. I can use it when Ed sings "The A Team" and everyone else has their phones held up. It'll be amazing.'

'Oh Greg,' Emma utters, rolling her eyes.

I go inside to get the torch and while I'm there, I ask Alexa to play "The A Team". Kathy loved it, we used to sing it together. It's a song I've not heard since she died. I hand Greg his Easter egg hunt find and we sit silently listening to Ed. Emma starts to sing along, I join in, feeling tears well up as we reach the chorus. When it's finished, we sit in silence. Emma puts her palms on the table, looks at Greg, then at me.

'That was beautiful. I'll be thinking of you and Mum when he sings it tonight. Come on, Greg, we need to get going. Dad, you be careful. Enjoy the concert, don't wait up.'

Emma stands up, I do the same and we have a big hug.

'Bye, Dad. You will be OK, won't you?'

'Of course, I'll be OK. Enjoy the concert.'

They get into Greg's car with the top down and head off, waving goodbye, shouting, 'Love you, Dad.'

I call after them, 'Love you too.'

I watch them go, change, grab a bottle of suitably chilled Sauvignon Blanc and head next door for lunch with Felicity and James.

Chapter 42

I'm not sure what I expected, but as I approach James's lodge, it's immediately obvious that I'm not the only guest they've invited. Outside, sat around a table on the decking are Mike, Julia and George. It looks like James and Felicity are going for a group "outing" of their relationship. Brave, I think to myself. James welcomes me, leads me inside and offers me a glass of wine. I note Paul bent down looking inside the cooker. He's overseen by Harvey.

'Hi, Harvey, Paul. Are you invited as well?'

'Hi, Max,' Harvey answers. 'No, it's a major emergency, the oven's not working. It keeps shorting. I think it might be creating a power overload. Not what's needed when you're having a lunch party.'

Felicity is busy making a large salad. It's all a bit chaotic.

'Hi, Felicity, that looks nice. Bad luck about the oven.'

'Tell me about it. My original plan was for salmon en croute, I'm making a salade niçoise instead. I had lots of tins of tuna in the cupboard, have been able to boil some eggs in the microwave and I'm using the salad we were going to have anyway with the salmon. You do like salade niçoise?'

'Yes, love it. George and Julia do too. I hope you're adding lots of olives.'

'Yes, I bought lots for pre-lunch nibbles. I'm using those.'

'George and Julia will be happy.'

Felicity gives me a mystified look as I wander out to join the others and seat myself between Mike and two empty chairs that I assume are for James and Felicity.

'This is nice. I didn't expect to see you three here.'

'Yes, we can't keep meeting like this. It almost feels as if you're stalking us,' George responds.

'I like to keep tabs on my neighbours, George. Wasn't it lovely at the Coastguards earlier?'

'Yes, we're lucky with the weather, it makes all the difference. Apart from tomorrow morning, it's supposed to be nice all week. How long are Greg and Emma here for?'

'Just the Easter weekend. They're at an Ed Sheeran concert today and not back until late tonight. They head off home tomorrow. It's been lovely having them here.'

'You're a lucky man, Max,' Mike says joining in. 'Family, it's what life's all about.'

I'm not sure how to take this. Mike's bitter about the break-up of his marriage, sad about not having had children and just coming to terms with losing his only sibling. I don't know whether it's genuine or self-pity and I'm not planning to find out. James and Felicity appear with bowls of crisps and nuts which they put on the table before joining us. George grabs a few crisps, puts them in his mouth and turns to Felicity.

'I'm supposed to be on a diet. You haven't got any olives, have you?'

'Sorry, I had to use them in the salade niçoise.'

'Ah, we're having salade niçoise, excellent. I haven't had one of those in ages.'

He winks at me. I watch Julia for the inevitable reaction. She looks at me, then George, then lets it go. I move things on.

'I asked George earlier, has anyone lost a torch? It's high spec. Greg found it yesterday under one of the bushes by the cliff edge.'

I wait for a response, but there's no answer so George jumps in.

'I'll have it then; I could use a good torch. I'll pick it up later.'

I'm still not letting him have it. 'I might hang on to it for a while, check if anyone else on the site has lost it. If not, I'll be handing it in to reception.'

George pouts, looks disappointed, stands up and excuses himself. I leave it a few minutes before doing the same. I catch him as he's leaving the bathroom.

'Was the dead crow a present from you?'

'Dead crow?'

'Yes, dead crow. It had been shot. Someone left it by my front door with a note. It had your name written all over it.'

'Well, it wasn't me. Scouts honour.'

He brushes past and I pop into the bathroom before heading back to the party. Harvey and Paul are outside waiting for a pause in the conversation so they can let James know they've fixed the problem. Harvey asks me to remind Emma to give him a call about their drink. I hate to break it to him that she's out today, then off home tomorrow. I nod and the two of them leave.

James disappears back inside and reappears with a tray on which sit six champagne flutes and a bottle of bubbly. He gives us a broad smile, pops the cork, pours the golden liquid into the glasses and we watch as several overflow with froth. Felicity sits down next to me, and I sense that we are all feeling slightly apprehensive waiting to hear what James has to say. He hands out the filled champagne flutes, taps a knife on his glass and remains standing as he waits for silence.

'Felicity and I have an announcement. We didn't want to say too much too soon as we know how everyone likes to gossip around here.'

George can't help himself and blurts out, 'Oh my God, Felicity, you're not pregnant?'

James gives him a killer look then delivers a decent riposte.

'No, George. Felicity is not pregnant. Being trite takes a moment, to be truly annoying takes a lifetime. Yours.'

George pretends to look sheepish. James continues.

'No, she and I are together. In fact, we are more than together, we're engaged.'

There is stunned silence. OK, so we're not just apprehensive now, we are shocked. George pretends to drop his glass. James carries on undeterred.

'I suspect it may come as a bit of a surprise, but we've been seeing each other for a number of months. In that time, we've become close. In fact, we've fallen in love. We want to spend the rest of our lives together. So, I would like to propose a toast. To Felicity, the love of the rest of my life.'

We stand, raise our glasses and repeat, 'To Felicity.'

George, being George, adds, 'The love of the rest of my life.'

I'm happy for the two of them but can't get over not having known or even suspected they were a couple until seeing them together at the restaurant. The walks, the chats of the past few days, not even a hint. It's impressive.

When James sits down, I turn to Felicity. 'Congratulations. You kept that under wraps well. It's wonderful news, a bit of a surprise, but wonderful.' I give her a hug, then continue. 'How have the children taken it?'

'Tom and Charlotte are fine, genuinely pleased. They've met James a couple of times and seem to get on well. You do, don't you, James?'

'What's that?'

'You get on well with Tom and Charlotte.'

'Yes, I think they like me. Felicity's grandchild Sophie is an absolute darling. It's lovely spending time with her. Isn't it, Flick?'

'Yes, the best bit is we can make a fuss of her then give her back to her mum and dad. All the joy and none of the responsibility.'

George pipes up again, saying, 'Well, Flick, we're happy for you both. It's nice to get some good news around here for once.' He then pauses before adding, 'Talking of which, is there any news about what happened to Gertrude?'

Julia rolls her eyes, but Mike answers anyway. 'The police think it was an accident. The post-mortem should be tomorrow. If all is straightforward, the funeral will be in a couple of weeks.'

George takes a mouthful of champagne and turns to me. 'Straightforward, Max? Any news on your theory about her having been pushed?'

'No, it's just a possibility, let's see what the post-mortem finds.'

'You can't really believe someone around here could have done that to her? Surely? It's not in our nature. Look at us, we're about to eat salade niçoise, for heaven's sake.'

'Who knows what's in our nature... what we're capable of.'

James joins in. 'I think man is capable of almost anything, especially when defending those we love, our family.' He pauses and adds, 'Or fighting for food, or shelter, or all the other things we had to go through to evolve to where we are now.'

Mike takes up the theme, making his point with an anecdote.

'Once, on safari in South Africa, I saw two cheetahs fly out of bushes like diving, outstretched goalkeepers. They landed simultaneously on either side of a young zebra whose mother had begun to run away with the herd. Seeing its offspring in trouble, it doubled back to fight the cheetahs off. It was fearless. Rearing up, kicking, biting. It was ferocious and incredibly persistent. The cheetahs eventually gave up and ran after a young wildebeest instead. Animals will do anything to protect their young. Man is no different. We'll do anything to protect our family.'

It triggers a story of my own. Having had a glass of wine and most of my champagne, my "appropriateness filter" has been disengaged. I begin to relate the story, only realising after I've started that it may not be quite right for such an occasion.

'A few years ago, Kathy and I were on safari in Tanzania. We were on a game drive and saw a mother warthog with her three, cute, adorable, "tails in the air" babies following behind her in a line. They disappeared into the bush, and we drove on. When we came around the next corner, we were welcomed by excited barking and loud piercing squeals. Our driver pointed to where one of the baby warthogs had been taken by a large baboon and was being carried up a tall tree. The monkey settled itself on a sturdy branch, looked down on us and munched a bite out of the back of the writhing baby warthog. We watched blood soak the baby's tiny defenceless body as the baboon tore it, still squealing, limb from limb. It was as if it was dismembering a barbecued chicken.'

I pause and look around the table. The others are understandably aghast. There is silence, several of the group take a gulp of champagne and Mike looks across at me.

'That's gross, Max. Could you not spare us the gory details? It's horrible. Anyway, what's your point?'

I gather myself and continue. 'My point is coming. The mother warthog was initially frantic but then, realising her other babies were at risk, fought off the rest of the baboons. It was heroic. She won single-handed and led her terrified family to safety. We were transfixed. The sharp squeals above continued for a few more minutes, then died away. The baby was finally out of its misery. I will never forget the bloodied face of the baboon nonchalantly looking down on us as if nothing had happened. I had no idea how brutal such a kill could be. I had no idea what our close relatives were capable of. So, who knows what man is capable of. What each of us is capable of.'

More silence greets the end of my story. Felicity comes to the rescue.

'Salade niçoise, anyone?'

Chapter 43

I reflect that my story was on message but not entirely appropriate and sit feeling mildly self-conscious. Everyone's avoiding eye contact with me. James tops up our glasses and Felicity fetches lunch to which we help ourselves. When we are all settled, I'm surprised by Felicity, who returns to my controversial theme.

'You know, Max, according to Steven Pinker, in his book *The Better Angels of Our Nature*, the world is becoming less violent.'

I know the title but not from the book. 'Isn't that from Abraham Lincoln's inauguration? I learnt the speech at school. "The mystic chords of memory, stretching from every battlefield and patriot grave to every living heart and hearthstone"... hang on, let me think, ah yes... "all over this broad land, will yet swell the chorus of the Union, when again touched, as surely they will be, by the better angels of our nature".'

'Well remembered, Max. I used to teach it in American history. Pinker tracked the data and concluded that violence has declined over time. He listed five inner demons that cause us to be violent: predation, dominance, revenge, sadism and… and one other. Hang on, it'll come… yes, ideology. These he claims are gradually being eroded by our four better angels: empathy, self-control, moral sense and reason. It's a nice theory.'

'Bullshit!' George exclaims, jumping in. 'Pure crap. Typical academic making it up as he goes along. We all know things are getting worse, much worse. We constantly hear about murders, assaults, rapes, terrorism, wars and the rest. What about 9/11? What about Ukraine? What about the Middle East, Yemen, Ethiopia? Which world is he living in? It's not the same as mine.'

Felicity shows her metal and defends Pinker. 'Yes, we know, George, they're all horrible, but Pinker says that our impression of violence has not followed the actual decline, possibly due to increased communication.'

George won't let it go. 'Oh really. Well, it's not the way I see it. It's nonsense.'

I'm no longer paying attention. I'm thinking about what Felicity has said about inner demons. If Derek's hit-and-run was deliberate and if Gertrude was pushed, I'm wondering which of the demons could have been responsible. I feel I can rule out sadism and ideology. I can't see anyone having much sadistic delight in, or ideological reason for, pushing Gertrude over a cliff or running Derek over with a car. That leaves predation, dominance, and revenge. I assume predation covers gain. As far as I can tell, the only person to financially gain from Derek and Gertrude's deaths is Mike. I suppose George might also be in this category, protecting his potential Sizewell C contracts. I'm not sure about dominance.

Possibly Tim wanting to put them in their place over the parking issue, although killing them does seem a bit drastic. Then there's revenge. Who would want revenge on Derek and Gertrude? Felicity, for them playing loud music. Really? I'm not sure Steven Pinker has helped much.

Mike tries to avoid a prolonged argument by moving things on. He looks from Felicity to James, and then back to her again.

'So, what brought you two together?'

'I was having problems with my boiler,' Felicity answers. 'James came and sorted it.'

I look around the table. I'm not the only one having to force back a smile. George can't pass up the opportunity.

'He sorted your boiler? I bet he did.'

A seemingly unabashed Felicity continues, 'Yes, he sorted it for me and did a range of odd jobs around the place. He had all the tools, knew what he was doing. I'm useless at that sort of thing. Peter did everything around the lodge.'

'I can do the basics, but I won't have anything to do with the electrics. I know what I can and can't manage,' James adds.

'Each time he sorted something out, we would sit chatting over a cup of tea. I suppose one thing led to another,' Felicity says, looking at James.

'We started having lunch,' he continues her thread, 'sharing bottles of wine, enjoying games of Scrabble.'

'You must have known it was getting serious when it led to Scrabble. There's no way back from that,' says George.

Felicity is sucked in. 'Yes, we both love playing. James is good, he taught me the value of maximising two-letter words. It transformed my game.'

'I'm more of a seven-letter word man,' says George.

'I was thinking you're more of a four-letter word man,' James responds with a smile.

A bit harsh but George had it coming. The conversation continues for another half an hour before Felicity and James clear the table, disappear inside, and return with pavlova, strawberries and ice cream. It's not been a heavy meal, but I need to save room for dinner.

'Mike has invited me to see Simon Rattle conducting the LSO at Snape tonight. We're eating first at Mainsail, so I'll go with the strawberries but skip the pavlova and ice cream, thanks.'

'The pavlova is my recipe,' says a disappointed Felicity. 'The ice cream is made locally. It's amazing. Come on, just one scoop? Live a little.'

'Oh, go on then,' I relent. 'Willpower has never been my strong suit.'

When I've finished dessert, I head inside, this time for a genuine visit to the toilet. James's lodge is well laid out, nicely decorated and spotless. I assume it's Felicity's influence. Well-taken photos of Southwold, Aldeburgh and Dunwich adorn the walls.

'Lovely photos, James. Where did you get them?' I say when I return to the table.

'Flick took them and gave them to me. She's been taking evening classes.'

'They're good.'

'Thanks, Max,' responds an appreciative Felicity. 'It's

something I started doing after I lost Peter. I'm not very talented but it's fun.'

'They're good. Atmospheric. You've captured the feel of the places. Lively, charming Southwold; arty, upmarket Aldeburgh; tiny, ancient Dunwich.'

'Thanks. Derek was a good teacher. I never liked the man, but he knew his photography. He used to say that truly creative art captures something, tries to interpret it, makes a statement about it. Art is not what the thing is, but what it creates in the mind of those who engage with it. If it creates nothing, it's not art. It's representation. Derek applied it to his photography. I learnt a lot from him.'

'Truly creative art is making that kind of stuff up,' George responds.

Everyone smiles but I'm thinking how much Felicity hated Derek and how he was run over having just given an evening class. A class she may well have been at.

Chapter 44

The lunch breaks up just before 4pm, which gives me time to have a short rest, take a quick shower and change before we leave for Aldeburgh. Mike drives us through sleepy Westleton, unusually quiet Leiston, then quirky Thorpeness where Easter holidaymakers are out eating cream teas, enjoying ice creams, feeding ducks on the green and rowing on the picturesque boating lake. We head south along the coast road running between the pebble shore on our left and RSPB marshes on our right and are fortunate to find a parking space just as we enter the town. It's not central, but parking spaces in Aldeburgh are like gold dust. We walk into the town along the seafront, past its four-hundred-year-old timber-framed Tudor Moot Hall. We split up to go our own ways, agreeing to meet at Mainsail restaurant at 6pm. Mike needs to do some shopping; I want to explore the town.

I always love wandering through Aldeburgh's narrow, characterful back streets infused with the light, scents and sounds that come from it nestling by the sea. I walk past the modern lifeboat station filled by the glossy, deep-blue hull and bright-orange cabin of its much-prized vessel and across Aldeburgh's wide, grey-pebbled beach. Derelict, clinker-built wooden fishing boats, not much different to those used by the Vikings, bask in retirement in the late-afternoon sun. They are holed, battered but proud, as they sit filled with lobster pots, ropes, nets and plastic boxes. I look out to sea at a fishing vessel patiently plying its way north, emitting a gentle, late afternoon hum. Returning up the beach, I continue walking along Crag Path. It runs the length of the town alongside the beach and is lined by holidaymakers sat on a concrete wall, savouring the view as they tuck into fish and chip suppers. The narrow road is overseen by colourful Georgian and Victorian seafront houses showing off pastel shades of blue, yellow, salmon and the odd vibrant maroon. I sit for a while opposite a lady playing a large harp. She is busking in front of an ice cream stall, plucking out Coldplay songs to admiring onlookers.

I check my watch; it's almost time to meet Mike at the restaurant. I work my way through the narrow back alleys and enter Aldeburgh's upmarket main street that is predictably full of restaurants, craft shops, fashionable clothing boutiques, galleries, ice-cream parlours, cafés and estate agents. I reach the double frontage windows of Aldeburgh Book Shop and stop to see what titles they're featuring. I'm reading about *The New Aldeburgh Anthology*, "a book for those drawn back year after year for the music, writing and arts, and for all who care for the landscape, the sea and the ongoing life of the Suffolk Coast", when my eyes catch a flash of red reflected in the shop window. My heart skips a beat. The woman in the scarf? I watch as her ghostly form walks past on the other side of the road and then turn around to follow her. She's gone. She must have entered the cinema that stands opposite. I cross over and expect to see her in the foyer. She's not there. She's vanished. Do I ask about her, look for her, see if it's Ann? Or do I let it go? I feel stupid and I'm running late for the restaurant. I leave. It can't be her. Surely, it can't be her.

Mike's waiting for me outside Mainsail and we enter together to be shown to a table that looks onto the high street. I grab a seat facing out. The restaurant is bright and airy, the tables fully occupied and the atmosphere happily relaxed. The walls are covered in local art with scenes of the town, sea, beach, boats and reed beds. Dotted around are maps of the River Alde and various items of fishing paraphernalia. We opt to share a dozen oysters followed by the sea bass.

I open the conversation. 'I love it here. It was one of Kathy's favourites; we used to come a lot.'

'Yes, it's nice. Gertrude and Derek were regulars.'

'How are you doing?'

'I'm OK, still shaken but coming to terms with it. Slowly. As they say, taking it day by day. The lodge seems empty. I keep making cups of tea for the two of us. I've never drunk so much of the stuff.'

'Yes, I was like that for months after I lost Kathy.' I pause and then ask, 'Have you thought more about her funeral?'

'I'm having her cremated in Halesworth. It's where she and Derek lived, where she had his funeral. She didn't leave any instructions but I'm sure she would have wanted to be close to him.'

'Yes, it seems right.'

Our oysters arrive in practically no time, and we enjoy gulping them down with shallot vinegar, lemon, and tabasco. Each one is a salty, creamy essence of the sea. In the back of my mind, I worry about the risk of food poisoning. It's happened to me a few times in the past from oysters, but I always think the benefit outweighs the risk. I think, come on, you love them, take Felicity's advice, live a little. My mind recalls a woman who sat in front of me a few years ago at a concert in Snape. At the start of the first movement of Rachmaninov's second piano concerto, she opened her handbag and gently, almost casually, puked into it. She snapped her handbag shut and acted as though nothing had happened. No one apart from me seemed to notice but the smell wafted across the hall, leading to a few concerned glances in our direction. I'm sure they thought it was me. I just shrugged a lot. I considered pointing the lady out but somehow it didn't feel the right thing to do. She sat through the remaining two movements before disappearing for good at the interval. I wondered at the time whether the highly evocative and deeply resonant opening to the second piano concerto had brought back some unpleasant memory or reopened an old wound in a previously broken heart. It occurs to me now that she may simply have eaten oysters for her pre-concert dinner.

Mike has a serious look on his face as though he's preparing to say something important.

'Max, can you do me a favour? Will you promise me you'll stop all this talk about Gertrude? You know, about the way she died, how she might have been pushed.'

I'm taken aback. Why would he ask me to stop? I down an oyster and dab my mouth with my napkin.

'It's only a theory. I don't have any proof. I just can't work out her injuries, not if she accidently slipped.'

'If the post-mortem finds it was an accident, please just leave it at that and move on. It's what I need to be able to do. I don't want months or years of conjecture, rumour and gossip. I want to be able to spend my time at Sunrise Park. I love it here. I don't want all the uncertainty and doubt hanging over Gertrude's memory. Or hanging over me.'

'Yes. But I believe she was pushed, and I need to know the truth. I think it could be connected to Derek's hit-and-run.'

'What makes you say that? What evidence have you got?'

'Nothing concrete, not yet. Just a feeling, a strong feeling.' I pause then add, 'Yesterday, I was in Leiston with Greg and Emma visiting Kathy's sister Sally. When we were leaving her house and crossing the road, I was nearly killed by a car that accelerated towards me out of nowhere. Greg pushed me out of the way. I'm sure it was deliberate. Someone's trying to stop me. They're trying to prevent me finding out what happened to Gertrude.'

Mike looks directly at me and there is a thoughtful pause during which we both swallow an oyster.

'Yesterday? Someone tried to run you down? You can't really believe that. You sound almost paranoid.'

'It's a quiet, narrow, residential street. There was no reason for a car to be driven like that. Even Sally, who lives there, thought it strange, asked if I had any enemies. And the burglary, what about the burglary? It's all too much of a coincidence.'

Mike prepares and downs his last oyster. 'I just don't see why anyone would want to push Gertrude off a cliff. She never harmed anyone in her life. Yes, she could be a bit caustic and would speak her mind, but it was never any more than that. Who would want to kill her? Why?'

'That's exactly what I'm trying to find out.'

We finish our oysters in silence then talk about music and birds as we enjoy our main course. I settle the bill and Mike drives us the six miles from Aldeburgh to the concert. We travel alongside the River Alde, passing a golf course, several pig farms and a nature reserve before reaching the tiny Suffolk village of Snape. Just outside the village is Snape Maltings, an attractively converted Victorian heritage site, whose centrepiece is Benjamin Britten's world-famous concert hall. It's an idyllic setting and, as we pull into the car park, I promise myself not to spoil the evening by thinking about Gertrude, the break-in, the crow or what happened in Leiston. I will simply try to enjoy the concert.

Chapter 45

There's time for a quick drink on the concert hall terrace overlooking a wide expanse of golden reed beds flanking the River Alde. It also overlooks large Henry Moore and Barbara Hepworth sculptures. It's a lovely setting. In the background, we hear classical music coming from the rehearsal rooms. A bell rings and we head into the hall past a converted red telephone box housing a defibrillator that caters for the older demographic that attends the classical concerts here. We enter a large concert hall, with massive brick walls, cavernous wooden roof and a huge wooden stage that combine to create the warm, reverberant acoustic that Britten sought for his operas. I feel a sense of privilege each time I'm here. The hall is full and there's an expectant buzz. The full symphony orchestra fills the wooden platform, brightly lit from above by a bank of impressive lighting. As the orchestra warms up, I read the programme notes.

Beethoven Symphony No. 6 in F major, Pastoral. Composed in 1808, and first performed in Vienna

on December 22nd, it is about the power of nature
to heal and restore the human spirit.

I can't help smiling to myself. It's exactly the reason I'm in Suffolk, in Dunwich. To heal and let nature restore my spirit. The orchestra quietens, there is silence and a sense of anticipation. Simon Rattle appears to thunderous applause before an expectant hush falls on the hall once again and the symphony begins. I hear the familiar and beautifully comforting notes of Beethoven's sublime first movement. I let the music flow through me, cleansing me of the stress, tension and pain of the past few days. Of the past few years. Then I feel an overwhelming sense of grief rising in me. If I don't stop myself, I'll be in tears. I focus instead on the joy in the music. It works and I put the grief back in its box for a later, more private, moment with myself.

By the interval, I'm feeling happily relaxed. We have an ice cream, discuss the concert and visit the gentlemen's facilities. I'm finished before Mike and wait for him outside the main hall entrance. I scan the other concert goers. We are a well-dressed bunch, almost distinguished, with an average age that must be close to seventy. And then my heart misses several beats. A woman in a red scarf is working her way through the throng towards me. I think: it's the colour of the telephone box. My pulse quickens as I watch her come closer. She reaches me, then walks on past. It's not Ann; of course it's not her.

Mike appears and we follow the woman into the concert hall. My mind, and then my pulse, settle again ready for Mendelssohn's *Fingal's Cave, The Hebrides* overture. I read the programme notes.

> *The overture consists of two primary themes; the opening notes of the overture state the theme Mendelssohn wrote while visiting the cave. This lyrical theme, suggestive of the power and stunning beauty of the cave, is intended to develop feelings of loneliness and solitude. The second theme, meanwhile, depicts movement at sea and rolling waves.*

I settle back in my seat. Immediately, the music begins. I'm with Emma and Greg in Mauritius, setting sail out to sea, heading for the coral island. Adventurers facing life together, overtaken by the storm with me looking after them, keeping them safe. My purpose, Kathy's purpose.

The final piece is one of my favourites, Ralph Vaughan Williams, *The Lark Ascending*. I close my eyes and am transported to Dunwich Heath, the Coastguard Cottages and the family bench. The sun is shining, the gorse is vivid yellow, the birds are in song and a skylark rises into a clear blue sky to begin its joyous, life-affirming recital. It takes me to the special place in my mind, a place that will always be there. The place where I'm with Kathy, Greg and Emma. The four of us, forever smiling, forever happy.

Chapter 46

The concert ends to rapturous applause. It's been a wonderful evening, and the music has freed my mind to wander through the good things in my life. It's reaffirmed in me the beauty, hope and joy in nature, the joy in us all. I feel as content as at any time in the past few years.

We join the queue of cars leaving and head back to Sunrise Park through Leiston and then Westleton. There is no traffic as we pass through Dunwich Heath but it's dark and Mike drives faster than I'm comfortable with. After a mile or so, he catches his breath, slams on the brakes and stops. Fortunately, there's nothing behind us. He reverses and switches his headlights to full beam. There, staring directly at us from the top of a fence post, sits a brown, cloaked figure with a ghostly, white, heart-shaped face. A barn owl.

We watch in silence.

'Beautiful,' Mike says in hushed reverence. 'You don't see them around here as much you used to.'

'Magnificent,' I reply. 'I recently saw one quartering

the fields at Eastbridge just as the light was fading. It was so graceful, so otherworldly.'

'Yes, twilight's the best time to see them. In Native American culture, they're thought to be a symbol of death, transformation, and rebirth.'

I have a feeling that I know what Mike's thinking.

'Gertrude?' I then can't resist adding, 'Or us? Maybe you need to slow down in case a deer jumps out and triggers our death, transformation, and rebirth.'

The owl flies off and we sit savouring the moment.

'Point taken,' he says, driving on more carefully.

When we get back to the site, Mike parks by his lodge.

'Thanks, it was a wonderful evening,' I say. 'Just what I needed. It's helped restore my faith in life.' As we get out of the car, I ask, 'Do you fancy coming across to mine for a coffee?'

'That would be nice,' he responds. 'You go in and put the kettle on, I'll get you those groceries of Gertrude's that I won't be needing.'

As I enter my living room, my heart sinks. The place has been trashed. Again. The shelves have been cleared, drawers emptied, and cupboards turned out. I walk around the lodge looking at the mess. I'm stunned. I feel sick. Whoever's done this has badly wanted to find something. I take out my phone to call the police. As I do, I head to the kitchen to put the kettle on. They will take at least an hour to get here, and I need something to calm me down. I'm more than upset, I'm seething. I'm tapping in the number when I hear a sound and sense something behind me. Turning to see what it is, I feel a sharp pain deep in my side. It's as if I've been punched hard. It takes my breath away. I see a face I recognise. A face full of hate. Then my head explodes. I gasp. Everything is spinning; I'm falling. Falling to the floor, falling into darkness, falling into Kathy's arms.

Chapter 47

Ed Sheeran finishes "Castle on the Hill" to a deafening roar as a packed Chantry Park crowd shows its appreciation. There's an expectant buzz as everyone waits, listening for what's to come. Emma gives Greg a hug as the instantly recognisable opening chords of "The A Team" ring out. Forty thousand people join in, singing together with their phone torches pointing to the stage. Greg holds his newly acquired flashlight aloft. He's swaying with the crowd, enjoying being part of the mass celebration of humanity. A vibration in his pocket alerts him that a message has come through on his phone. He ignores it. What can be more important than Ed Sheeran? More important than "The A Team"?

A string of notifications follows, each one vibrating as it arrives in his pocket. He's being bombarded. Curious, he finally checks to see what can be so important. There are five of them; they're short, all from his dad and all saying the same thing: *Urgent. Please return to lodge.*

Greg holds the phone up to show Emma. She looks at the messages, frowns then takes the phone from him for a closer look. They don't make any sense. What could be so urgent they need to leave an Ed Sheeran concert? He must know they'd still be here. She turns to Greg, moves closer to him and shouts in his ear.

'I don't understand what he wants. Anyway, why's he messaging? He never messages.'

'A joke? Maybe he's had a few too many?'

'Funny kind of joke.'

'Hang on, I'll text him back.'

Greg texts, *What's up? R U OK?*

The response is immediate.

You need to come back.

'I don't like it, I need to call him,' Greg says, turning to Emma.

Greg phones but it goes through to voicemail. He can't understand why his dad's not picking up. He's worried. He texts again and receives the same response. Now he's very worried.

'I think we should go,' Greg mouths to Emma.

'What… now?'

'What if something's happened to him?'

'Like what?'

'I don't know but I'm worried. We should leave.'

'OK, let's go. With everything that's been going on, I hope he's alright.'

They fight their way out of the tightly packed crowd accompanied by "Sing". Taking a last reluctant look at Ed performing in the distance, they head quickly for the car and waste no time in setting off. Emma calls their father; there's no answer. She tries again. Just voicemail. She leaves a message then turns her head to Greg.

'Dad's still not answering, nothing, just voicemail. It's not like him to make a fuss. Why would he ask us to come back? It doesn't make any sense. Oh God, I hope he's OK.'

Greg's mind is working overtime. 'I don't like it. Why isn't he answering our calls?'

He can't work out what his dad is playing at. Why do they need to return and why the urgency? He likes to drive fast and there's no holding him back. They sit in silence, each imagining what might have happened. The road from Ipswich is dual carriageway and Greg knows that there can be speed traps. He doesn't care. They need to get back. They turn off the A12 and he scares Emma as he speeds through the narrow road past Dale Farm. The drive through Westleton is pitch-black, as is the road across the heath. But as they approach Sunrise Park, flashing blue lights penetrate the darkness. Emma feels sick, physically sick.

'My God, Greg, what's happened?'

'Don't panic, it's probably nothing.' But he knows it's something.

They arrive at the Sunrise Park entrance and find it cordoned off with police cars parked either side of the gates and the area swarming with uniforms. Greg stops, winds his window down and an officer leans in.

'Are you staying here tonight?'

'Yes, we're with our dad, lodge sixty-six.'

'Dr Max Middleton?'

'Yes, that's right.'

'Please can you both come with me? Park the car inside the entrance and then follow me.'

He removes the cordon, beckons Greg into a parking place, waits as Greg and Emma step out of the car and then leads them into the main site reception. They are taken to an office where a policewoman in uniform is sitting in front of a desk. She's facing them, behind her sit two boxes of tissues and two glasses of water. Two empty chairs wait close to her. She stands to greet them.

'Hello. I'm Officer Patel. Fatima Patel.'

Emma is ashen, her heart is racing and she's feeling even more sick than before. Greg is apprehensive, confused, disbelieving of what's happening. They're encouraged into the empty chairs and the woman begins to speak. Slowly, softly.

'Can I confirm that Dr Max Middleton is your father?'

'Yes,' they respond nervously as one.

'Is this him?'

She shows them a photo of their father. It's the one of him and their mother that he keeps on his bedside cupboard. They look at each other. They nod.

'Then I am afraid to have to tell you that your father was attacked earlier tonight in his lodge. He was found by a neighbour with a stab wound and a head injury. I'm sorry to say that he passed away from the injuries he sustained.'

Fatima waits in silence for the news to begin to sink in and, after a prolonged pause, adds, 'I'm so sorry for your loss.'

Chapter 48

Greg looks at Emma, Emma looks at Greg. They can't believe what they've just heard. The words, they can't believe the words. They don't want to believe the words.

'No, there must be some mistake,' Greg utters. 'It can't be him. Are you sure it's him?'

But he knows, he's seen the photo. Emma feels a chasm open in her stomach, she struggles to breathe, her heart pounds, she feels dizzy. She looks at Greg, reaches out for him, tries to stand but is shaky and needs to grab on to the desk. Greg gets up and goes to her. They hug, he holds her close. She's trembling, crying. He just feels numb. They comfort each other, gently swaying from side to side. Fatima offers Greg and Emma the tissues and water before watching and waiting patiently for when they are ready for her to move things on. Eventually, she feels the time is right.

'Can I get you anything? Contact anyone for you?'

'What... what happened?' Greg asks.

'When you're ready, DI Lawton will see you and explain what we know so far.'

Emma sits down again. Tears stream down her face, and she holds a tissue against her increasingly red nose. Greg looks at her. He feels for her, he really does, but he needs more information.

'They want to know if we're ready to speak with an officer. Find out what happened.'

'What, now? Here? Now?'

'I need to know what happened.'

'I suppose so.'

Greg nods to Fatima. 'Yes, let's do it now.'

Another man, dressed in a light-blue shirt and dark-blue tie, enters the room. Fatima introduces him as Detective Inspector David Lawton. He moves close to them, sits them down and speaks to them in a respectfully calm, matter-of-fact voice.

'I am sorry for your loss. I understand you wish to know what's happened to your father. Is now alright? We can do it another time if you would prefer. There's no hurry.'

Greg and Emma agree to proceed. They're in shock, going through the motions. It's easier just to go with the flow.

'This is what we know so far. Your father and his neighbour, Mike Butcher, returned from a concert this evening. Your father invited Mr Butcher in for coffee and Mr Butcher watched him enter his lodge. Mr Butcher then went into his own lodge to collect some unwanted groceries that he'd offered your father. On returning, he saw someone rush out of your father's front door. He shouted after them, but they ran away up the track. There are footprints, we're checking them out. Mr Butcher went to see whether your father was OK and found him lying on the floor of the living room with a stab wound to his side and an injury to the back of his head. We suspect it was caused by being hit with a vase. Mr Butcher tried to stop the bleeding, but it was too late. I'm afraid to say your father was already deceased when the ambulance arrived. There was nothing anyone could have done.'

Emma sits in silence. She listens to the man but does not really hear what he says. Greg takes it all in. He needs more.

'Does Mr Butcher, Mike, have any idea who it was? Who did it?'

'It was dark. Mr Butcher didn't see enough to identify the assailant. We have a team looking for evidence and any signs of who it may have been, what might have happened. They'll be taking photos, dusting for fingerprints, collecting samples. We haven't found the weapon, but it was probably a knife. We are making urgent inquiries and speaking to anyone who was in the area. Other lodge owners, campers, caravaners.'

'Do you need us to do anything? Can we help?'

'No, not tonight. You'll need to formally identify your father's body, and we will need to interview you, so it would be helpful if you could remain in the area for a few days. But for now, you need to get some rest. I'm afraid the lodge is a serious crime scene, so you'll need to sleep somewhere else for a while. Is there anyone locally you can stay with for a night or two?'

'An aunt in Leiston,' Greg answers. 'I'm sure she'll put us up. I'll call her.'

'OK, we've got your mobile number, if you need anything at all, here's mine.'

DI Lawton hands Greg and Emma his card and leaves the room. Fatima then asks if she can do anything. Emma switches to autopilot.

'Is it OK if we pick up a few things from the lodge? Sponge bags, toothbrushes, a change of clothes.'

Fatima has to play it by the book. 'Sorry, it's a crime scene. No one unauthorised can go in or out for now.'

'Can you pick stuff up for us?'

'Sorry, it's all potential evidence. You will need to make do this evening and buy essentials tomorrow.'

The conversation upsets Greg. It's all too callous, and it's too soon. His dad's dead and they're talking about toothbrushes. He snaps himself out of it and calls his aunt.

'Aunt Sally, it's Greg.'

'Greg, it's late. Is everything OK?'

'No, it's not. It's Dad, he's dead.'

'What?'

'Dad, he's been attacked, stabbed and hit over the head. He's dead.'

There is silence, a long deafening silence. It sounds as if his aunt has dropped the phone. Then Greg hears Sally's shaky voice.

'Your father's dead? He can't be. Not Max.' There's further silence before she adds, 'When?'

Greg's answer is matter-of-fact. 'Earlier this evening, in the lodge, after he got back from a concert.'

'Oh my God. Really? Max is dead. I can't believe it.' More silence. 'How are you? How's Emma?'

'Aunt Sally, can you put us up for a while? The lodge is

a crime scene, we can't go back there. We need somewhere to stay.'

'Of course. How will you get here?'

'I should be OK to drive. Or the police can give us a lift.'

'When will I expect you?'

'I'm not sure, don't wait up.'

'I won't sleep, not now. Oh, how awful.' Greg hears his aunt begin to cry.

'I need to go now, Aunt Sally. Thanks.'

Greg rings off and lets Emma know that their aunt is happy to put them up. He then turns to Fatima.

'I'm having problems taking this all in; it doesn't seem real. Can we see the lodge? It might help us start to process things, begin to make sense of it.'

'I can take you, but you will need to remain outside of the police cordon.'

Greg turns to Emma. 'Do you want to stay here or come with us?'

'I'll come with you. Will Dad be there?'

They both look at Fatima.

'No, they took him away a short while ago.'

'Where to?' Emma asks.

'Ipswich Hospital, the coroner's mortuary. There will need to be a post-mortem.'

'Can we see him?'

'Yes, tomorrow. You will need to identify his body.'

Chapter 49

Fatima leads Greg and Emma by torchlight along the main gravelled site road before turning into the track leading to their father's lodge. The area around the lodge is cordoned off and brightly lit. A small group has gathered to watch from outside the cordon. Around the lodge, people are going about their business, some in police uniform, a few in plain clothes, others in white boiler suits. The scene is like something out of a TV crime detective drama. There's no doubt they're treating their father's death seriously. Greg thinks, *If only they'd taken Gertrude's death as seriously*. He wonders when to tell the police what he knows, what he suspects. That his father's death is probably tied to what happened to his neighbour. And possibly to Derek. He decides now's not the time.

Emma feels a hand on her shoulder, hears a familiar voice and turns around to find Harvey standing behind her.

'Emma, you poor thing. It's such a rum do, it's awful. I can't imagine what you're going through. If there's anything you need me to do, just ask, anything at all.'

Greg's upset but he still can't help thinking to himself that this would be a good time to ask Harvey to fix the cupboard door in the lodge that keeps coming off its hinges. He thinks it's the kind of thing Dad would have thought, maybe even said. He then thinks, *Oh God, Greg, stop it. Dad's dead.*

Emma's red eyes look Harvey in the face. She doesn't really know him. She breaks down crying. Harvey tries to give her a hug, but she pulls away. Turning towards Greg, Emma reaches out and wraps her arms around her brother. Greg pulls Emma in tight and kisses the top of her head.

'Do they know what happened?' Harvey asks.

'He'd been to a concert at Snape with Mike,' Greg answers. 'When they got back, Dad let himself in to his lodge and Mike went to get groceries that he'd offered him. They were going to have a night cap. When Mike walked towards Dad's lodge, he saw someone run out of the front door. He went in and found Dad lying on the floor. He'd been stabbed and hit on the back of the head. He was gone by the time the ambulance arrived. That's it, that's all we've been told.'

'Did Mike catch sight of who did it?'

'I don't think so, the police don't seem to think so.'

They stand silently looking at the scene, trying to take it in.

After a while Harvey sighs then says, 'I'd better be off, I've an early job in the morning.'

They watch as he walks away to be replaced by an ashen-faced Mike who has worked through the onlookers to get to them.

'Emma, Greg. I still can't believe it's happened.'

'Mike, I'm sorry you had to find him like that,' Greg says. 'It must have been awful.'

'It was. Shocking. We'd had a lovely evening. Really lovely. We'd enjoyed the concert. He was happy, as happy as I'd known him. It's just wrong, so wrong, so senseless.'

They stand in silence watching the activity unfold in front of them. Mike feels the need to tell them what happened.

'I saw someone running away from his lodge. I didn't know whether to chase them or check on your dad. I had to make sure he was OK, so I went in. He was lying on the floor in the kitchen. He was unconscious. There was a broken vase in bits around him. It looked like he'd been hit on the head. He was covered in blood. Not just his head, his shirt. It was soaked. He'd been stabbed. I tried to stop the bleeding, but I couldn't. I just couldn't. It was horrible. I can't get the sight of it out of my head... but you don't need to hear this, he was your dad, for heaven's sake.'

Greg shivers as he tries to picture the scene. 'It must have been awful. The police say they've spoken to you. Have you spoken to anyone else, have you been offered support?'

'I've given a statement, but they say they'll need to interview me again. They say a counsellor will be in touch. My God. I just can't believe it. I need to go, it's too upsetting. I won't sleep, not with what's happened. But I'm not much use here. Let's speak when you're ready, maybe we can help each other try to make some sense of it. Call me.'

Mike gives them his number and heads for his lodge which sits just outside the police cordon. Greg and Emma watch as he walks up the steps to his porch decking and in through the front door. His head is bowed, his shoulders are hunched. He looks weary, broken. Greg thinks, *First Derek, then Gertrude, now Dad. Poor man.*

Chapter 50

By the time they arrive at Aunt Sally's house, it's well into the early hours of the morning. Greg parks on the left to ensure he, not Emma, gets out of the car into the road. He checks carefully to make sure there's no one else around, no driver waiting to mow them down. They walk to the front door, ring the bell and are greeted by their aunt. She immediately gives them a big hug. She's been crying and Greg's not sure whether the hug is for them or for her. He concludes it's for both.

'Oh Emma, Greg, it's so awful,' Sally says. 'You must be heartbroken. I can't believe it, I just can't. He was such a nice man, such a good man. Who'd do such a thing?' She sighs deeply and dabs her eyes with a tissue. 'Come through, I'll make us a pot of tea.'

They follow their aunt through the hall. The lights are dimmed; it's dark, matching their mood.

'Thanks, Aunt Sally. Thanks for putting us up,' Emma says.

'Of course, of course. You must stay for as long as you need, my home is yours. Your dad was like a brother to me. He was so good to Kathy, she doted on him. It's all so sad, so senseless.'

They stand together watching steam rise out of the kettle. Greg sees Emma's eyes staring, then they begin to moisten and soon she and her aunt are holding each other, leaning on one another, crying. He leaves them to it, sits at the kitchen table and puts his head in his hands. Sally pours the tea and, when she's finished, she looks up just as Greg does the same. Their eyes meet and he notices how similar hers are to his mother's. He'd never seen it before, not really. She hands out the cups and resorts to the only practical comfort she has.

'There's chocolate cake in the tin. I think we could all use a large slice.'

'It's the early hours of the morning,' Emma replies.

'If not now, when?' Sally says, before cutting them each a slice.

For once, no one's really interested. They sit staring at their cake. Sally fiddles with her piece, then looks from it to Greg and Emma.

'What did the police say? What do they think happened?'

'Dad and his neighbour Mike had been to a concert at Snape,' Greg answers. 'You know Mike, Gertrude's brother, the lady who fell off the cliff. They got back and Mike saw Dad let himself in before going to get some groceries he'd promised Dad. When he returned, he saw someone run out of the lodge. He went to investigate and found Dad lying on the kitchen floor. He'd been attacked. Stabbed and hit over the head. Mike tried to help but it was no use. He called an ambulance, but Dad was already... already... you know.'

'That's just awful.'

'Mike is beside himself,' Greg adds. 'Finding Dad like that after what happened to Gertrude.'

'Poor man. He's having such a terrible time. He's been so unlucky.'

'Unlucky? I don't think so. After what happened outside here yesterday, I think it's all connected. It must be. He's not unlucky, he's the target of some madman. Dad was too.'

'Your dad a target? Why?'

'I don't know, but I'm going to find out. It's what Dad would have wanted. I won't let him down. I'm going to finish what he started.'

Emma gives her brother an anxious look.

'Oh Greg, you need to be careful. First Mum then Dad, we can't lose you as well. Please leave it to the police.'

'I can't stand by doing nothing. I need to help. I need to do something.'

'But please be careful, say you'll be careful.'

'Of course I will. Of course I'll be careful.'

'That's what Dad said. He thought he'd be OK.'

'Come on, Emma, I won't do anything stupid, I'm too much of a wimp.'

'You're not, you've never been a wimp. I can't see you starting now. Anyway, please can we not talk about it anymore, not now. Not tonight.'

Greg nods and they sit silently at the kitchen table, sipping tea, nibbling at their chocolate cake, trying to make sense of it all.

Chapter 51

The next morning is damp and gloomy. Greg looks out of the window of his aunt's kitchen to a small, tidy, well-stocked back garden. A fine drizzle falls from a cloudy, grey sky. He stirs his tea slowly, sadly. He doesn't feel like having anything to eat. Breakfast is not always his thing and it's certainly not today. He turns his head and looks across the table at Emma. She's sitting in a generously sized dressing gown borrowed from her aunt, staring at her phone looking tired and drawn, as though she's been crying for most of the night. She almost certainly has. Greg is curious.

'What are you looking at, Em? Messages?'

'No, photos. Of Dad. Mum and Dad.' She keeps scrolling on her phone, pauses, then adds, 'I keep looking through photos of them, of us. We had so many good times together. I can't believe they're gone, that we'll never see them again. We'll never be together again. I feel so sad. It was awful when Mum died, but somehow this is worse. I'd got myself prepared to lose Mum, but this time it's like something's suddenly been ripped out of me. It's left a gaping hole. I feel so empty, so flat. Not angry, just flat. Like I'll never feel happy again, can never feel happy again.'

'I know, it's sucked the life out of me too. Give it time, we need to give it time.'

'Maybe. But how much time will it take when we've lost them both so close together? The way Mum died. The way Dad died. I just don't know.'

'Me neither, but we have each other. We need to trust in each other… and time.'

'Do you think they'll want us to identify Dad today?'

'Probably, it's what Fatima said last night. Anyway, I want to tell them what we know… what Dad knew. They need to hear it.'

Sally joins them in the kitchen, she also looks tired and drawn.

'I thought I heard the two of you in here. You're up early. I can't say I'm surprised. Did you get much sleep? I know I didn't.'

Emma continues looking at her photos, she's not ready to engage with her aunt.

'I got a bit,' Greg responds. 'It all kept going around in my mind. I was turning things over, trying to make sense of it. I can't believe it's happened.'

Sally sits down, removes a tissue from her sleeve and blows her nose.

'Neither can I. Max was so well liked. I keep thinking about the car that almost hit him and about what you said last night. That he was the target of some madman.'

Greg furrows his brow and taps his fingers on the table.

'It's just a feeling. A feeling that what happened to Derek, to Gertrude and now Dad is somehow all connected. It doesn't make sense though. Maybe someone did have it in for Derek and Gertrude, but I can't see why they also had it in for Dad. He didn't arrive at the lodge until after Derek had been killed. All I can think is that it was to do with Dad trying to find out if Gertrude had been pushed.'

Sally pours herself a cup of tea.

'You know, your dad reminded me of your Grandfather Eric. They were similar. Both good men, kind men, and both like a dog with a bone. When they thought something wasn't right, they'd want to get to the bottom of it. They would keep going no matter what. They were both fearless, almost reckless.'

'Maybe, and maybe he was right to keep going. Maybe whoever did it was trying to shut him up, stop him looking into things. Maybe they're behind the burglary, the close shave with the car... now his... his... you know.'

Emma looks up from her photos and stares at Greg. 'So, if it's all connected, if we can find out what happened to Derek, we might get an idea who did it? Who killed Dad?'

'We might do. We, Emma? I thought you wanted me to back off. Now it's we?'

'I thought about it last night. Dad would want us to find out, wouldn't he? What he said about you playing football, about being fearless. He wasn't going to be put off. We mustn't be. I've come to terms with it, I'm not afraid. Not now. The worst has already happened; we've lost Mum and Dad. It's just us now, us and our memories.

Our precious stones. We need to find out who did this or those won't mean much. Will they?'

Sally frowns. 'That's all very well but if what you suspect is true, there's a serial killer on the loose. It's not for the two of you to go after them, you need to tell the police what you know. You need to leave it to them, let them do their jobs. It's what they do, what they're good at.'

Greg takes issue with this. 'Good at? I can't see they were good at following up on what happened to Derek. They didn't seem particularly bothered about Gertrude and they weren't overly concerned about the burglary. OK, what happened last night they will have to take seriously. But good at? Really?'

'At least tell them what you know, work with them. You must.'

'Of course, I was planning to tell them today. I wasn't sure whether to call them or wait for them to contact us. I've got the number for the detective we spoke to last night. I could give him a call.'

'Yes, do that, but first let me make you breakfast. Are you up to eating anything?'

Greg and Emma settle for a piece of toast and another mug of tea. Greg phones DI Lawton.

'DI Lawton, it's Greg Middleton, Max Middleton's son. You said last night to give you a call if we needed anything. There are things Emma and I need to tell you about Dad, about what he was doing, what was happening. Can we meet with you?'

'Of course, I was about to call. We need you and Emma to formally identify your father. He's at the Ipswich Hospital mortuary. Are you OK to do it today?'

Greg turns to Emma and tells her what DI Lawton has asked. She nods.

'Yes, it's OK,' Greg answers.

'You're in Leiston, aren't you? I can give you a lift. We can go together and talk in the car. I'll pick you up around eleven.'

Greg agrees and gives him Sally's address. It seems the police are taking his father's death seriously. Unlike Derek and Gertrude, there's no doubt this is murder.

Chapter 52

Before DI Lawton arrives, Greg and Emma decide to walk the short distance into Leiston town centre to pick up some essentials. The rain is spitting. It's still overcast and gloomy. It reflects their mood. They need to get out of the house. They need the physical exercise, the normality of shopping, having something to do. They pass the site of the old engineering works where they once made traction engines. It's been converted into offices. It used to be the heart of the town. Emma and Greg walk past The White Hart Hotel and The Mechanic's Arms pub where, not many years ago, they lined up rows of lunchtime pints for the workers. Greg used to smile morbidly at the thought of how many limbs might have been severed by mechanics having had too many lunchtime pints at The Arms. Today, he suppresses the thought.

They reach The Long Shop Museum dedicated to the history of the works and head to the Co-op, passing a bookie, a barber, two hair salons, a cheap grill, a Chinese takeaway and several charity shops. The High Street looks tired, untidy and unloved. Greg can't help thinking that although Sizewell C might be a disaster for the local environment, it could be a much-needed boost for Leiston. As they reach the crossroads at the top of the High Street, they see a familiar face. Paul's crossing the road walking towards them. He's not paying attention, and they almost collide. Just in time, he glances up and does a double take.

'Oh Emma, Greg.'

They stand facing each other. There's an awkward silence that's broken by Paul.

'I heard about your dad. I'm sorry.'

'Thanks,' Emma responds, 'we're trying to take it in. It's such a shock.'

'It must be, I can imagine. Well, I can't really, not what you're going through. I was expecting to lose my Jean.'

More silence.

'What brings you to Leiston?' Paul asks.

'We're staying with our aunt while the police are at the lodge. She's got a house in Margareta Crescent,' answers Greg.

'I know it, I used to have a school friend who lived there. It's a quiet road. It's not far from the old works.'

'Yes, that's it. We're just on our way to the Co-op to get a few things to tide us over.'

'Well, if there's anything you need, let me know. I'm Leiston born and bred. I can get you anything, if not, I know someone who can. I need to get going, see you around. I'm so sorry about Max.'

Paul gives Emma a hug and pats Greg gently on the shoulder before walking on. Greg and Emma continue up the High Street before stopping outside Sizewell C Information Centre. Glossy posters in the windows display how the new power station will, "help tackle climate change, provide local jobs, and supply decades of low carbon electricity".

'I had no idea this was here,' Emma says.

'Nor me. I can't help thinking about what Dad thought of Sizewell C and how much he hated the idea. How he knew we needed the power but couldn't accept it had to be nuclear.'

'And had to be here.'

'Yes, had to be here. He had a point.' Greg pauses, thinking. 'It was George who stood to gain from the contracts, wasn't it?'

'Not just George, lots of people. Practically the whole of Leiston.'

'Dad said Derek was against it, actively fought it. I wonder if that had anything to do with his hit-and-run?'

'I can't see it. Lots of people are against Sizewell C and lots are actively fighting it. Those who hate the idea of nuclear power, those who hate the loss of the local environment, those who hate the local community being disrupted and those who just hate the whole non-renewable power industry. Why go after Derek? It makes no sense.'

'Unless it was personal. Remember, Dad told us about Derek finding out about the accidents at George's company.'

'And the cover-ups. That would make it personal.'

'But why Gertrude and then Dad?'

'Because they both knew, were both talking about it?'

'Possibly. We need to tell the police. DI Lawton needs to investigate. Let's go in and find out more.'

'Not now, Greg, not now.'

The Co-op is the major shop in town, and they find most of the essentials they need before buying a change of clothes from the factory shop next door. They walk back to Aunt Sally's in silence. They are thinking about Sizewell C, about George and about their father. They are thinking about finding who killed him. Their grief is turning to anger and the anger is focusing them on finishing the job their father had started.

Chapter 53

Emma and Greg have time to shower, change and sort themselves out before DI Lawton arrives. When he does, he looks as if he's had a long night. Emma gives him a once-over, as if she's seeing him for the first time. She hadn't been in a fit state last night to notice anything. He's tall, lanky, possibly early forties, with a long, serious face and short, dark hair. Greg sits in the front of the car next to him, Emma takes a back seat, and they set off on the twenty-mile drive to Ipswich. It's the nearest large town and closest major hospital. DI Lawton opens the conversation as he pulls out of Margareta Crescent and heads towards the A12. He speaks slowly and carefully.

'How are you? Did you get any sleep? It can't have been an easy night.'

Greg turns his head towards the inspector. 'A little, it wasn't easy. I think we're both in shock.'

'That's understandable. We have people who can help, let me know if you want me to put you in touch.'

'I don't think we'll ever get over it… can ever get over it.'

'I know, of course. You'll need to give it time.'

There's silence. DI Lawton concentrates on driving before, after a considered interval, resuming the conversation.

'I need to run through what happens next and I believe you want to tell me a few things. We need one or both of you to formally identify your father's body. You will appreciate your father's death was violent and unnatural. As such, the coroner has prioritised a post-mortem to determine the cause. It's scheduled for this afternoon. The sooner we get things moving, the better. We need to find out what happened and catch whoever did this. The post-mortem will determine whether an inquest is needed. It's a legal investigation into the circumstances of his death.'

'Surely,' Greg says, 'the way he died, stabbed, hit over the head... surely, there will need to be an inquest.'

'Probably, but I've learnt never to pre-judge a post-mortem. I leave it to the experts and take it from there.'

'Will we get to see the outcome of the post-mortem?'

'Yes, you'll be told the cause of death. There will be a full pathologist's report which you can have access to if you wish. There may be a fee.'

'Really? A fee for a report on how our father was murdered?'

DI Lawton doesn't respond. There's a long silence.

'What happens when we identify him?' Emma asks.

'We don't need you both to do it. One of the mortuary staff will show you a photo of your father and ask you to confirm it's him. If it is, they will lead you into another room where your father's body will be laid out covered up to his chest with a sheet. You will be asked to formally identify him. You will be able to hold his hand if you wish.'

Emma dabs at a tear that has formed in the corner of her eye.

'Yes, I'd like that.'

Greg nods and agrees, mumbling just loud enough for DI Lawton to hear. There's more silence before he feels the time is right to say his piece.

'You know, Dad had a concern about how Gertrude fell. He thought it might not have been an accident, as her injuries weren't right. She didn't have them to her forehead, face, wrists or hands. He thought it was likely that she fell backwards, that she might have been pushed.'

Greg looks across at the inspector. If he's shocked, he doesn't show it. Greg then tells the inspector what his father had found out about Mike, James, Felicity, George and Tim. He runs through their potential motives for pushing Gertrude over the cliff. He tells DI Lawton about the possible connection to Derek's hit-and-run, the burglary, the dead crow and their father's close shave with the Land Rover. The inspector listens in silence and waits for Greg to talk himself out. When he senses Greg has finished, he responds gently but firmly.

'Well, that's quite some story. I'm not saying it isn't true, but the idea that Gertrude's death was anything more than an accident does seem like speculation. I'm not sure we can do anything until we get the results of her post-mortem. I believe it's happening this morning, probably as we speak. It should tell us whether she fell frontwards or backwards. Even then, if it was backwards, it could still have been an accident. Linking Gertrude's fall with your father's death, connecting them with what happened to Derek, it does seem unlikely. I'm not saying they're not connected but we'll need evidence to convince us. We have to take this one step at a time. If you come into the station at Leiston, we can take a statement. Meanwhile, first things first, someone needs to formally identify your father.'

When they arrive at the hospital, they take a lift to the basement, walk down a long corridor and pass through large, double, wooden doors to the mortuary visitor suite. It's clinical, clean and tasteful. The lighting is subdued and there's a silence that echoes. They are met by one of the mortuary team who introduces herself. She's very formal; pleasant but formal.

'Good morning, I'm May Lin. Please can you sign in? I'll shortly be taking you through to another room. It's where your father's laid out. You will be able to touch him and stay with him for as long as you wish to say your goodbyes. First, though, I need you to look at this photo and confirm to me that it's him.'

Emma and Greg both take a quick look at the photo, turn to May Lin and nod. Emma wells up but manages to keep from breaking into tears.

'Yes, that's Dad.'

May Lin gives her a sympathetic look.

'Are you OK to go in now and identify him?'

They both nod again, and May Lin leads them into the viewing room. Greg sees his father and goes straight over to be at his side. Emma is more reticent. She hangs back and looks around her. The room is uncluttered with white walls, wood flooring, a cream fireplace, a small vase of flowers perched to one side of the mantelpiece, a tasteful picture and an armchair in the corner. May Lin leads her to where her father is lying, covered by a sheet that reaches up to his chest. His face, arms and hands are visible. It's him; of course it's him. Greg and Emma stand either side of their dad, each holding one of his hands. His cold, hard hands.

Emma sobs quietly. 'I love you, Dad.'

She looks closely at her father's face. He is Dad, but somehow, he's different. He's fixed, set. Gone is the smile, the smiley emoji face she used to joke about. They all used to joke about. What she would give to see that face again. Not this one, not like this. She wants him back so badly. She wants to shake him, wake him from this sick joke.

'Bye, Dad, bye. I'll always love you.' She starts to cry, and then turns away. She can't look back.

Greg tries to remember the last thing he said to his dad, but it won't come. Maybe it was, 'I love you.' He hopes so. He really hopes so. He wants to capture this moment, his last with his dad. To say thanks for all the encouragement, the help with homework, the words of advice, the lifts to rugby matches, Spurs, the holidays, the bad jokes, all the time they spent together.

'Thank you, Dad. Thank you,' he whispers, before looking at his father for the last time. 'I will find out who did this. I will. I promise.'

Chapter 54

DI Lawton drops Greg and Emma back at Sally's and offers to keep them updated on developments. Their aunt opens the door, gives them a big hug, and leads them through the hall to the kitchen where they are greeted by the comforting smell of home baking.

'You must be hungry,' she says. 'I've made leek and potato soup and there's fresh bread just out of the oven. You need to keep your strength up. How was it? It can't have been easy.'

'Hard,' Emma responds. 'We didn't know what to expect. He was just lying there. He looked so alone. I got upset. We both got upset.'

'It's natural. When Graham died, it was awful seeing him there like that. Laid out, cold, on his own. I'll never forget it.'

Emma and Greg sit at the kitchen table while Sally remains standing, her mind deep in thought. She shakes her head before dishing out bowls of hot soup with thick slices of warm, freshly baked bread. They sit watching the steam rise off the soup. Their aunt joins them at the table and looks across at Greg.

'What happens now?'

Greg blows on his soup. 'They're doing the post-mortem this afternoon. They should get the results quite quickly. Inspector Lawton promised to keep us updated.'

'Did you tell him about what Max thought? What he'd found out?'

Greg tears a slice of bread in two and dips half in his bowl. 'Yes, but he didn't seem to take it very seriously. He wants to get the post-mortem findings before progressing things further.'

'Well, I suppose he has procedures. The police can't just jump to conclusions.'

Greg puts the soup-soaked bread in his mouth and swallows it. 'I know, I get that. But I don't think we need the results of the post-mortems to reach a perfectly obvious conclusion. They were both murdered. The issue is, by who? I just think they're wasting time. Why can't they start investigating now? Why wait? Well, we don't have to, we can start now.'

Emma looks at him, frowning worry lines adding to her already tired eyes. 'I said I'd help you, but how do we go about it? And will they let us? We've told the police what we know, won't they want to follow it up and not want us getting in the way?'

'Maybe. But I'm not waiting until we've given a written statement, they've processed it, decided whether it's relevant, developed a plan and celebrated Christmas. I promised Dad I would find out who did it and I will.'

'When did you promise Dad?'

'Earlier, when we were with him at the mortuary.'

'Really, you promised him?'

305

'It was the last thing I said to him before we left. I can't not keep my promise. I wouldn't be able to live with myself.'

'Oh Greg.' Emma sighs.

'I'm going to speak to the other lodge owners just like Dad did. Ask them what they know. Find out where they were when Dad was… was… attacked. Find out what they were doing. Find out who could have done it.'

'But it could have been anyone. Anyone on the site, a lodger, a camper passing through, one of the site team, even someone who has nothing to do with the place.'

'Then I'll just have to work on narrowing it down. Dad suspected Mike, George, Felicity and Tim. They're probably my best bets to begin with. I'm going to the site. I'm going to pay them a visit.'

'Today?'

'Why not? After lunch.'

'I can't let you do this alone. I'll come with you.'

'Are you sure?'

'I promised Dad I'd look after you. Yes, I'm sure.'

Sally places her hands flat on the table, studies Greg and looks him closely in the eyes.

'If only Dad – your Grandfather Eric – was here now. He'd know what to do. How to gather the information, read the clues, put the pieces together. Investigating murders, it's what he did. It's what he was good at. Kathy and I helped him solve one of them to do with the family of a school friend. Mum didn't want us to get involved, didn't want him to put us in danger. I feel like that about the two of you now. Have you thought this through?'

'What do you mean?' says Emma.

'I can't say I'm happy about what you're going to do.

If you must speak to people, you need to be careful. One of them could be a murderer. Your father could have been killed trying to find out what happened to Gertrude. If they think you're picking up where he left off, they could do the same to you. This is real, not some TV crime drama. Are you sure you want to do this?'

'I'm sure,' Greg answers. 'But I can't speak for Em.' He furrows his eyebrows and taps his fingers on the table, before looking at his sister for a sign. Emma doesn't hesitate in responding.

'If you're going ahead, I am too. You promised Dad and you need me.'

Sally breathes out a long sigh; she knows when she's beaten. 'Then you must stay together. Maybe have a code word between you. Warn each other if one of you thinks things are getting out of hand.'

Greg considers this. He likes the idea. 'Yes, a code word for when one of us thinks the other is getting in too deep, asking questions that could provoke the killer or giving too much away.'

Emma buys in to it. 'How about "red", like code "red". One of us says it if we're worried or think it's becoming dangerous.'

They agree the code is "red" and finish lunch. Sally gives them a spare set of house keys and they set off for Sunrise Park. When they arrive, the police manning the site entrance recognise them and immediately wave them through. They leave Greg's car in the main car park and walk to their father's lodge. It's still cordoned off and a team in white boiler suits remain busy at work. Emma looks at the holiday home her father so loved. She has a vision of him sitting on the patio peering out to sea, drinking his decaf. She sees them playing Scrabble, laughing, eating chocolate, drinking wine. She remembers them singing "Sunday Morning". When was it? Two days ago? She feels herself well up again.

Greg suggests they approach Mike first, so they climb the steps to his decking and ring his doorbell. He answers almost at once.

'Greg, Emma, how are you doing?'

'Not great, didn't sleep much,' Emma responds. 'It's not really sunk in. I can't believe it's happened. I can't believe how it happened.'

Mike looks to the ground then back up at Emma. 'I know what you mean. It's so awful.' He pauses and then says, 'I was just going for a walk along the beach to clear my head. Do you want to come with me?'

Greg turns to Emma, who nods back at him.

'Yes, thanks, we could use some sea air. It might help us start to take it all in,' he says.

'I was thinking of heading up the beach to Dunwich.'

'Yes, the wind will be behind us. It's not as gloomy as this morning.'

As they walk, dark clouds work their way ahead of them up the coast and the sea rolls in grey with occasional white tops. The air is bracing, but not cold. The wind is fresh. They walk along the firm sand close to the froth that comes off the waves that break on the shore.

'This is just what I need,' says Greg, breathing in deeply. 'I've been feeling like I'm in a dream. The sea, the breeze, the salt air, the sound of the waves all cut through the haze.'

Mike picks up a pebble and throws it hard into the sea. 'I know what you mean. Gertrude and now your dad. I can't take it in, I just can't. He was a good man, your dad. I didn't know him well but after what happened to Gertrude, we spent quite a bit of time together. Went for walks, shared a few meals, the concert last night. You know, he told me he thought Gertrude might have been pushed. I didn't believe him. I do now. I just wish I had then.'

'Why would you?' Emma joins in. 'Not before the post-mortem findings. He was right though. Otherwise, why would anyone want to burgle him, try to run him over, kill him?'

'And he told me about the close shave with the car in Leiston. I told him he was being paranoid. I'm so sorry. He was right, he must have been. I'm so sorry.'

'It's not your fault, you weren't to know what was to happen.'

'Did your dad say anything more about who he thought might have been responsible?'

Emma turns to Greg, and he senses that she's not sure how much to share with Mike. He's happy to continue.

'Not really. He did mention something about how he thought it might be connected to what happened to Derek.'

'I hadn't thought about that, it all seemed so far-fetched.'

'It probably was far-fetched. Until last night. Now it seems highly possible. In fact, anything seems possible.'

'But why would someone want to do that to your father? Even if it was about Derek and Gertrude, what has that got to do with your father?'

'He was a GP. He saw Gertrude's body and had a theory she'd been pushed. He was talking about it, spreading the idea, was obsessed with it. Maybe the killer got spooked, maybe they wanted to shut him up.'

'Yes, but he'd already told people what he thought, it was too late. And why the burglary?'

'Maybe he had something they were worried about, maybe his notebook?'

Emma's been listening closely. She thinks about the notebook. Then another thought crosses her mind.

'It could have been the notebook, but what about the torch? Maybe it belonged to whoever did it. What if they'd had it when they pushed Gertrude? Maybe that's when they lost it. What if they knew he'd found it and were trying to get it back?'

They stop walking. Greg and Mike look at Emma.

'Yes, of course, the torch,' Greg responds. 'That would make sense. Gertrude might have tugged it out of their hand when she fell. It could have rolled under the bush and been left there in the storm.'

'Why would it matter?' asks Mike.

'Maybe it could be traced. It could have Gertrude's fingerprints on. And theirs. I still have it. It's in the car.'

Emma frowns, then chooses her words carefully. 'It's red, isn't it?'

'No. It's black,' answers a bemused Greg.

'No, red. It's red.'

The penny drops. Greg gets the message.

'Oh yes, I see. Yes, it's reddy-black. In fact, it's not in the car. I forgot; I handed it in to DI Lawton.'

Mike misses the look between Greg and Emma.

'That all makes sense, but we only knew he'd found the torch when we were at lunch with James and Felicity. That was yesterday, the burglary and close shave with the car were earlier. I don't get it.'

Greg's mind is in overdrive.

'True, but maybe the burglar wanted to find out how much Dad knew. The notebook could have told them. Maybe the car incident was to warn him off and stop him following up on his theory about Gertrude.'

'It doesn't get us any closer to who did it,' Mike says. 'I was wondering about the connection with Derek. Who would have a grudge against both Gertrude and Derek?'

Greg and Emma only know what their father has told them. Greg decides to share this with Mike.

'Dad thought a few people on the site had issues with them. They argued with Tim over his car parking, were actively against Sizewell C, upset Felicity with their loud music and they both knew George's company had safety issues.'

'I suppose so, but could any of them really have killed your father? I'm not sure they have it in them.'

'Who knows what we're capable of?'

'Yes, that's what your dad said. But why run away up the track after attacking him? I don't think whoever did it saw me. It was dark and my lights were off. Why wouldn't they go back to their lodge? Why run all the way up the track?'

'Maybe they panicked, wanted to put as much distance as they could between them and what happened. Maybe it was someone staying somewhere else in the park.'

'Or outside it. A local?'

They reach Dunwich and turn inland to walk back to Sunrise Park. A woodpecker drums high up in one of the silver birch trees. Mike immediately picks up on it.

'Great spotted woodpecker. One of your dad's favourites. I should have brought my binoculars.'

'It's a lovely looking bird,' Greg says. 'But Dad once saw one carefully make a large hole in a tree in our garden and, instead of nesting there, it let a family of blue tits move in. When the young were nearly ready to fledge, the woodpecker returned to pluck them out one by one. Like a fresh food larder. He assumed it had taken them back to feed its own chicks.'

'Probably, nature is clever that way. Parents are capable of anything to ensure they successfully raise their young.'

Chapter 55

When they get back to the site, Mike continues to his lodge while Greg and Emma go back to their car to compare notes. They sit looking ahead through the windscreen.

'I don't think it could be Mike,' Greg says, 'he seems so genuine. He's keen to help and not at all evasive. I can't believe he made up having seen Dad's attacker running away; and anyway, DI Lawton said there were footprints.'

Emma turns her head towards Greg. 'I suppose so. You worried me when you mentioned having the torch. If he'd killed Dad for it, why wouldn't he do the same to us?'

'Yes, sorry. Thanks for the warning. If it's him, he'll be thinking the police have it, and it's just a matter of time before they find his and Gertrude's fingerprints.'

'Maybe, but they lived together so it would be easy for him to explain away. They will need a lot more than that to link him to pushing her over the cliff.'

Greg thinks about this; his brow is furrowed and he's tapping his fingers on the steering wheel.

'Why would Mike have wanted to kill Derek? Getting rid of them both to claim an inheritance seems unlikely. He would need to be a complete psychopath. It makes no sense.'

'Come on, let's get the torch to the police. We can drop it off at Leiston station before heading back to Aunt Sally's. Hopefully, DI Lawton will be there and will take our statement. I'll give him a call.'

DI Lawton picks up at once and tells Emma that the Leiston police station is unmanned but he can meet them there in an hour. It gives them time to kill, so they decide to take a drive to the Coastguard Cottages for a quick cuppa. They would normally turn right out of Sunrise Park towards Leiston but, instead, turn left and head along the narrow road that ends at a pair of open double gates that mark the entrance to Dunwich Heath. They soon reach a large National Trust car park, behind which sit the Coastguard Cottages.

The weather has picked up and late-afternoon sun shines across the trestle tables, benches and play area outside the café. Emma picks a table with a good view of the clifftop while Greg queues inside for cups of tea and the café's renowned cheese scones. He returns with his tray of goodies, and they sit with the sun warming their faces, enjoying the view. Greg butters his scone while Emma pours the tea. As she does, she sees a now familiar face heading towards them. It's Paul.

'Emma, Greg. What a surprise coming across you here. The weather's picked up from this morning, it's nice now. I've been doing a job here, I'm about to head off back to the site.'

Emma asks whether he would like to join them; he accepts before going to the café to get himself a cup of tea. He returns and sits opposite them.

'How are you doing?'

Emma puts her cup down and looks at him. 'Oh, you know, trying to come to terms with it. We've just been for a walk by the sea and have come here to chill for a bit. It seems strange, though, being here without Dad.'

'I understand. Your dad and I spoke about this place a few days ago. I love it here. It's somewhere you can clear your head, think, work things out.'

'Yes, Mum and Dad loved it, they used to bring us all the time. It's where we scattered Mum's ashes. There's a bench on the clifftop where you can look out to sea, along the beach and across Minsmere to Sizewell. They dedicated it to Nana and Grandad.'

'Yes, your dad told me. I know the bench, it's where I proposed to my wife, Jean. Our special place.' Paul looks down and sits in silence. He then looks back at them. 'Any news on what happened?'

'To Dad? Seems Mike found him, he'd been stabbed and hit on the back of the head. At least it must have been quick. He probably didn't know a thing.'

'Do they have any idea who did it?'

'No, not yet. But we'll find out, won't we, Greg?'

'Yes, I promised Dad.'

'You promised him? When?'

'When we identified him in the mortuary.'

'Ah, I see. Well, if there's anything I can do, let me know.'

They sit in silence for a while. Greg thinks about Gertrude and what Mike asked about the connection with

Derek's death. Maybe the key to what's been happening might lie in what happened to him. He looks at Paul.

'Do you know anything about what happened to Derek?'

'Derek?'

'Gertrude's husband.'

'That Derek. No, I don't know anything about it. I do know a few people didn't much like him.'

'Who? Why?'

'George had it in for him over Sizewell C, Tim didn't see eye to eye with him because of the parking, Felicity blamed him for her husband's heart attack. That's three right there. There could have been others.'

'Not popular then.'

'Not really. Anyway, no one ever proved it was deliberate. It was probably an accident. The driver just didn't have the guts to stop. It wouldn't be the first time.'

'Yes, but Dad wasn't convinced. He thought it might all be connected. After what happened to him, it does now make sense.'

Paul sits for a while, reflecting on this. 'I guess the police will be looking into it. Anyway, I'm off. I've a job at the site to be getting on with. Look after yourselves.'

Paul finishes his tea, rises to his feet and heads off. Emma uses her phone to prepare bullet points for their statement, every so often checking with Greg. As they get up to go, Emma looks around her. Soft sunlight sparkles on a calm sea, gorse bushes glow bright yellow, swallows and sand martins criss-cross in the cloudy sky above. She thinks how much her father would have loved it.

Chapter 56

They pull up at the recently opened, state-of-the-art, economically combined Leiston fire and police station. Further savings come from it not being permanently manned. There's an out-of-hours phone connected to the Suffolk Constabulary on the front wall and a PIN-coded door entry system. The only sign it is in any way connected to the previous, recently decommissioned Leiston police station is an old blue lantern marked "Police" that hangs on the wall by the side of the front door. Greg and Emma wait in their car until DI Lawton shows up. He's exactly on time. Their father's death is a priority.

DI Lawton clutches what looks like a notebook, Greg holds his recently acquired torch, and Emma has her mobile phone with her statement notes. DI Lawton shows them into the police station. They are the only ones there. It's clinical. It reminds Emma of the waiting room at the Ipswich Hospital mortuary. The entry hall has a pale-oak, laminate floor with white walls and cream paintwork. Multiple uninviting wooden doors lead from it. DI Lawton ushers them through the first door on the right and into a compact windowless room that contains a table and four chairs. He sits them down before offering them tea, coffee or water. They opt for water. DI Lawton opens the discussion.

'I thought you might like this. It's your father's journal. We found it in his backpack. There's nothing controversial, but I thought you would want it.' He hands the journal to Emma and then turns to Greg. 'What's the torch for?'

'We found it during an Easter egg hunt on Sunday, it was under a bush close to the top of the cliff where Gertrude fell. We think it could be important. It's possible that Dad's killer was looking for it.'

'Thanks. I'm surprised the team didn't find it when they found Gertrude.'

'It was well hidden, deep in the bush. Maybe they didn't look very hard, everyone thought Gertrude's fall was an accident. Even Dad. It was only later he thought it suspicious.'

'I understand she had dementia and was out on her own in a raging storm. It's not an unreasonable conclusion. We should get the results of the post-mortem in the morning. We'll know more then.'

Greg takes a sip of water and says, 'Meanwhile, could you check the torch for prints? Just in case. It will have my prints on, but it could also have Gertrude's and those of the killer?'

DI Lawton looks at Emma, then back to Greg.

'Maybe you watch too many detective series. Life's not like that. In nearly all cases, the obvious conclusion is the right one and the obvious conclusion in this case is that Gertrude fell by accident. I'll take it back to forensics though; after what happened to your dad, you never know what they might come up with.'

There's a lull in the conversation during which DI Lawton pours himself a glass of water before resuming the interview.

'So, you want to make a formal statement about the events leading up to your father's death?'

Emma speaks for her and Greg. 'Yes. It's what we ran through with you in the car on the way to Ipswich. We just want to get it all down on record so it's clear. It's what Dad would have wanted.'

'Have you managed to obtain any evidence?'

'Not really, but he told us what he found out and we think it makes sense.'

'OK. If you write out what you would like to put on record, we'll have a look at it and assess how best to follow it up. Please understand though, without solid evidence, there's not much we can do.'

'We know, you said, but we still want to get it all down. We want it taken seriously.'

DI Lawton gives them advice on how to structure their statement. Emma pauses, takes a breath, then starts writing. She consults the bullet points on her phone, every so often reading the statement out for Greg to comment. It takes the best part of an hour. DI Lawton spends his time on his phone. When the statement is finished, Emma reads it out to him. He asks her and Greg to add their signatures. Emma can't help feeling they're going through the motions. That DI Lawton is humouring them. *No matter*, she thinks, *it's best to have it in writing. Just in case anything happens to her and Greg. Who knows what their father's killer might do next?* They finish off at the police station and head back to Sally's.

On the short journey across Leiston, Emma lets Greg know her thoughts.

'I don't think the police are taking what we've told them seriously. They're treating Dad's death as murder, but I still don't think they're connecting it with Gertrude's fall, or the burglary.'

'Or Derek, or Dad's close shave with the Land Rover,' Greg adds.

'Or the dead crow,' responds Emma. 'What do we do next?' she asks. 'I wonder what Dad would have done. Or Grandad Eric. What would he have made of this? What would he be thinking?' She remembers when, as a girl, she spent time with their grandad. 'Do you remember him reading *Sherlock Holmes* to us before bed? Do you remember the quotes? I'll never forget, "You see but you do not observe".'

'"There's nothing more deceptive than an obvious fact",' Greg adds with a smile.

'"Once you eliminate the impossible, whatever remains, no matter how improbable, must be the truth",' responds Emma. 'I've not heard that in years. I reckon Grandad would have told us to work out who couldn't have done it and see who's left.'

'That sounds like good advice. We haven't yet spoken with James and Felicity, or Tim. Perhaps we should go to The Six Bells tonight for dinner and see if they're there. Even if they aren't, we might pick something up from the staff, or whoever else is about.'

'Let's hope Sally hasn't already prepared dinner.'

When they arrive at their aunt's house, it's obvious they are too late.

'Aunt Sally, we're back, something smells amazing,' Emma calls out.

Sally welcomes them and takes a sip of what looks like sherry. 'Boeuf bourguignon with baked potatoes. I used a nice bottle of Burgundy. It's how your dad loved it. It'll be ready in twenty minutes if you need time to change.'

They haven't got the heart to turn her down.

'Change of plan,' Greg says to Emma. 'The boeuf bourguignon does smell good. We can go for a drink at The Six Bells after we've eaten.'

The boeuf bourguignon is as good as it smells and the apple pie that follows is just as tasty. Sally is looking after them in the way she knows best. After dinner, they mention their plan to go to The Six Bells for a drink and tell her not to wait up. She seems disappointed they are not staying to keep her company, but it can't be helped. As they leave, she tells them to be careful. It's what she said to their father the last time she saw him.

Chapter 57

When Greg and Emma arrive at The Six Bells, they look around and note most of the usual suspects. Tim is with Harvey, chatting to Becky, who's behind the bar. George and Julia are standing further along the counter with recently outed James and Felicity. They are talking and laughing loudly, nicely oiled by a couple of hours' drinking time. It noticeably quietens as Greg and Emma approach the bar. There's an awkward silence. The subdued mood is accentuated by R.E.M's "Everybody Hurts" playing in the background.

James breaks the spell. 'We are all so upset about your father. Max was a good man, everyone liked him. I can't believe what's happened, it doesn't make any sense.' He pauses and then adds, 'How are you doing?'

Emma can't think how to respond.

'Just getting over the shock,' Greg says. 'It's not really sunk in. I'm not sure it ever will. Not the way he died.'

James puts his hand on Greg's shoulder. 'I understand. It's awful. I can't imagine who would do such a thing. Was it another burglary? I honestly can't see what they would have wanted so badly. There must be a local madman.'

'Or someone who knew what they were doing,' Greg replies. 'Dad was convinced Gertrude had been pushed over the cliff. As soon as he starts asking questions, he's burgled, is delivered a dead crow, nearly killed by a car coming out of nowhere, then murdered in his lodge. It can't all be coincidence.'

There's a lull in the music; everyone at the bar has been listening. Tim comes across to where they are standing.

'Not you as well. You can't be serious. You're as bad as your dad. I know he's gone, so we need to be respectful, but he was slightly crazy. What possible motive could anyone have to murder both Gertrude and Max? Sunrise Park is full of all sorts of malicious gossip. This is just adding to it.'

'Come on, Tim, that's too harsh,' James intervenes. 'They've just lost their dad. Max was a good man, and he certainly wasn't crazy.'

'I've no idea if Gertrude was pushed,' Felicity adds, 'but what happened to Max must have been deliberate. I just can't believe it was one of us. We need to let the police do their job, let them catch whoever did this.'

'Do you think your dad suspected one of us?' James asks.

'Yes, he suspected several of you,' Emma replies.

'Did he have any proof?' Tim jumps in. 'We all know Gertrude fell and we all know it was an accident.'

Greg puffs out his cheeks in exasperation.

'But what about Dad? Someone stabbed him and hit him over the head. That was no accident.'

'What about a surprised burglar?' Tim snaps back. 'Maybe the same one as before, back for the stuff he didn't get the first time.'

'Or one of you looking for something,' Greg adds. 'Maybe the torch we found where Gertrude went over the cliff?'

The group look around at each other. George smiles, it's almost a smirk. It's as though he's about to reveal a winning poker hand.

'Most of us were in here when it happened. Simon kept the bar open late. That rules him, me, Julia, James and Felicity out for starters.'

'And me, I was here with Harvey,' Tim quickly adds.

George thinks for a bit. 'You were earlier, but you left just after Becky finished her shift.'

'Yes, but I came back.'

'After an hour or so. Long enough.'

'Long enough for what?'

'Long enough for what happened to Max.'

Tim looks shifty, as though he's trying to work out what to say next. 'It couldn't have been me. I have an alibi.'

George won't let it go. 'Oh yes, and what's that?'

'Mind you own business.'

The group falls silent and exchange glances with each other. Tim's looking decidedly uncomfortable. Fleetwood Mac's 'Oh Well' strangely adds to the moment. George can't leave it there.

'I think we can all guess what your alibi might be. Has anyone spoken to Joyce recently? Any good gossip?'

James, Felicity and Harvey break out in grins. Julia splutters into her Sauvignon Blanc. Becky gives him a long, hard stare. Greg and Emma feel as if they're missing out on a shared joke. The air is thick with tension. Tim stabs his finger into George's chest.

'Why don't you fuck off?'

George isn't intimidated. 'I'm just asking.'

'Well, just fuck off. We all know what you're asking. Another word and you can join me outside.'

'Keep your hair on.'

Becky moves closer to Tim on the other side of the bar and looks him in the eyes.

'Calm down. It's OK, let it go. It's not worth it.'

'This is the Tim we all know and love,' George adds, smiling.

Tim shoots him a vicious look and drains the last drop of his whisky. He turns to Becky.

'Give me another malt. A large one.'

'You've had enough,' Becky responds calmly. 'In fact, you've had too much. You don't want to do something you might regret. It's time to leave. Please.'

Becky looks Tim hard in the eyes. He looks back at her. He's about to say something, stops himself, turns around and storms out of the bar. Emma and Greg have no idea what's going on. They are about to ask when Harvey announces he's also off home. Before he goes, he takes Emma to one side.

'Your dad was a nice man, a good man. Let me know if you need to talk.' He pauses then adds, 'Or a shoulder. I'm told I'm a good listener.'

Emma's going to be around for a while and spending time with someone like Harvey might be just what she needs. Anyway, he may have some useful information.

'That would be good. Lunch tomorrow?'

Harvey can hardly believe his luck. He gets his phone out, checks his diary, and mentally shifts a site job from early to late afternoon.

'Yes, I can do lunch. I've got jobs all morning, but it looks like I'm free for a couple of hours from one to three. How about here just in case an urgent job comes up?'

'Sounds good. One o'clock here, see you then.'

'Yes, see you t'amara.'

'T'amara?'

'Tomorrow – it's local.'

Harvey heads off home to Leiston. There's a prolonged silence.

'Tim can be such a dick,' James observes after a while. 'I reckon he could pick a fight in a monastery. If anyone pushed Gertrude over that cliff, it was probably him. He's nasty enough, probably crazy enough.' He then looks at Greg and Emma and adds, 'Ignore Tim, he's an arse. Always has been, always will be. A drunken arse.'

'He doesn't help,' Emma replies, nodding. 'We lose Mum, now Dad. It's like our lives have been ripped apart, shredded by some heartless lunatic. The last thing we need is a fight with Tim.'

She looks at Greg, covers her face with her hands and breaks down in tears. Her brother puts his arms around her, gives her a hug and asks if she wants to leave. Emma nods, dries her eyes with a tissue and they make their excuses.

'Sorry, it all got too much,' Emma says as Greg drives back to Aunt Sally's. 'Tim being so nasty. I thought I could handle things. I guess I wasn't ready.'

'You're only human. After what's happened, of course you're fragile. Perhaps you should take it easy for a bit, let me follow things up.'

'No, I'm OK. We need to do this together. Anyway, tonight was useful. Remember Grandad's *Sherlock Holmes* quote, "Once you eliminate the impossible, whatever remains, no matter how improbable, must be the truth." I reckon that puts Simon, George, Julia, James and Felicity in the clear. When Dad was attacked, they were all drinking in The Six Bells bar.'

'Maybe, assuming they didn't all do it and are covering for each other.'

'Like in *Death on the Nile*? But that's impossible, isn't it?'

'It's *Murder on the Orient Express*. Improbable, yes, but not impossible.'

Chapter 58

The next morning, Emma wakes to the smell of cooked breakfast wafting up from the kitchen, gets out of bed, uses the bathroom and heads downstairs in her aunt's dressing gown. Sally is frying eggs, bacon, sausages and mushrooms while Greg sits at the table looking at messages on his phone.

'Morning. How did everyone sleep?' asks Emma.

'Better than Monday night, that's for sure,' Greg replies, glancing up at her.

'Me too. I was shattered. I fell asleep straight away. That smells good, Aunt Sally.'

'You need to get something inside you. I know when I lost my Graham, I didn't want to eat for days. I couldn't be bothered to make anything for myself. You don't have to, you've got me.'

They sit around the kitchen table as Sally hands them their fry up, together with tea and toast.

'How was last night at The Six Bells?' she asks. 'Was anyone there you know?'

Greg pours his tea and starts to butter a piece of toast.

'Yes, quite a few of the other lodge owners. We nearly had a fight. Tim, from the lodge closest to the cliff edge opposite Dad's, got upset with George. He threatened him. I couldn't work out what it was about. One minute, we're talking about a late drinking session they'd had the night Dad… Dad… well, you know, that night, the next moment, Tim's wanting to take George outside. He'd had a few, but even so, he's a headcase.'

'It was strange,' adds Emma. 'I'm seeing Harvey for lunch. I'll find out what it was about. He should know.'

'Harvey, do I know him?' Sally asks.

'He's the site handyman,' Greg answers. 'He's young, local, nice. I think he's from Leiston. He lives with his parents.'

'What's his surname? I might know him or his family. Leiston's a small town.'

'Sorry, no idea. I'll have to ask him,' Emma replies.

'Just be careful. Anyone could have been responsible for what happened to your father, even Harvey.'

'Of course. We're meeting at The Six Bells, there'll be lots of people around.'

'Good. What about you, Greg, what are your plans?'

'I've got things to catch up on. How's your Wi-Fi?'

'Good. Bill sorted it out for me.' Sally points across the room. 'The password is on the router over there. How is work?' Sally asks.

'Good, busy but good.'

'And you, Emma, what have you been up to? How are the amateur dramatics going?'

'I'm playing Ophelia in a local production of *Hamlet*.'

'*Hamlet*, the revenge play. Fancy giving us a line?'

Emma thinks for a while. She tries to find something that feels right but can only think of a song. She doesn't want to use it, but it won't go away. It's been going around and around in her head since she found out about her father. It needs exorcising.

'And will he not come again? And will he not come again? No, no, he is dead; Go to thy deathbed; He never will come again...' Emma's voice fades, then stops. She can't continue. Tears trickle down her cheeks.

Sally gets up and gives Emma a hug. Greg picks at a sausage. He's no longer hungry. But it smells nice. It smells warm and cosy. It smells like normality. But he knows things are not normal. Things will never be normal again. His stomach is churning. It's not the churning he feels before throwing up. It's a more subtle churning in the depths of his guts that weighs his whole body down and sucks the life from his mind. He stares out of the window at the birds flitting on and off the seed dispensers. He thinks of his father. What he'd said about blue tit parents flying one hundred miles. He wishes he could be like them. Focused solely on the job of feeding their young. Going back and forth with their ten thousand tiny caterpillar deliveries, not feeling, not thinking. Just doing.

Chapter 59

Greg and Emma spend the morning on their phones, catching up on emails and messaging friends. They wait expectantly for a call from DI Lawton with the result of their father's post-mortem. They hear nothing. Just after midday, Greg drives Emma to Sunrise Park and drops her off at The Six Bells for her lunch date with Harvey. The place is full of campers, caravaners and lodge owners enjoying meals outside on the terrace. Harvey has booked them a corner table. Emma sits facing outward on to the children's play area. As she waits for Harvey, she watches small girls and boys enjoying themselves on the swings and climbing across a monkey bridge. Others are kicking a football around. She's had a reasonable night's sleep but is still deeply weary. The sun is on her face, and she absorbs the heat gratefully as she lays her head on the wooden trestle table.

'Are you OK? Can I get you anything?' It's Becky.

Emma orders an apple juice with ice. Looking around, she sees happy, smiling faces enjoying their Easter holidays. She'd been so looking forward to spending time with her dad and brother. And it had been so nice. She remembers moments from the time they spent together. The walks along the beach, exploring the heath, crabbing in Southwold, dinner in Aldeburgh, singing "Sunday Morning" on the lodge decking.

She's brought back from her thoughts by a soft Suffolk voice.

'Hi, Emma. Sorry I'm late.'

It's Harvey, standing looking down at her. He's changed out of his usual work overalls into a light blue shirt and dark blue chinos.

'Hi, Harvey. I only just arrived myself. I've ordered an apple juice.'

'Good idea, I don't drink when I'm working. Alcohol, that is.'

Becky arrives with Emma's apple juice. Harvey sits opposite Emma and orders a pint of orange and soda. They look at the lunch menu. Emma has a cheese omelette with salad; Harvey has a cheese toastie with chips. They smile at Becky as she leaves and then look across the table at each other.

'Not very glam for a first date,' Harvey says. 'I'll make it up to you next time.'

Emma raises her eyebrows. 'Next time? You're making quite an assumption.'

'No, sorry, I didn't mean – well, I suppose I did.'

'It's fine. I'm teasing. I've been watching the children play. They're so happy, not a care in the world. One day, they'll be sitting here wondering where the time went. How it vanished so quickly. Why they didn't make more of it when they could, more of being with their family, their parents, their grandparents.'

'Wow, deep.'

'Sorry. I'm not usually so serious. Just recently, you know.'

'Of course. You and your dad seemed close.'

Emma takes a sip of her apple juice.

'We were. Daddies and daughters; it's special. I loved Mum, we got on great. But Dad was Dad. Funny, kind, supportive. There was one time when I'd split up with a boy. Charlie. We'd been together about six months, which was a record for me. I was in pieces. Dad was so understanding. We chatted and he made me feel good about myself, made me feel like I was the centre of his world. Like I was special. Like I could be the centre of another boy's world. I miss him so much. Already.'

'My dad died when I was young,' Harvey says. 'My mother remarried. Jim, my stepdad. We get on OK, but it's not the same. It's like I need to keep proving myself. We're good, but it's not as easy.'

Emma takes another sip and looks at Harvey. 'Dad was fun. He made such awful jokes. They were often bad taste, but he seemed to get away with them. He made me laugh, made us all laugh. He wasn't the same after Mum died. He blamed himself, couldn't come to terms with not picking up on her cancer. It was stupid. He did everything he could for her.'

'I'm sure he did. I liked him. He seemed kind, thoughtful.'

'He was. He was.'

Emma feels herself begin to well up. She doesn't want Harvey to see, so she turns away just as Becky arrives with their order. Harvey smothers the chips in salt, vinegar and ketchup, effectively preventing Emma from picking at them. By the time they are ready to eat, her emotions are back under control. After a few mouthfuls Emma puts her knife and fork down.

'Harvey, what was all that about last night in the bar?' she asks.

Harvey stops eating and takes a gulp of his orange and soda.

'All what about?'

'Tim threatening George. I didn't get it. Why the reaction when Joyce was mentioned?'

'Ah, the barney. You really don't know?'

'No, I don't. I wouldn't be asking.'

Harvey leans in closer to Emma. 'It's a bit sensitive, we need to keep our voices down. Tim and Becky are playing silly buggers.'

'Silly buggers?'

'You know, having an affair.'

'Oh. Becky? Waitress Becky? With Tim? He's old enough to be her father. My God. And what was all that about Joyce?'

'Joyce's a blabbermouth. She's snouty. She caught them at it in the bushes by the cliff path. Tim threatened her to keep her quiet, but she can't help herself. She can't keep her mouth shut. She must have let on to half the site.'

'No wonder Tim's upset.'

'Just a bit. He's already picked fights with a couple of those who've mentioned it. He nearly added George to the list.'

'He does seem aggressive.'

'He is, especially when he's had a few drinks. That's pretty much every night. He's a rum 'un.'

'How was he with Gertrude?'

'Gertrude? Same as with everyone. They argued. She kept accusing him of blocking her view to the sea with his car. I once heard him tell her to piss off. She had a go back, gave as good as she got.'

'Could he have pushed her?'

'Over the cliff?'

'Could he?'

'Maybe. Paul says Tim was drunk, he heard the two of them having a shouting match on the doorstep that night.'

'Paul?'

'Yes. He was there sorting Tim's lights out. They went out in the storm.'

Emma makes a mental note to speak to Paul. She doesn't like what she's hearing about Tim. He's violent, was drunk on the night Gertrude fell and he argued with her. It doesn't take a genius to jump to the conclusion that he could have pushed her.

'What were they fighting about?'

'Paul says she was having a go at Tim about his affair with Becky. She must have heard about it from Joyce. She was shouting at him, calling him a paedophile. He told her to mind her own business. When she carried on, he shouted back, was getting angry, but she wouldn't stop. Being Gertrude, it wasn't going to happen. Who knows what went on after that.'

'Do you think he could have attacked Dad?'

'No idea. I can't think why he would, unless your dad had something that proved he'd pushed Gertrude. Maybe your dad arrived back when he was in the lodge nosing about. Maybe he was disturbed, panicked and attacked. It's possible; who knows. He did go missing from The Six Bells that night.'

Emma needs to find out more about Tim, but first, she wants to find out more about Harvey. They discuss his family, his job and his plans. Becky arrives to clear the plates, and they order another round of drinks. After what she's just been told, Emma can't help looking at their waitress more closely. She's young, pretty, has a pleasant smile and a confident manner. She seems far too nice for Tim. Still, there's no accounting for taste.

Harvey asks about Emma's job, her acting, where she lives. It's easy, relaxed. She likes him, maybe she will let him buy her a meal somewhere more glam. When their drinks are almost finished, she takes out her phone and looks across at Harvey.

'I need to give Greg a call to have him pick me up to take me back to Aunt Sally's.'

'Don't worry about that, I can drop you off. I don't need to be back on site for a while.'

'Great, thanks.' She pauses before asking, 'Do you know where Paul lives?'

'Leiston. Why?'

'I want to go and talk to him about Tim. About that night. I need to know what happened with Gertrude and... Dad.'

'Isn't that what the police are doing?'

'I know, but I need to find out. I can't help it. I need to do something now. I'll go crazy just waiting for news from the police.'

Harvey is silent for a bit. He looks across at the play area. Then down at the table. He's struggling with something. He's avoiding making eye contact with her. Emma can't make it out. Eventually, he looks directly at her.

'There's something you need to know. I've been meaning to tell you. I just couldn't work up the courage. Don't think too bad of me.'

'What?'

Emma's worried. She can't think what he's about to say.

'I'm so sorry. If I'd known what was to happen to your dad, I wouldn't have done it.'

'What? Done what?'

'The dead crow. It was me.'

'The crow?'

'Yes, on your dad's decking. George asked me to do it.'

'You? George?'

'He'd seen your dad at the Sizewell protest, then, when they had lunch, they had a run-in over the new power station. I've been doing some bits and pieces for him. He gave me the "Jobs not Snobs" poster with the crow that he'd shot that morning. He asked me to leave it in front of your dad's door. He said it would be funny, a prank. He didn't want your dad to know it was from him. I didn't want to do it, but he insisted. I'm so sorry.'

'How could you?'

'I thought it was just some joke between them. After what then happened to your dad, I'm not so sure. I had to tell you. Please don't think too badly of me.'

They sit in silence. Emma's mind is wondering whether

if George had paid Harvey to plant the dead crow, maybe he also paid to have her father killed. But not by Harvey, he wouldn't do it. Would he? And why would he have told her about the crow?

They pass on dessert and Emma offers to share the bill. Harvey won't think of it. He settles up and looks her in the eyes.

'Let me drive you to Paul's, it's the least I can do to make up for what I did.'

Emma thinks twice before accepting his lift, but she needs to see Paul and she can't believe that Harvey is dangerous. Not Harvey.

Chapter 60

Greg spends his time reading his father's journal. He can't find anything in it that sheds light on who the murderer might be. He wishes he had the previous one. The one that was stolen. And he reads the press reports. There's a lot of coverage about what happened to his father, but little about Gertrude or Derek. None of it is helpful. He thinks about calling Emma to see whether she's ready for a lift when the doorbell rings. He hears Uncle Bill's voice, picks up his phone and heads downstairs.

'Uncle Bill, how's things?'

'I've been to see Orla. I thought I'd pop in on my way home.'

'How was she?'

'She had a bit of a fall yesterday but just bruises, nothing broken. I heard about your dad. I came to say how sorry I am.' He pauses and then adds, 'We'll all miss him. He was a good 'un, great sense of humour, kind, caring, generous. It's so sad.'

'Thanks, I'm still trying to get used to him not being

here. It's happened so suddenly. One moment we're having Easter together, the next he's… he's… you know.'

Sally sits them around the kitchen table, puts the kettle on, removes a chocolate cake from its tin and sets it out on a plate in front of them. She cuts three slices, places them on plates and hands them out. They each look down at their slice. Greg thinks back to them all eating cake together on Easter Sunday. It was such a short time ago.

'I hope you don't mind me asking, but what happened?' Bill says.

'What happened?'

'To your dad.'

Greg takes a sip of tea, pauses, and looks across at Bill.

'He was attacked when he got home to his lodge on Monday night. Stabbed and hit over the head. He was dead before the ambulance arrived.'

'My God. I've heard some rum things. Who would do that?'

'No idea.'

'I'm buggered if I can see why anyone would do such a thing. To Max! Max, of all people.'

'The police are waiting for the forensic post-mortem report. It must have been murder. Especially after what happened to Gertrude. Then there's Dad's burglary, the dead crow, and the near miss with the car here on Sunday.'

'What? I know about Gertrude, but what burglary? What dead crow? And what near miss? What haven't you been telling me, Sal?'

Chapter 61

As Harvey drives Emma to Leiston, she thinks about what she will say to Paul. She needs to find out if Tim could have killed her father. She needs to find out what he was like when Gertrude came to his lodge that night. Whether he got violent with her. Whether he could have walked Gertrude to the cliff and given her a push. She needs to find out what Paul knows. She wonders about calling Greg but decides to wait until after she's seen Paul. There's no point getting her brother involved just yet, not until she has more evidence on Tim. She wonders if Paul might go with her to face him. Tim has a history of violence. It could get nasty. Perhaps it would be better to call DI Lawton and let the police handle it. *No*, she thinks, *I need more evidence. Paul will help.*

As they enter Leiston, Harvey's phone rings. He speaks briefly, rings off and lets Emma know that someone's lock is broken; they can't get into their lodge. He needs to be back on site. He drops her off on the corner of a narrow street off the main road to Sizewell with instructions that Paul lives at number forty-two. It's a 1960s estate handily sited for the town centre. She passes a string of small semi-detached houses, some with immaculate front gardens, others in need of serious attention. Paul's is run-down and tired, but not one of the worst.

Emma lets herself in through a low gate and tentatively walks up a short path flanked by tiny squares of grass. She rings the doorbell, waits, senses he's out and wishes she'd thought of phoning ahead. She's about to leave when she sees the front room curtains twitch. Someone's in. She knocks on the window. One of the curtains is pulled back and a surprised-looking Paul peers out at her. He comes to the front door, opens it and looks her up and down.

'What are you doing here?'

'I need to speak with you. Can I come in?'

He shows her through the hall into a small kitchen. 'Coffee or tea?'

Emma opts for a white coffee and watches Paul as he boils the kettle. The back door is open, and she looks out on to an untidy garden with a rotary washing line set in the centre of a small lawn. Items of children's clothing are swaying in the breeze. Well-worn jeans, shirts, knickers and socks.

'So, what's up?' he asks.

'I just had lunch with Harvey; he brought me. I need to talk to you about Tim and what happened with Gertrude that night. I need to talk to you about Tim and Dad.'

'What about them? What about Tim and your father?'

Paul hands her a mug of instant coffee and they sit at a small, round kitchen table. She looks at Paul. He's leaning forward and his stocky frame fills the chair he's perched on. Emma decides to dive straight in; there's no point wasting time on small talk.

'Harvey told me you were there at Tim's the night Gertrude fell over the cliff, the night she died. Dad thought she'd been pushed. Harvey said you told him you heard them arguing. What happened?'

Paul pauses and looks closely at Emma. He appears to be weighing her up, deciding whether to answer. Deciding how much to tell her.

'Tim called me; his lights had gone out in the storm. I was already on site as others had been having the same problem. When I got there, he was drunk. He likes to drink, that night was no different to usual. I got to work on the lights – they'd fused. The rain gets in the outside switches in some of the lodges. I heard someone knocking at the door. Tim didn't answer at first, but the knocking kept on. It was insistent. Eventually, he got up, opened the door and I heard him speaking. Then I heard Gertrude's voice. She seemed upset. They started shouting at each other, it got nasty. I couldn't exactly make out what they were saying, but it wasn't nice. Tim was very angry.'

'Harvey said something about Gertrude accusing him of being a paedophile because of his affair with Becky. Is that right?'

Paul looks surprised. 'Oh, he told you about that? Well, yes, I didn't want to mention it. Tim can get upset. He gets angry, sometimes violent.'

'Do you think he could have pushed her over the cliff?'

'I heard him tell her to go away, I heard him shut the door. He may have gone after her, I don't know.'

343

'What about Dad? Did he ever say anything to you about Dad?'

'Like what?'

'Anything about being upset at Dad for looking into what happened to Gertrude?'

'No, nothing. I was there in The Six Bells when they argued about it. I thought they would come to blows.'

'We found an expensive torch under a bush close to where Gertrude fell. Do you know if Tim had one? Might it have been his?'

Paul peers down into his mug, takes a gulp of coffee and looks back at Emma.

'Possibly. I might know if I saw it. Where is it?'

'Greg handed it in to the police. They're running fingerprint tests, trying to find out who it belongs to.'

Paul looks thoughtful. 'He gave it to the police. How long have they had it?'

'Since yesterday. They should have the results soon, maybe today.'

Paul repeats, 'Today?' Then he drains his mug and gets up. 'I need a pee, make us another cup, will you?'

Chapter 62

Sally looks down, feeling guilty about not telling Bill about the burglary and Max's near miss. She's also wonders about the crow.

'It's all happened so fast, Bill. I'll let Greg explain.'

Greg turns from his aunt to Bill, sighs and decides to give the potted version. When he's finished, Bill leans back and takes a deep intake of breath.

'Have you told the police about all this?'

'We've given them a statement. They say they need to wait for Gertrude and Dad's post-mortems. They need solid evidence. I handed in a torch… it was really a flashlight, we found it by the cliff close to where Gertrude fell.'

'You found a flashlight. How might that help?'

'It could have fingerprints on. It was a good one, looked expensive. It's surprising whoever lost it didn't go back for it. Something must have happened.'

'I've sold a couple of top-quality flashlights recently. I don't sell many.'

'It's zoomable, rechargeable, waterproof, with an adjustable focus.'

'Yes, that's it. One was to a guy I didn't recognise. He said he worked in security at Sizewell.'

Greg processes the information; his pulse quickens. He thinks that it could be Tim.

'What did he look like?'

'Hard to recall. Youngish, maybe in his thirties, tall, slim.'

It doesn't sound like Tim. Greg wonders whether Bill has remembered correctly.

'Did he have a paunch?'

'I don't think so. He was driving one of those new electric cars.'

'Who bought the other one?'

'Paul, local lad, electrician. I've known him for years. He came in on Saturday.'

Greg leans forward, spreads his arms on the table and double checks what he's just heard.

'Paul who works at Sunrise Park?'

'Yes, that's him. One my regulars. He's had a rum time of it. His wife was hit by a car and nearly killed. It left her in a bad way. She never recovered, died six months or so back. It was terrible, they never caught who did it. Paul was distraught. He's got two young girls who he dotes on. He worries about them all the time, not knowing how they'll cope without their mum. We chatted about them when he came in for the flashlight. He said he'd lost his. He also took a lock for one of the lodges and had extra keys cut. It took a while, so we had a good catch up.'

'Paul? Harvey fitted a new front door lock for Dad after the burglary on Saturday. The day we arrived. I assumed that he bought it. And Dad had just one spare key.'

'No, this was Paul. He had two spare keys cut. Three in all. I didn't sell any more locks or cut any other keys on Saturday. Just the ones for him.'

Greg leans back, puts his hands behind his head and purses his lips. His mind usually produces thoughts that ripen over time into workable ideas. It's as if his brain is like a slow cooker. He puts in the facts, lets them bubble away and, eventually, up pops the solution. Sometimes, though, he simply connects the dots, and the answer is clear. Paul bought a torch and a lock. And had three sets of keys. Dad was only given two.

Paul? Could it be Paul? What if he thought Derek had run down his wife and got away with it? What if he'd done the same to Derek, run him over, killed him in revenge? Maybe he also pushed Gertrude? Killed Dad to keep him quiet or get his hands on the torch. Oh God, Paul. He needs to let Emma know. He's beginning to feel sick. There's a murderer on the loose and it could be Paul.

Greg tells Sally he needs to use the bathroom, heads out of the kitchen and calls Emma. There's no answer.

He whispers down the phone, 'Pick up, Emma, pick up,' but there's nothing. He needs to call Harvey but hasn't got his number. He phones Sunrise Park reception pretending to be a lodge owner with an issue that needs a handyman. They give him Harvey's number; he makes the call and is relieved to immediately hear his voice.

'Harvey, it's Greg.'

'Greg, how are you? What can I do you for?'

'Is Emma still with you? Can you let me speak with her? She's not answering her phone?'

'No, I took her to Leiston a while ago. I'm back at Sunrise doing a few jobs.'

'Where did she go?'

'To see Paul. She wanted to ask him a few questions about Tim.'

'Paul? About Tim, why Tim? It's not Tim she needs to worry about, it's Paul.'

'Paul? Why Paul?'

'We found a flashlight torch close to where Gertrude fell over the cliff. We think it was Paul's.'

'So, he could have just lost his. I can't see it means he pushed her.'

'Did you buy Dad's replacement lock on Saturday?'

'No, I asked Paul. He was in Leiston.'

'How many extra keys did he have cut?'

'Just one for the key safe. It's all your dad asked for.'

'I thought so. We're with Bill – you know, from the hardware supplies shop. He says he sold Paul a new torch on Saturday, together with a lock. He cut him two spare keys. He had three in all.'

'Three? On Saturday. Are you sure?'

'Yes, three. Paul must have kept one. It's how he got into Dad's lodge the night he was attacked.'

'Why would Paul want to kill Gertrude and your dad? Bugger if I can see why he'd do that.'

'Paul's wife was run over and nearly killed. She died six months ago. They never caught who did it. We wonder if he thought it was Derek and got revenge by running him over, then pushing Gertrude over the cliff.'

'Paul did get upset with Derek after the accident. He saw his car had a new dent and accused Derek of running down Jean. Derek denied it and then avoided him. Paul was convinced it was him, he used to talk about it all the time. I told him it was all squit, but he kept on. He eventually went to the police. They turned him away as he had no evidence. By then, Derek had fixed the dent. Oh my God, he hasn't, has he? But why go after Max?'

'I don't know, maybe he wanted to stop Dad investigating what happened to Gertrude? Maybe to get the torch? It doesn't matter, we need to find Emma. What's Paul's address?'

'Leiston, forty-two Neill Street.'

'Harvey, Emma's in danger, can you meet me at Paul's?'

'Of course. I'm on my way.'

Greg rushes back to the kitchen. 'I haven't got time to explain; I think Emma's in danger. Bill, come with me. I have a feeling there could be trouble. I might need backup.'

'What, now?'

'Now, come on.'

'Of course. Let's go.'

Sally frowns, purses her lips, and follows them as they disappear into the hall. She shouts after them, 'I won't ask but please, please let me know what's happening. Go, if Emma's in danger, go.'

Chapter 63

They rush to Greg's convertible, dive in and accelerate off to Paul's house. They are in luck; the lights turn green just as they reach the junction in the centre of Leiston. Greg puts his foot down, then brakes hard as a car pulls out in front of them. It's run the red light, is travelling far too fast, and its tyres screech as it takes the sharp corner into Saxmundham Road. Greg recognises it at once.

'Black Land Rover, silver tow ball – that's the car that nearly ran Dad down.' He makes a split-second decision. 'I'm going after it.'

Bill is taken by surprise, both by the near collision and by Greg's reaction.

'What about Emma?'

'There's two in the car, it could be Emma and Paul. Harvey's heading to Paul's.'

Greg does a rapid U-turn and follows the Land Rover towards Saxmundham. He has his foot to the floor. They soon catch it stuck behind a van. Greg flashes his headlights, the Land Rover pulls out, overtakes the van on a blind corner and speeds away. Greg waits for a straight stretch of road, also overtakes, and soon catches the Land Rover again. He sits on its tail flashing it to pull over. The road twists and winds through a series of sharp bends. It's flanked by hedges either side and is just wide enough for two cars to pass. Greg pushes his new car to the limit. Bill is terrified. A car coming towards them just manages to slow in time to pull tight into a hedge before hooting as they speed past. After what seems like an eternity to Bill, the Land Rover slams on its brakes and abruptly turns into a farm track. Greg overshoots, stops, reverses and follows. At the end of the gravel track is a circular drive that sits in front of an old, thatched farmhouse. They pull up behind the Land Rover just as two figures emerge. Greg is expecting Paul and Emma to get out, but, instead, it's two beefy lads. They stride purposefully towards the convertible, fists clenched, chests bulging. Greg and Bill leave their car and stand facing them. Greg is ready for a fight. He sizes the lads up; he's not confident but he's not afraid. Bill is more relaxed. He speaks first.

'What the hell, David… and Ian. I might have guessed. Greg, meet the twins David and Ian Stewing. I used to manage them when I ran Leiston Rovers youth set-up. Good footballers but mouthy, always in trouble. This is their dad's farm.'

The taller of the two lads responds. 'Oh, it's you, Bill. Are you alright? Why are you chasing us? What's up?'

'You two, playing silly buggers. Driving around scaring folk. That's what's up. I suppose it's your idea of a laugh.'

'Not us, Bill. You must be confusing us with someone else.'

Greg steps forward. 'You nearly killed me and my dad on Sunday. It was your car. I saw it. I had to push him out of the way, or you would have run him down. You gave us a real shock, not to mention grazes and bruising. And you just ran a red light. If I hadn't braked in time, you could have killed us. You're out of control. What's going on?'

'What a load of squit, there's nothing going on.'

'It's not nothing, you scared the hell out of us. Do you want me to get the police involved?'

'It was just a bit of fun. That was you on Sunday? Great tackle.'

'It's no joke. We could have been badly hurt.'

'But you weren't, were you.'

Bill also steps forward. 'You will be if you do it again. I know your parents. I imagine it's your dad's car. How is Brian? Any more trouble, I'll tell him, and you won't have the chance to scare anyone else. Maybe I'll see if he's in now, that'll learn you.'

'No need for that. We get it, we'll go easy.'

Greg's not sure whether to be upset or relieved. So, the attempted hit-and-run was nothing of the sort. It was just local lads being morons. They needed to get to Paul's, not waste time discussing parenting with Brian. He abruptly cuts things off.

'OK, just don't do it again. Come on, Bill, let's get out of here.'

'Yes, get yourselves going before we have a real barney.'

They ignore the last remark and jump back into the convertible.

'Bastards,' Greg mutters to Bill as he accelerates away back to Leiston and Paul's house.

'I'll have a word with Brian,' Bill says. 'We go way back. He needs to know that his lads are out of control. They need reining in.'

Greg is seething and he's worried. 'What a waste of time. I just hope Emma's OK.'

Chapter 64

Emma puts the kettle on and, while waiting for it to boil, checks out the kitchen. There's a collage of photos of Paul's daughters on the wall. Two sweet, young girls growing through the years. With them are Paul and a lady who she assumes was Paul's wife. Emma remembers Paul saying she was called Jean. There are three photos of the four of them at the Coastguards. In one, they are by a wooden climbing frame; in the second, they are sitting at a trestle table eating ice creams; and in the third, they stand in front of the cliff with the sea stretched out behind them. And on the kitchen dresser there is another of Paul with his arm around Jean sitting on a bench looking out over Minsmere. She can't be certain, but it could be her family bench. The one with the memorial plaque dedicated to her grandparents.

When Paul returns, Emma makes them both another cup of coffee and they sit back down.

'Your girls are so sweet. What are their names?'

'Karen, she's twelve; Kylie, she's ten. They are sweet – they were sweet. It's been hard on them since their mum died. They play up a lot now.'

'Oh, I'm sorry. Where are they?'

'With Jean's mum. She picks them up from school, gives them tea when I'm working. She helps when she can. She's good with them but she's got her dad to look after. He's not been well. It's not ideal, they miss their mum.' Paul pauses, looks at the photo collage and adds, 'We all do.'

Emma is silent, wondering what to say next. She opts for the awkward but obvious question.

'What happened to Jean?'

'Hit-and-run. She was badly injured, never recovered. Died six months ago.'

'I'm sorry, that's awful. It must be difficult losing her. Having to look after the girls on your own.'

'It is. I feel empty, it gets me down.' He pauses then adds, 'But the girls keep me busy, keep me from thinking about it too much.'

They sit together in silence. Emma looks out of the back door at the clothes hanging on the washing line, then at the photo on the dresser of Paul and Jean sitting on the bench. She thinks of her being run down. She then pictures her father nearly being hit and remembers what happened to Derek. Three hit-and-runs in Leiston in under a year.

'Leiston seems to be a hotspot.'

'A hotspot?' Paul says, looking confused.

'Yes, for hit-and-runs.'

Paul crosses his arms and leans back. 'What do you mean?'

'Well, three, it seems a lot.'

Paul raises his eyebrows and leans forward. 'Three?'

355

'You don't normally hear of them. Three is a lot, it's strange. It feels more than a coincidence.'

'What are you saying?'

'Nothing, I'm not saying anything. It's just that your wife, Derek, my dad. All hit-and-runs and all in a short space of time. It seems odd.'

Paul furrows his eyebrows and taps his fingers on the table. It reminds Emma of when Greg is confused or worried.

'Your dad?' he questions.

'Yes, someone tried to run Dad over on Easter Sunday. Here in Leiston, outside my aunt's house. It can't all be coincidence, can it?'

'Well, it could be. It's not impossible.'

'Improbable though,' Emma says, thinking of her grandfather.

Paul spreads his hands on the table, leans back, sighs and then leans forward again. 'Maybe, but why do you care?'

'Someone tried to run my dad down. Now he's dead. Of course I care.'

'No one tried to run your dad down.'

'They did, I was there.'

'No, not on purpose. They didn't.'

'Yes, they did. I saw it happen.'

Paul's face is red, his fingers tapping. He's jiggling his right foot and avoiding her gaze. Emma wonders why.

'What's up, Paul? Is everything OK?'

'Why?'

'You seem agitated.'

'I'm not, and I didn't try to run your dad down.'

'I never said you did.'

'Why did you and your family have to get involved?'

'It was Dad who found Gertrude.'

'I know, he shouldn't have stuck his nose in. Now the police have the torch, it's all going to come out. It's not right.'

Emma's scared, she knows where this is going. It's not Tim, it's Paul. She's sitting with Gertrude's killer, probably her father's killer, and he knows he's given himself away. Her mind is racing. She needs to leave. She tries her best to appear calm.

'I need to go now. Thanks for the coffee and the information on Tim.'

She gets up from the table and starts to leave, but Paul is too quick. He gets up, moves to the dresser, opens a draw and pulls out a large-bladed knife. He points it at her, waving it, forcing her to sit back down. He closes the back door and sits opposite her.

'You're not going anywhere. I need to think.'

Paul stands up again. He's shaking, the knife is shaking. He's moving it one way, then the other. Emma sees the blade glint as it weaves from side to side. She wonders if it's the one that killed her father. Paul makes his decision and grabs Emma's wrist.

'You're coming with me.'

Emma tries to ask where they're going but her mouth won't work. The fear has struck her dumb. Paul drags her up out of her chair with his left hand, his right still holding firmly on to the six-inch blade chopping knife. He walks her through the hall, collects the keys to his house and van, takes her outside and shuts the front door behind them.

Chapter 65

Greg and Bill arrive at Paul's, jump out of the car and rush to the front door. Greg rings the bell. There's no answer. He tries again, knocks, then hammers on the door. Nothing. They peer through the windows; there's no sign of anyone. Bill pushes on a gate that leads to a side passage. It swings open and he leads the way around to the rear of the house. Greg tries the back door; it's unlocked. He enters to find two half-finished cups of coffee on the kitchen table, a chair in the middle of the room and the top dresser drawer pulled open.

'Looks like they've not been gone long. Something's happened. They left in a hurry. I don't like it. My God, Emma. I hope she's OK.'

'We need to find them,' Bill says rapidly, just as worried. 'They could still be in the house. I'll check upstairs, you look down here.'

They search but they aren't there. Greg tries to call Emma again, but it goes through to her answerphone. He leaves her a message, but he knows it's too late. He tries to think where they might have gone, but nothing comes to him. They hear a car pull up outside and open the front door. It's Harvey, who double parks alongside Greg's car and jumps out.

'Sorry, I was held up by the poo lorry doing its stuff blocking the site road. It took forever. Are they inside? I can't see Paul's van.'

'No, it looks like they were here then left in a hurry,' Greg responds with an obvious sense of urgency. 'There's no one about. Emma's not answering her phone. I'm convinced it's Paul. He's a killer and he's alone with her.'

'If his van's not here, where are they?' asks Harvey.

'No idea,' answers Greg. 'We need to think. If Emma has challenged Paul about the killings, he'll be spooked. He'll want to go somewhere he knows.'

'How about Sunrise Park?' suggests Harvey. 'If it is him, it's where he pushed Gertrude and killed your dad. Returning to the scene of the crime.'

Greg's not sure. 'Do you remember passing Paul on your way here?'

'No, but he may have taken the back route.'

'It's possible,' Greg answers. He pauses, thinking, then adds, 'Grandad used to be a detective. I remember him saying that some murderers return to the scene of the crime but for most, it's the last place they want to be. Harvey, you go and check the site. Bill and I will try to work out where else he could have taken her. We need to look around the house. There might be a clue.'

Bill takes the living room; Greg heads for the kitchen and looks for inspiration. He wonders what Grandad Eric would be thinking. *What would he have done?* Greg closes his eyes, tries to let his mind relax. He remembers his grandfather's smile, his smell, the way he used to set him and Emma puzzles to solve. He recalls the Sherlock Holmes quotes: "Once you've eliminated the impossible…", "there's nothing more deceptive than an obvious fact…", "you see but you do not observe". He sees the photo collage, stares at Paul's face and wonders, *If I was you, where would I take her?* He looks closely at the photos and thinks, *You see but you do not observe.* Then he sees the photo on the dresser. The scene seems familiar. He knows it, he's been there. Recently. The Coastguards, the family bench. Greg thinks, *The obvious, it's obvious where he's taken her.*

'I've got it, I think I know,' Greg shouts to Bill. 'It's in the photos. There's a place, our family bench up at the Coastguard Cottages. It overlooks the sea, overlooks Minsmere. Paul loves it. It's where he proposed to his wife. He told me and Emma it was his special place, where he goes to think. The Coastguards will be closed now, they'll be on their own. I can't think where else he'd have taken her.'

Chapter 66

Emma's mouth is dry, her heart pounding, her mind racing. Paul is driving fast along Minsmere Road. She thinks about jumping out, but it would be suicide. He heads towards Sunrise Park but as they reach the entrance, he speeds past, taking them on towards Dunwich Heath and the road to the Coastguard Cottages. They reach the entrance to the National Trust heathland but it's past 6pm and the road gates are locked. The area is closed. Everyone has left. Paul parks the van up on a patch of grass. He's still holding the knife. He gets out, opens her door, and waves it at Emma. He tells her to get out, grabs her by the arm and walks her into the heath. No one else is around. It's eerily quiet apart from the rumble of the sea beneath the cliffs and the birds who are disturbed as they pass. Their tics and clicks and scolds each somehow magnified by her terror. Paul walks Emma along the sandy path, the sea to their left and the Coastguard Cottages ahead. As they get close to the buildings, he skirts around them and takes the path closest to the cliff. She knows where they're heading now. *Of course,* she thinks, *where else would he bring me?* They reach her family bench. Paul and Jean's bench. Waving the knife, he pushes her down and sits next to her.

'This is where I proposed to Jean. It was our favourite place. We used to come here in the early evenings as the light was fading. Just like now. We would watch the sun disappear together. Before Derek ran her over. After that, she couldn't come. When she couldn't get here, she just gave up.' Paul stares out at the view and adds, as much to himself as to Emma, 'Look how the light glows and sparkles on the sea. Look how it shines on the power station and across Minsmere. It's magical.'

As Emma listens, she senses Paul becoming less agitated. Less angry. As he calms, so does she. She thinks, *maybe I can get through to him.* She speaks slowly.

'This is our family bench, Paul. My grandparents' ashes were scattered here and my mother's too, last year. Now Dad's will be, I suppose. There's a plaque on the side.'

'I know. We used to read it when we came here. Jean always wanted it to be our bench. We used to talk about what we'd have on a plaque if we could. She wanted, "For Jean, loving wife and mother". I only found out it was anything to do with Max when he mentioned it while I was fixing his lights. It made me hate him even more.'

'Why did you hate him so much?'

'I didn't. Not at first. But he kept telling everyone Gertrude had been pushed.'

'Was she? Did you push her?'

'No, but I was glad she fell. She was telling people I ran Derek over. The police were investigating. I was going to just wait and see what happened, but I heard her at Tim's door that night, heard them shouting at each other.

She left just as I finished. I followed her. She was walking close to the edge of the cliff. I shone my torch on her. She turned, saw my face and recognised me. She screamed that I was the one who'd killed Derek. Tried to attack me. Grabbed my torch. I tried to pull it from her, but she just clung on more tightly. She had her back to the sea pulling me towards her, towards the cliff. Eventually, I had to let go. If I'd hung on, we'd have both gone over the edge. She toppled backwards. Just like that. I didn't mean for it to happen, but it did. It just did.'

'And Derek? Did you run him over?'

Paul sits thinking, looking at the knife, turning it over in his hand. Eventually, he answers.

'Yes. You may as well hear it all. I was driving out of Leiston, it was dark, no one else was about and he was crossing the road into the car park. I was sure it was him that had hit Jean. I knew it. I didn't set out to run him over, he was just there in front of me. Jean had been in so much pain. It was all his fault; he just left her. She could have died when he hit her, might have been better if she had. The girls wouldn't have had to see their mum suffer so much. I put my foot down. I couldn't help myself.'

'What made you think it was Derek that ran her over?'

'Jean couldn't remember anything but I noticed that his car had a dent. It was in the right place. I saw it when I was doing a job at theirs just after Jean's accident. I'd been looking at his car a week before when I was doing another job for them. I was thinking about getting one myself. It didn't have a dent then, this was new. I challenged him about it. He said he didn't know how it had been done. He blamed Gertrude. But I never saw her drive, ever. He looked guilty and asked me to leave. He wouldn't speak to me again after that. I just had a feeling – have a feeling – it was him. I can't prove it, but I know it was him.'

'So, it was revenge?'

'No. Well, yes, I suppose so. I couldn't help myself, I just couldn't. But not Gertrude, that was an accident. Derek, yes, it was revenge and hate, bitterness, grief. All the things that build up in you when someone takes away what you love most. It wasn't planned, I didn't set out for vengeance. But revenge, yes, I suppose so. I wanted to hurt him like he hurt my Jean. Kill him, like he killed my Jean. Payback. I don't know where it came from. I'd never been violent before, it was just in me waiting to come out, waiting for the right moment. Waiting for Derek.'

'But why Dad?'

'He wouldn't let it go. I heard him say he thought Gertrude had been pushed. I needed to know if he had any evidence that I'd been there. He discovered her, was first to see her. And I needed to find the torch. I was sure it had been lost over the cliff when Gertrude fell. They didn't find it when they recovered her body, so I thought I'd got away with it. It would have had Gertrude's fingerprints on… and mine. I needed to get it back. I looked for it the day after she fell, but it was nowhere. He could have found it; I needed to know. I thought if I could see his journal, it would tell me. But there was nothing about the torch. Just him thinking she'd fallen backwards, maybe been pushed. Lots of stuff about what people had told him and who she'd argued with. Who had a reason, who might have done it.'

'Was it you who tried to run him over in Leiston?'

'I don't know anything about that.'

'Really?'

'Why would I lie? I killed your father, I admit it. But I'm not a liar.'

'So, why did you kill him?'

'He just wouldn't shut up. Harvey asked me to have a spare key cut when I bought the lock he replaced for your dad after I'd broken in. I had an extra key made just in case. I heard about him having found the torch when I was at James and Felicity's helping to fix the cooker. I went to your dad's lodge to find it. I let myself in and looked everywhere, but I couldn't see it. I figured he would have it with him when he got back. He didn't. I just snapped. I hated him, the bench, the torch, everything. I'd been thinking about what would happen to the girls if the police found out about me and Gertrude. Whether they would believe it was an accident. Whether they would link it to what happened to Derek. What would happen if they put me away. If I couldn't look after Karen and Kylie. They'd just lost their mother, they were in a bad place, they couldn't lose me too. It would have destroyed them. They're everything to me, all that's left of me and Jean. I promised her I would look after them. I was there for an hour stewing, waiting for him, endlessly waiting. When he finally got back and he didn't have the torch, I couldn't take it. I had to stop him, stop it all. He came in and was making tea with his back to me. There was a knife in a block on the side. I grabbed it, came up behind him and stabbed him. He started to turn so I hit him with a vase. It was just there; I grabbed it, and it smashed. I can still see it breaking into pieces. Lots of pieces. He collapsed and I ran out. It was all so quick. After the waiting, I couldn't get away fast enough. It was crazy. I was crazy.'

Emma feels numb, she can't believe what she's just heard, and she can't get the image of the shattered vase out of her mind. She thinks of her father's head being smashed into pieces. She shudders.

'So, why have you brought me here?'

'You're like your father: you won't let it go. I can't do it anymore. I'm going to end it now. It's all your family's fault. You're coming with me. We're going over the cliff together, here at your family's place. Jean's place.'

'But your girls need you. If you do this, what will they think of you when they grow up? What will it do to them? You must see it. I know it's hard, it's hard for me. I've lost my mum, now Dad. Both gone in a year. You've lost Jean. Killing us won't undo any of that. It'll just make it worse for your girls. I sort of understand, others will understand. You were protecting your family.'

'You do? You understand?'

Emma thinks back to what her father had told her about what animals will do to ensure the survival of their young. She searches for an example that might get through to him.

'A few years ago, Dad told me something about Indian hornbills. The males are incredibly protective of their families. They seal their mates in tree hollows with mud, sticks and bird droppings. It's where she lays the eggs and tends to the chicks. Only the bills of the female and her young can get through the opening to receive the male's food offerings. It's thought this protects the young until they're ready to fledge. When they are, the male releases them from their prison. I get it, it's natural. You want to protect your girls until they can take care of themselves. But not like this. How will this help?'

Paul turns his head; something's got his attention. Emma looks around and sees two figures approaching. Paul stands to face them, pulls Emma up and puts the knife to her throat. It's Greg and Bill, they're about fifty feet away.

'Stop. Stop there,' Paul shouts.

'Emma? Are you OK?' Greg shouts back. 'The police are on their way.'

'I'm OK,' Emma responds. 'Don't come any closer. Paul and I are talking, working things out. Aren't we, Paul?'

'Stay back or she's coming over the cliff with me.'

Emma takes control.

'Paul, look at me. Don't think about them, think about your girls. You said it yourself, it's hard for them losing their mum. They're so young, they can't lose you as well. You're all they've got. They need you. They need to know you're alive. You've brought them here, haven't you? I've seen the photos.'

Paul removes the blade from Emma's throat, and they sit back down again on the bench.

'We used to come before Jean's accident. They would play on the wooden climbing frame by the Coastguards, we'd have a drink, maybe an ice cream, then we'd come here and sit on the bench. We'd often sing a song by that Hawaiian singer. His ukulele medley with "Over the Rainbow" and "Wonderful World". We'd play it on a phone and sing along. The girls loved it. We were so happy. I bring them here now to remember those times. To remember Jean.'

'If you do anything silly, it will spoil it. Ruin it for them. They won't be able to come here to remember their mum. They will just think of what you did.'

'Maybe.'

'Killing someone creates an unpayable debt, it's taking what can never be given back. They can never have their mum back, but they do have their memories of her. Of being here with you and her, of being together as a family. Don't take this place away from your girls. Why not come home with me and Greg? Tell the police what happened.'

'I don't know.'

'The sentence might not be so long, what with losing your wife, the grief, the girls. You would be able to see them, they could still come here.'

'I don't know. I just don't know.'

'Give me the knife. Please.'

'The knife?'

'Please, Paul, for Karen and Kylie.'

'For Karen and Kylie?'

'And Jean. We could put a plaque on the bench dedicated to Jean. The girls could come here and read it out, they could remember her. And think of you. They would still have this place, still have the good memories of the four of you together. Happy memories.'

'You would do that? After what I did to your dad?'

'I would need Greg to agree, but yes, I would. One day, you, Karen and Kylie might be able to be here together again. You could read the plaque out to them, "For Jean, loving wife and mother". Let Greg come over; we can ask him. But give me the knife first.'

Paul rocks back and forth, thinking. Turning over the knife, thinking. Close by, a nightingale begins to sing. Softly at first and then more resonant as it builds momentum. They listen in silence to its melodic churrs and chortles and whistles. It's as if nature is speaking to Paul and guiding him. It's wrapping its soothing blanket around him, helping him make his decision. Slowly, tentatively, he hands Emma the knife. She gently takes it, sets it on the ground by the side of the bench away from Paul and calls to her brother.

'Greg, we have something to ask you.'

Epilogue

Greg and Emma sit on the family bench looking out across Minsmere. In the distance, Sizewell B's gleaming, white dome looks back at them. An endless expanse of sea to their left shimmers brightly, sparkling in the sun. Gulls cry, waders on the scrape cry, Greg and Emma cry. A lark rises into the clear blue sky, until, high above them, it answers their cries. An answer full of hope, an answer full of the joy of being alive. Greg opens Max's journal and reads aloud his last entry. It's the one his father wrote sitting on the bench while he and Emma were paddling along the shoreline.

'I look out over the gently rolling sea, the wildlife-rich marshes, the wide-open, mind-calming heathland. I see Sizewell B and think of Sizewell C and the inevitability that man will soon overreach himself. That the wonderful journey through cultivation, industrialisation then digitisation will eventually self-destruct. Through need or greed or plain stupidity. But I know that nature will survive, revive and regain ascendency. I know that the spirit of Kathy, of Greg and of Emma will continue as part of the cosmos where man and nature and time are one. We are only here for the briefest of moments. A temporary collection of atoms that will soon disperse to be reborn as part of the ever-changing universe. I'm lifted knowing that we will be together again. It's why I love open spaces. Mountains, deserts, the sea, the heathland, here. Places where I sense I'm part of something more, something spiritual, something eternal. Places where I sense the consciousness of all around us and that death is just a journey back to that.'

Emma then recites from Hamlet. Not as Ophelia, but as Hamlet's mother, Gertrude.

'Thou know'st 'tis common; all that lives must die, passing through nature to eternity.'

Greg and Emma sit for a while, in silence. They get up and walk towards the cliff edge. The wind is blowing away from them and out to sea. Emma holds a scatter tube and casts some of her father's ashes into the air. The coarse grey dust dances in the wind and disappears over the cliff. She hands the tube to Greg, who does the same until the container is empty and Max is set free. The sun shines down on them. And it shines down on the bench behind them. And as it does, it illuminates two new brass plaques.

One that reads, "For Jean, loving wife and mother".

And the other that reads, "For Olive, Eric, their daughter Kathy and her husband Max. They loved this place".

Acknowledgements

I would like to thank all those who supported me in writing this, my first murder mystery novel. In particular, those who reviewed the many drafts of the manuscript to give their invaluable feedback and those who gave encouragement through their positive comments. Above all, huge thanks to my wife Rosie for her attention to detail through the many re-reads, her insightful suggestions, incredible patience and constant support.

Thanks also to all at Troubador for their dedication and skill in the publication of this novel, and to William Morrello for his wonderful cover painting of the Dunwich bench looking across Minsmere. It captures well the beauty and serenity of what is a truly magical place.

All That Lives Must Die is a murder-mystery roller coaster but it is also a nod to the power of the natural environment to support those with mental health issues. Above all, it is a love letter to the largely unspoiled Suffolk Heritage Coast. My final thank you must go to those who are fighting to keep it that way. My hope is that this book will swell our ranks.

About the Author

Ivor Eisenstadt, having studied zoology and physiology at university, and spent much of his career within healthcare publishing, is keen to share his personal experience of the healing power of nature through this murder mystery novel set on the idyllic Suffolk Heritage Coast. It is where his wife Rosie grew up and where they have a lodge from which they enjoy walking, swimming, birdwatching and spending time with their family.

Ivor also enjoys watching sport and his first novel *Final Score* is about a day in the life of a sports addict:

You don't have to play sport to be a sports addict. Ivor Eisenstadt's timely novel details a momentous day in the life of David, an 'active spectator' so immersed in the thrills, stories and unpredictability of sport that it takes over his life and he is unable to control his behaviour. If you doubt this constitutes a true addiction, Final Score *will set you straight. A captivating and thought-provoking read.*

Phil Hammond, NHS doctor, writer and broadcaster.